Rupert
on the Leeward Island of Nevis. The seventh generation of an English colonial family, Mr. Gilchrist is the first to break away from plantation life. After attending preparatory school in Rhode Island, he studied on the Continent.

He has travelled extensively in Africa and the Far East and now lives in Montserrat, in a 17th century captain's house, which he has faithfully restored himself. His hobbies include horses, skin-diving, collecting African artifacts and tuning the engine of his Lamborghini.

Also by Rupert Gilchrist

THE HOUSE AT 3 O'CLOCK (Slaves Without Masters Volume One)
A GIRL CALLED FRIDAY NIGHT (Slaves Without Masters Volume Two)
THE GUNS OF DRAGONARD
THE SIEGE OF DRAGONARD HILL
DRAGONARD RISING
DRAGONARD BLOOD
THE MASTER OF DRAGONARD HILL
DRAGONARD

and published by Corgi Books

The Wrong Side of Town

Slaves Without Masters Volume 3

Rupert Gilchrist

CORGI BOOKS

THE WRONG SIDE OF TOWN
A CORGI BOOK 0 552 12430 3

Originally published in Great Britain by
Souvenir Press Ltd.

PRINTING HISTORY
Souvenir Press edition published 1985
Corgi edition published 1985

This book is set in 10/11 pt Sabon

Corgi Books are published by Transworld Publishers Ltd., Century House, 61-63 Uxbridge Road, Ealing, London W5 5SA, in Australia by Transworld Publishers (Aust.) Pty. Ltd., 26 Harley Crescent, Condell Park, NSW 2200, and in New Zealand by Transworld Publishers (N.Z.) Ltd., Cnr. Moselle and Waipareira Avenues, Henderson, Auckland.

Made and printed in Great Britain by
Hunt Barnard Printing Ltd., Aylesbury, Bucks.

Contents

Historical Note

Prosperity in America at the turn of the last century eluded the vast majority of its Black citizens who, less than forty years earlier, had still been in slavery. In the decades following the Civil War, freed Negroes gladly accepted the most menial jobs offered them, endangering health and imperilling family life for any chance of work. Powerful vigilante groups such as the Ku Klux Klan strove to keep the Black population suppressed and uneducated, helping to create the shameful situation of a great nation having slaves without masters.

R.G.

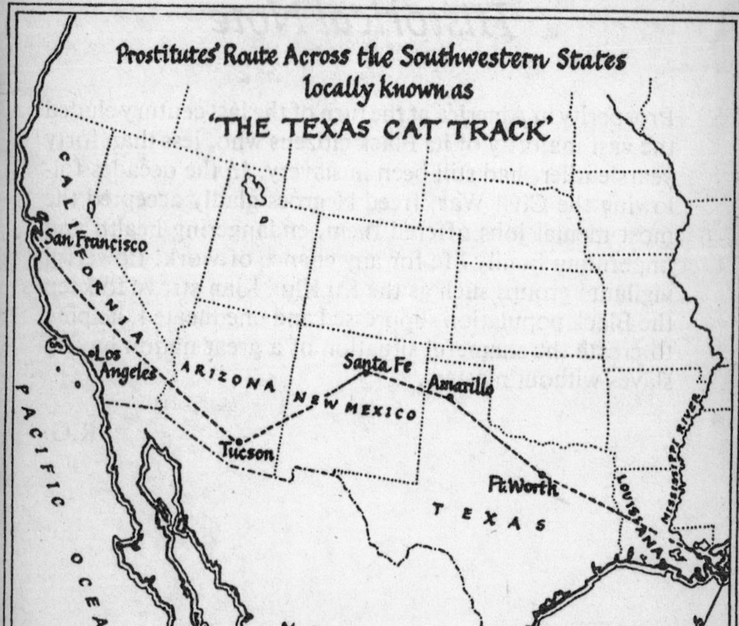
Prostitutes' Route Across the Southwestern States
locally known as
'THE TEXAS CAT TRACK'
CALIFORNIA
San Francisco
Los Angeles
ARIZONA
Tucson
NEW MEXICO
Santa Fe
Amarillo
Ft.Worth
TEXAS
LOUISIANA
MISSISSIPPI RIVER
New Orleans
PACIFIC OCEAN
MEXICO
GULF OF MEXICO

PART ONE

NOB HILL

Chapter One

THE INTERVIEW

'Men usually come to a brothel looking for pleasure, Mr Summers, not work.'

Lady Elizabeth Raleigh was more refined than Smoky Summers had expected a San Francisco madam to be. She wore a blue woollen skirt with a long rope of pearls knotted over a white silk blouse. Her black hair was streaked with grey and piled on top of her head like a schoolmarm's. Her handsome, distinguished appearance was enriched by a crisp British accent.

Lady Elizabeth's brothel surprised Smoky, too. It was located in the best part of town, on Nob Hill, a big house furnished with antiques, silver candlesticks and oil paintings, not crowded with gold cherubs and swags of scarlet velvet which Smoky had imagined he would see in a whorehouse.

He was even more astonished that Lady Elizabeth should address him as 'mister' and not 'boy', that she did not treat him like dirt under her feet. Maybe White folks were nicer to Black people out here in California than back home in Louisiana.

* * *

Lady Elizabeth paced the Oriental carpet of the bordello's upstairs parlor, trailing her skirt's fashionably long hem as she held one hand clasped to a garnet brooch pinned to her high-necked silk blouse. 'I won't insult you, Mr Summers, by offering you a job in the stables or kitchen. But I'm afraid I have no other vacancy at the moment.'

Smoky tried not to look disappointed, while thinking

that he could have stayed in New Orleans and fed horses and washed dishes for a living.

A pretty girl, with skin the color of milky coffee, sat forward on a stool by the grey marble mantelpiece. 'Excuse me, Lady Elizabeth, mam. But Rob Johnson's planning to leave next week for Oregon. His job'll be empty."

Lady Elizabeth glanced sharply at the girl. 'When I need your suggestions, Petal, I'll ask for them.'

The Black girl persisted. 'But, mam, you said there's no work here except kitchen or barn chores and –'

Lady Elizabeth lingered in front of the window. 'Petal, that's enough.'

Petal shrugged her thin shoulders and sank back on the stool.

Bewildered, Smoky looked from Petal to Lady Elizabeth, wondering who this Rob Johnson fellow was and what kind of a job he was leaving in a whorehouse. Was it something he could do?

Lady Elizabeth stood with her back to Smoky, staring out of the window at the uneven rows of rooftops spreading down to San Francisco Bay. 'You must forgive Petal, Mr Summers. She's an impetuous girl. But what she says happens to be true. The position of bartender might be available. Now, remember, I say "might".'

Smoky sat alert on his chair. 'Bartending's fine with me, mam.'

Lady Elizabeth surveyed the rooftops – steep cedar roofs, slate mansard roofs, flat tarpaper roofs down in the jungle of the Barbary Coast. 'Have you served drinks before, Mr Summers? Are you able to mix fruit punches? Open champagne without losing half the bottle in foam? Shake a bottle of beer to fill two schooners without making it so frothy that customers complain?'

Smoky's head nodded eagerly. 'I know all the tricks of bartending, mam. I learned bartending in New Orleans.'

Lady Elizabeth studied Smoky as if making a mental note of his features: black hair cropped closely to his skull; skin the color of golden caramel; high cheekbones, small nose, thin lips; an eager, almost little-boyish manner to him – a polite, personable young man who could have been called a 'Fancy' back in the old slave days of Confederacy. She noticed, too, a glint in his eye which told her he was a devilish young man despite all his 'Yes, mams' and 'No, mams'.

She asked, 'Where did you work in New Orleans, Mr Summers?'

'Mam, the last place I worked was –'

Smoky thought of the bordellos and sporting clubs where he had tried to find jobs but from whose back doors he had been turned away like an undesirable pedlar, sometimes even a dog. 'At Wilma Starett's place on Basin Street, mam,' he lied.

'Wilma Starett?' Lady Elizabeth's crisp British accent disappeared. 'Wilma Starett's got a place on . . . The Line?'

A knock sounded on the parlor's mahogany doors. One door slid open and a short maid with curly blonde hair bustled across the carpet to whisper into Lady Elizabeth's ear.

Listening, Lady Elizabeth nodded. 'Thank you, Mo.'

Turning to Smoky, she rose, apologizing, 'Forgive me, Mr Summers, but an urgent problem has arisen. I must leave you for a few minutes.'

Remembering the good manners his grandmother had taught him, Smoky sprang to his feet as Lady Elizabeth left the room with her maid.

* * *

Smoky felt more relaxed when the maid had slid the door shut behind Lady Elizabeth. Looking back to the Black girl, Petal, seated on the low stool next to the mantelpiece, he said in a light easy voice, 'Thanks for trying to help me get a job. You could have lost your own job speaking out like that.'

Petal's hair formed a soft black halo around her coffee-brown face, and her yellow dimity dress showed her buxom figure to its best advantage – high fulsome breasts, a slim waist, firmly rounded hips.

Looking up at Smoky with dewy brown eyes, she teased, 'I just want to help a nice down-home boy like you find work in the wicked, big city.'

Smoky guessed from Petal's accent that she also came from one of the Southern states. But he could not tell yet if she was one of Lady Elizabeth's prostitutes or some kind of housemaid or companion.

Cautiously, he asked, 'How long you lived in San Francisco, gal?'

'My best friend, Alicia, and me, came out west from Georgia two years ago.' Petal clasped both hands over one knee and leaned back on the stool. 'What about you, pretty boy? Where you from?'

Smoky had not been with a woman since he had arrived in San Francisco three weeks ago. He tried to avoid staring at the way Petal's breasts strained the small pearl buttons of her dress, to ignore the way her eyes studied him.

Reminding himself that Lady Elizabeth would soon be returning to the room, he cleared his throat. 'I live with my grandfolks north of New Orleans,' he answered. 'Ever hear of Longchamp Parish?'

'Can't say that I have.' Petal's sparkling brown eyes dropped slowly down the front of Smoky's navy blue suit. 'But I sure enough recognize you.'

'Recognize . . . me?' Damn it! Who was she? Some fancy girl who remembered him from New Orleans? Why was she teasing him like this?

Mockery in her eyes, she said, 'You come out to California looking for fame and fortune, ain't you, country boy?'

Smoky bobbed his head, sticking both hands into his trouser pockets. 'Yeah, is it that . . . obvious?'

Petal's smile dimpled her cheeks. 'You Black bucks the same as White boys. All you young bucks come out here to California looking for gold mines or silver mines – or some rich old widow who owns one.'

Smoky jerked his head, angered by the inference that he was an opportunist. 'I'm not after some old woman's money. Fact is, I don't want anything for nothing. I'm strong and willing to work hard for my pay.'

Petal angled her head, a pretty smile on her red lips. 'So what makes you come to Pleasant Street looking for work? Why don't you try down on Cunningham Wharf? Or go see if you can get hired for the Sutton Street trolley if you've got such a strong back and willing spirit?'

'I tried to get construction work,' Smoky protested, pushing out his chest. 'I tried for dock work. For road work. For everything, gal. But I didn't have any luck. Nobody's interested in hiring Black boys in this town. There's too many Chinamen. Then I looked at a copy of that little book called *The Gentleman's Guide to San Francisco's Pleasures*. It says that this place is the most famous, most expensive whorehouse in all San Francisco. That gave me the idea of trying to find work here. I figure customers who come here do more than make love with the pretty gals. I figured that there's other jobs going here, jobs for waiters and doormen and bartenders.'

Petal began to speak but, checking the words, she rose from the stool and put her elbows on the mantelpiece, standing with her back to Smoky, shaking her head.

Surprised by her sudden change, Smoky stepped forward. 'What's the matter, gal? What'd I say wrong?'

Petal shrugged her shoulders. 'Nothing.' She began toying with a crystal teardrop dangling from a silver candlestick, explaining in a softer voice, 'It's just that I don't meet many nice boys like you. Not pretty boys from down home. Well-meaning bucks itching to make their way in the world. It makes me come over – oh, I don't know what the heck it does to me!'

Smoky stepped closer, his voice softening. 'Aren't you happy living here? Don't you like working in this . . . house?'

Petal continued toying with the candlestick's crystal teardrop. 'Sure, I'm happy living here. Lady Elizabeth, she's no slave driver. The other girls, they ain't so bad, even if they're all White gals except for me and my friend, Alicia, and one Chinaman gal named Chickie Ling. Oh, sometimes the men customers, they get out of hand. But –" Petal's laugh was empty. '– but pretty bucks like you, they *never* get out of hand . . . dang it!'

Glancing at the sliding mahogany doors across the room, Smoky knew that Lady Elizabeth would be returning shortly to resume interviewing him for a job. Should he try to make some kind of date to meet Petal later, to have a rendezvous with her away from the house?

Moving behind her, he began, 'You know, gal, I don't have much money.'

Petal shrugged again, mumbling, 'What for I care about your money, boy?'

Smoky's hardening penis bolstered his courage. 'I also got me another problem, gal.'

Petal stood facing the mantelpiece, tracing a long red fingernail around the base of the candlestick, a pout on her lips. 'What's your problem, boy?'

Slipping one hand around her waist, he murmured, 'How does a guy get to know you better without getting into trouble with the boss lady?'

Smiling, sliding back against him, Petal rubbed her buttocks against the front of his trousers. 'Sometimes a boy's got to take chances with a gal.'

Smoky pushed harder against her. 'Can you feel *that* chance?'

'Hmmm.' Petal pressed more tightly against him. 'I'd have to be wearing iron britches not to.'

Smoky cupped a hand over Petal's breast. 'For a little thing, you're pretty well fixed yourself.'

'You don't know half of it –' Grabbing his other hand, she moved it down the front of her skirt, holding the finger on the firm mound between her legs.

Pressing his fingertips against the thin dimity, Smoky could feel that she wore no underclothes. Pressing harder, probing for her cleft, he found the rise and began stroking her as the head of his penis crept down the inside of his leg.

Glancing towards the parlor doors, he whispered in a rush of nervousness, 'Isn't this a little bit risky, sweet potato?' He didn't want to risk his chances of getting the bartending job.

Petal, bolder, turned to face him, pressing her breasts against his chest, looking up into his twinkling brown eyes. 'Just keep those big fingers working, dumpling. I like how you stir my dish.'

A dimple deepened in Smoky's chin. 'You're a chancy little thing, aren't you, gal?'

'I ain't chancy enough to let you pass me by.' Petal kept her eyes on his as she dropped one hand to his trousers, moving her finger over the bulge of his crotch, feeling for the end of his penis.

Standing upright, she stared at him in amazement. 'Boy, what you got stuffed in those britches? Some big chunk of dago salami?'

'That's all me, gal. That's all Louisiana lunchmeat!'

Laughing, Smoky pulled her towards him and planted a kiss firmly on her red lips as his penis crept farther, thicker, down the inside of his blue serge trousers.

* * *

'His prick, you silly little goose! Stand back and let me see his prick!'

Lady Elizabeth hid in a small storeroom adjoining the upstairs parlor, muttering as she pressed her eye to a peephole drilled through the plaster wall. The maid, Mo, stood alongside her holding a flickering candle.

Watching Smoky and Petal beginning to explore one another's bodies in front of the fireplace, Lady Elizabeth thought of her lover, wondering if Cory Roper was making love to someone, perhaps had become romantically involved with another woman. He had been due back in San Francisco last week and still had not arrived.

Reminding herself that she had more important things

to worry about than a lover's unfaithfulness, she told herself to think only about a young man who might be eligible to work in her bordello.

Lady Elizabeth always interviewed – inspected – men in the same way. She began by informing them that no work was available in the bordello, saying that she wouldn't insult them by offering a job in the kitchen or stables. The interviews were always conducted in the same, small upstairs parlor. One of her six prostitutes was invariably present at the interview. The prostitute interrupted Lady Elizabeth to say that the bartender, Rob Johnson, was leaving for Oregon, that his job was soon going to be available. After Lady Elizabeth reprimanded the prostitute for speaking out of turn, the maid entered the room and whispered a message into Lady Elizabeth's ear. Excusing herself, Lady Elizabeth left the young man alone with the prostitute while she adjourned to the adjoining storeroom to watch the prostitute seduce the young man, providing her with a clear view through the peephole.

Lady Elizabeth was not interested in hiring anyone to work as a bartender. Nor in the livery stable or kitchen. She was only interested in luring young men into becoming male prostitutes on Pleasant Street.

* * *

One floor above Lady Elizabeth, the Black woman, Alicia Fargo, paced the floral carpet of her bedroom, wondering if she had at last found a way to free herself from being a prositute, perhaps even a way to get money to buy her and Petal the love nest they had always wanted back home in Georgia.

Alicia and Petal had come to San Francisco as lovers two years ago – in 1904 – from Savannah, Georgia. Lady Elizabeth, impressed with the two young Black women's beauty, had immediately hired them to work for her on Pleasant Street.

Tall, long-legged, with a complexion the color of ripe

plum, Alicia Fargo was the more exotic of the two Black girls, and had quickly become one of the most popular prostitutes in the house. Cool, aloof, arrogant, her speciality was being insolent to men who enjoyed abuse, insulting them, acting frigid with them in bed, sometimes even physically punishing them, pretending that she was their nursemaid, a stern governess, a strict teacher at school.

Having worked on Pleasant Street for two years, Alicia had learnt that Lady Elizabeth was a shrewd, clever woman. Alicia especially admired her for having the good business sense to keep at least one male prostitute on the premises. Why should men be the only ones to come to a whorehouse? Why shouldn't females – those women who enjoyed making love to men – be able to find lovers in brothels too?

As Lady Elizabeth was clever at finding new ways to make money, she was also adept at getting people to work for her, at keeping them working for her, taking advantage of their poverty, their homelessness, whatever reason had made them drift into prostitution. She also took advantage of their greed.

It was a house rule that all the girls dressed in the latest fashion. Because they did not often leave the house, Lady Elizabeth had shopkeepers come to Pleasant Street to show their latest fashions to the girls in the parlor. The girls chose the gowns, shoes and bonnets they wanted, letting Lady Elizabeth pay for them and deduct the money from their wages. The inflated prices kept the girls indebted to her, preventing them from flitting from house to house as so many prostitutes did, even from town to town, state to state.

A prostitute's life was short, Alicia knew, especially at a top house like this. Drinks were expensive and customers expected a girl to drink them if they paid for them at such exorbitant prices. A prostitute could soon become puffy and blotchy, her body loose and flabby.

Besides alcohol, laudanum took its toll on a woman, not

so much in her face as by killing her when she wanted to dull her mind to forget about the life she was leading. Sometimes an overdose was accidental, sometimes not.

A lover was often a prostitute's one consolation. But the men who wanted prostitutes for lovers were mostly pimps, men too lazy to work, who only wanted to live off a woman's earnings.

Alicia and Petal, like many prostitutes, discovered love with another female. Alicia had taught Petal that women didn't need a penis for love-making. There were other thrills.

Mouths. Fingers. Tender caresses. Kissing and tonguing and nibbling. Probing and poking one another's love buttons. Using the friction of knees: Alicia called the act 'slick-legging'.

Pacing the bedroom floor, Alicia thought how Lady Elizabeth was jeopardizing their love. Alicia was not jealous of Petal going to bed with her customers. They were usually old, selfish White men, men who just wanted to use a pretty Black girl and forget about her. But Alicia had always dreaded that one day nineteen year-old Petal would find a man she enjoyed making love to, a man who treated her with respect, whom she enjoyed in bed.

Thinking about Petal being with a country boy one floor below her, an attractive Black boy from the South, Alicia felt pangs of jealousy.

Should she go downstairs? Should she burst into the parlor and pull them apart?

Or, instead, should she confront the culprit?

Lady Elizabeth had come to Petal's room little more than an hour ago, saying that she wanted Petal to help interview a Black bumpkin who had knocked on the front door of the house. In her excitement, Lady Elizabeth had pulled the scarf from her neck and Alicia had caught sight of a blue scar, a small tattoo, about the size of a silver dollar, on her throat. Recognizing the shape of the tattoo, Alicia had suddenly realized why Lady Elizabeth always wore a brooch or scarf at her neck. She was hiding a secret sign.

Should she confront Lady Elizabeth, say she had seen the tattoo on her throat? Should she expose her secret in public? Ruin Elizabeth's standing as Nob Hill's most elite brothel-keeper? Alicia laughed at the idea of the so-called 'Lady Elizabeth' being reduced to sucking cock for a quarter down on the Barbary Coast. The third alternative was blackmail.

* * *

Petal's yellow dimity dress hung unbuttoned from her shoulders as she clenched her bare legs around Smoky's naked buttocks, his penis bared and erect and driving into her furry oval.

Standing with his trousers dropped to his ankles, Smoky used the palms of both hands to hold Petal over his naked midsection as he drove his hips rapidly against her, sinking himself into her contracting vagina, revolving his thickness inside the stretched pinkness of her womanhood.

Petal, forgetting about Lady Elizabeth watching them through the peephole, mindless about Alicia waiting jealously upstairs for her to return, tossed her head back and forth, begging, 'Stir me, pretty boy! Stir me! Stir me with that big fat black dick of yours, honey boy. Stir my little pussy!'

'Shhh.' Smoky glanced at the sliding doors. 'Keep your voice down, baby.'

Clinging tightly to Smoky's neck, Petal pushed and contracted and expanded her feminine warmth around him. 'Don't you worry, baby. Don't you worry. She ain't coming back. Not for a while yet.'

Perspiration pouring down his forehead, Smoky raised Petal up and down on his standing penis, gasping between drives. 'Why you so sure, honey? Why you so sure she's not coming back any second?'

Petal covered Smoky's face with kisses, squeezing and relaxing her brown thighs, enjoying his penis stirring deeper and harder inside her velvet-smooth walls.

"Don't stop, honey,' she pleaded. 'Don't stop . . . Don't stop. I'm just getting there . . . I'm getting there . . . My little pussy's starting to *cry*, baby . . . My little pussy's starting to *shout* . . .'

Smoky's excitement was also cresting. But worried about being discovered by Lady Elizabeth, he said honestly, 'I don't want to lose my chances of getting that bartending job, honey.'

'Finish *this* job, baby,' Petal urged as she dug her heels into the base of his back, helping the head of his penis pump further, harder, deeper inside her. 'Finish *this* job, baby. Finish *this* job.'

'But, sugar . . .'

Grabbing the back of Smoky's head, Petal rose higher against his chest, shoving his face towards her bare breasts, arching her back to stopper his words with a plump raspberry-black nipple.

Chapter Two

PLEASANT STREET

The early morning rain beat against the leaden panes of Lady Elizabeth's bedroom window. Snuggled in the cosy warmth of her tester bed on the bordello's second floor, she told herself it was time to rise and begin another busy day. It seemed as if she had only seen the night's last customer to the door before coming upstairs and collapsing into a deep, delicious sleep.

Cinching a rose moiré silk robe around her waist and tying it securely at the neck, Elizabeth crossed the dark room and pulled back the thick Flemish draperies to let in the light of a dismal, wet San Francisco day.

Standing by the window, looking down through the pelting rain, she felt a sense of pride as she saw the two neatly trimmed bay trees flanking her front iron gates.

Hers was the finest house on Pleasant Street, a row of vanilla-washed private residences tucked between Jones and Taylor Streets on Nob Hill. The neighbors had long ago stopped complaining about a bordello on their street when they learned that Elizabeth ran a discreet, exclusive establishment, a house to which the majority of them would probably be denied admittance.

Like a private morning prayer, Elizabeth lingered at the window, thankful she had managed to survive as a business woman in San Francisco. Her house had come to be considered more elegant than Sally Thigpign's Oriental Palace two blocks away on Pacific Street; more discerning than Ruth Birchwood's red brick mansion on Turk Street; far more accommodating to bizarre sexual tastes than the so-called 'specialty' houses bordering the Barbary Coast. There were still many improvements to make, though, new battles to fight.

For instance, what about finding the right male prostitute to work for her? Rob the bartender frequently satisfied a lady patron. But Elizabeth needed a house bull, a full-time stud.

Women were complex, demanding customers, often more difficult to please than men. And men made such bad whores! A man either wanted to screw, screw, screw. Or else he reached an orgasm too quickly, taking valuable time to recover his potency.

Turning away from the window, Elizabeth crossed to the Carrara mantelpiece on the far side of the bedroom and pulled the blue silk bell cord for Mo to bring her tray of *café au lait* and brioche, a morning ritual she had begun years ago when she had lived – and worked – on Basin Street in New Orleans.

Tugging the cord a second time, she surveyed the row of silver-framed photographs lining the mantelpiece. She picked up a sepia picture of a moustached man with deep-set eyes.

Cory Roper was more than Elizabeth's lover. He was her adviser, her counsel, her guide to survival in San Francisco. Cory likened San Francisco to a woman with dung on her ballgown, a town little more than a generation away from being a rugged mining settlement.

It had been Cory Roper who had first told Elizabeth about the importance of screening the customers she allowed into her house. He had taught her to serve only the finest wines, vintage champagnes. To demand that her girls be beautiful, exotic, dressed in the latest European fashion. He had told her the importance of taking the girls out to smart restaurants so that the public could be dazzled by their beauty. And, above all, he had told her to insist that all the girls be healthy and clean.

It has also been Cory Roper who had suggested to Elizabeth that she herself dress older than her forty-three years. He had told her to comb premature grey streaks into her hair, to avoid the colorful ruffles and garish feathers sported by other bordello-keepers, to present a matriarchal image of soft tweeds and pale silks to the public, to appear as a lady of quality. San Francisco strived to be the cultural centre of the American's West so, Cory told her, be the most cultured madam west of the Mississippi!

Elizabeth had adopted the title of 'Lady Elizabeth Raleigh' before she had come to San Francisco. Cory disapproved of the title, believing it was unnecessary, even troublesome, to burden herself with a counterfeit title, to invent stories which were difficult to remember. He also considered the practice to be oldfashioned, belonging to the bygone Gold Rush days when rustic madams had dubbed themselves 'Countess' and 'Princess'. He agreed that Elizabeth should continue using the title only to avoid suddenly appearing as a charlatan, to risk admitting openly that, yes, she had once called herself by a fake title.

Remembering how innocent and naive she had been when she had arrived in San Francisco sixteen years ago, Elizabeth wondered where she would have been today if she had not met Cory Roper. Would she be performing tricks down on the Barbary Coast? Be some two-bit street-walker? Perhaps have drifted back to New Orleans?

Thinking about New Orleans reminded her that Cory was there, and that his return was two weeks overdue. The jealousy she had felt a few days ago about him meeting other women had turned to concern for his physical safety.

Cory had gone to Louisiana to secure controlling shares in the *Natchez-Pacific* Railroad. But he refused to travel by train, insisting on riding horseback as he had done so many times as a younger man, saying that he would soon be too old to enjoy the freedom of an open range, of country roads dotted with livery stables and farmhouses. Elizabeth loved Cory for being an incurable romantic.

The route between San Francisco and New Orleans passed through Nevada, Arizona, and Texas, and because so many prostitutes travelled between the two cities, frequenting gambling houses and tough saloons along the way, the route had become known as 'The Texas Cat

Track', the haunt for low, scurrilous characters. Thieves. Murderers. Pimps. Renegades.

With the consoling thought that Cory had been a Mississippi riverboat gambler in his early days, that he still carried pistols, Elizabeth again rebuked herself for wasting valuable time worrying about him. She had the day's work to consider.

Regular customers. New visitors referred to her by satisfied men. Saturday night's party to prepare. Judge Douglas's usual visit on Thursday afternoon. There were a million things to do.

There was also the task of preparing the new boy, Smoky Summers, to work in the house, or to send him packing and find another young man to train as a stud.

It had been Cory, too, who had first told Elizabeth about hiring young men to work as whores. But men were proud animals and Elizabeth had learnt over the years that it was best not to *ask* a young man to become a whore. It was wiser to seduce him, to inveigle him into accepting the job, slowly tell him the advantages, sometimes even entrapping him.

Waiting for the appropriate moment to inform Smoky Summers why she had hired him, Elizabeth had assigned him to work in the downstairs parlor, helping the bartender, Rob Johnson, before Rob presumably left for Oregon.

Tugging on the rope for Mo to hurry with the morning tray, Elizabeth wondered if she was wasting her time by trying to make a prostitute out of the Southern boy. Smoky Summers was young, devilishly handsome, endowed like a stallion. She had seen, too, that he knew how to use that big prick of his.

Elizabeth had noticed, however, that Smoky was not as thick-headed, as dumb as his southern accent and easy-going manner led one to believe. It was obvious that he had been raised to say 'please' and 'thank you' and, with that kind of good background, she guessed he would have a very sensitive conscience. He would probably make love to customers happily for a few weeks and then become suddenly guilty that he was a whore. Such behaviour would be bad for an investment of time and money. Studs were supposed to screw, not think.

Another fact against Smoky was his color. Elizabeth wondered if it was too soon for White women to accept Negroes as lovers? Had too little time elapsed since Black people had been emancipated from slavery? Hmmm. She would see.

* * *

Three days had passed since Smoky Summers had been hired to work on Pleasant Street. He had brought his paste-board suitcase of clothes from his uncle's apartment on Jackson Street and, for the past three nights, had been sleeping on a narrow metal cot over the stables. Rising at six o'clock in the morning, he washed, dressed, and crossed the flagged garden to the kitchen where he ate breakfast with the apple-cheeked cook, Emma Goodhew, two Irish cleaning women, Mo the parlor maid, and the big, sandy-haired bartender, Rob Johnson.

Smoky had met all the prostitutes in the past three days but never saw them at breakfast. Petal had avoided him after their first meeting in the parlor. Smoky never saw her out of the company of the prostitute, Alicia Fargo, a tall Black woman who reminded him of the drawings of primitive African sculpture which his grandmother had shown him in books.

In the house were five other prostitutes: Ava Wells, a full-busted White woman with copper colored hair; Chickie Ling, a little Chinese girl with delicate features; Lillian Benoit, an energetic girl who claimed to be French and said she did the best *soixante-neuf* in town to prove it; Dorothy Carlson, a freckle-faced blonde who laughed a lot when she was in the kitchen but spent most of the day reading romances in her room.

Smoky had seen very little of Rob Johnson in the past

three days. He had learnt that Rob was two years older than himself and had come south to San Francisco from Seattle on a logging boat. Rob was not overly friendly to the other people working in the house, keeping to himself, reading the *Police Gazette* or disappearing upstairs at various moments throughout the day and early evening. Smoky wondered what the big, quiet lumberjack did on those brief visits to the upper floors? Did he go and take a nap? Or was he meeting one of the girls in her bedroom?

Smoky decided to broach the subject of Rob's departure for Oregon, to find out when the job of bartender would be free.

Finishing his last cup of coffee at the kitchen's pine table, he thanked Mrs Goodhew for the breakfast of fried ham, eggs, and hashed brown potatoes, complimenting her that only his grandmother could have made such a tasty meal. He left the kitchen to follow Rob Johnson into the main parlor.

Smoky's first job of the day was to collect empty bottles from around the house, putting them into a gunny sack while Rob made an inventory of spirits.

Dropping an empty rye bottle into the bag, Smoky called across the mahogany panelled parlor, 'Started your packing yet?'

Rob stood with his back to Smoky, facing a line of glass shelves with a small black notebook in one hand.

'Packing for what?' Rob's voice was full, rich, coming from deep within his broad chest.

'Oregon.'

Rob licked the tip of a stubby lead pencil. 'Oregon? Why you say that?'

Picking up two Golden Dane beer bottles from the closed top of the shiny black Bechstein grand piano, Smoky tried to sound casual. 'I was told you were leaving any day now for Oregon!'

Rob jotted in his notebook. 'Who'd tell you a thing like that?'

'Lady Elizabeth.' Smoky dropped a beer bottle into the sack.

'Did she?' Rob's voice remained calm as he raised his pale blue eyes to the bottles of berry liqueurs lining the top shelf. 'What exactly did she tell you?'

Dropping the second bottle into the bag with a clank, Smoky called, 'She said I'd be getting your job when you took off for up north!'

'What else she say?'

'What else?'

'Yeah. For instance, did Petal promise you something, too?'

Smoky looked over his shoulder at Rob, knowing that the big lumberjack was not as dumb as he was pretending to be. The false pose irritated Smoky and he demanded, 'What could Petal promise me?'

Rob continued jotting notes. 'Oh, promises get mighty generous when a man and a woman are alone together in a room.'

Smoky turned and stood looking at Rob's back. 'What you know about me and Petal being alone in some room?'

Rob closed his black book and faced Smoky. Both men were tall, wide-shouldered, strongly muscled. Rob had a milky complexion with a tangle of soft brown hair; Smoky's dark hair was cut short to his cinnamon-brown skin.

Resting his weight on one boot, Rob began, 'Kid, the last boy who asked me when I was leaving for Oregon was German. He claimed that the boss lady had promised him my job. Do you believe a guy would say such a thing? But before him I heard the same story from an Italian guy. And before him, from a Swede kid. They each swore up and down that the boss lady had promised them they could take over my job as soon as I left for Oregon. But do you know what else, kid?'

'What?' Smoky knew when somebody was pulling his leg, leading him on.

Rob's blue eyes twinkled. 'The boss lady, she never hires nobody to take over my job. No. Any guy who gets hired here is hired to do the same thing upstairs as those –' Rob raised his eyes. ' – as those party gals do in bed.'

Smoky surprised Rob, knocking him back against the glass shelves.

Falling to the floor in a clatter of bottles, Rob fended off Smoky's driving blow, clipping him on the jaw with his right fist.

Smoky stayed on top of Rob, jabbing his right hand towards his face, his left hand clutching for his throat.

Rob jolted his stomach, bucking Smoky to the floor, and raised his right foot, kicking to drive the boot between Smoky's legs.

A voice shrilled behind them. 'Stop it!'

Ignoring the voice, Smoky grabbed the sole of Rob's boot, twisting his foot, turning him over onto his stomach.

A china vase crashed to the floor. 'I said stop . . . it . . . right . . . *now!*'

* * *

'What's the meaning of this?' Elizabeth stood in the archway, her grey-streaked hair hanging loose to the shoulders of her dressing gown. Gripping the robe tightly to her throat, she looked from Smoky to Rob sprawled on the floor. 'I will not have brawling in my house! Do you hear me? I will not tolerate this kind of behavior under my roof!'

'Oh, yeah?' Smoky wiped a rivulet of blood from the corner of his mouth. 'Well, he said you hired me to be some kind of whore!'

Turning on Rob, Elizabeth's eyes became large, dark, flashing with anger. 'Did you say that?'

Gulping to catch his breath, Rob nodded, 'Sure I did. Because I'm getting tired of these guys always hounding me about when I'm leaving –'

'Enough!' She interrupted. 'I'll deal with you later, Rob Johnson.'

'Yes, mam.'

'And don't forget. June Myles has an appointment to see you at eleven, mister!'

'No, mam.'

Smoky, stepping forward, grabbed her forearm. 'So you *don't* deny you hired me to be some whore!'

Shaking off his hand, Elizabeth pulled back from him, shrieking, 'How dare you touch me! How dare you speak to me in that tone of voice!'

Smoky thumbed his chest. 'I'm not working in any cathouse like some party gal!'

'But you don't mind if some "gal" works here!'

Smoky sniffed. 'That's different.'

Elizabeth glared up into his square face. 'And what's different about it, mister?'

'Men expect to find gals in a cathouse.'

Jabbing a forefinger at his chest, she ordered, 'Well, you listen to me and you listen good, mister. First of all, I didn't ask you to come here. You came knocking on my front door. Out of your own free will. Remember? Secondly, as soon as I turned my back on you, you didn't wait one minute before you pulled out that big fat dick of yours and started wagging it in front of Petal.'

'How do you know that? Petal tell you that?'

'Petal didn't have to tell me anything! I saw you!' Elizabeth's accent had become broad, flat, totally American in its twang.

'Saw me? How could you see me? You'd left the room.'

'For somebody who thinks he's so smart, Mr Summers, you're very, very stupid. But then I suppose that comes from being so greedy. So selfish. So concerned about your . . . your . . . valuable manhood!'

'Say what you want about me, lady, but I don't want to be some whore!'

'No, but you're ready and willing to get a free poke at

one of my girls as soon as my back's turned, aren't you? You don't even bother to lay her down on the sofa or floor. Some gentleman you are!'

'She tell you that? Petal tell you all that, lady?'

'Petal told me nothing. I watched you from the next room.'

'You some kind of Peeping Tom or something?'

'Yeah!' Elizabeth gave a quick nod of her head. 'So what if I am?'

Smoky's upper lip curled with disapproval. 'You're disgusting.'

'And you're not?' Elizabeth stepped closer to him, looking up into his angry face, beginning in a lighter voice, 'Stop fooling yourself, kid. You're nice looking but you're no god. You're sweet but what's that going to buy you? You're also having a hard time finding a job. Don't forget, I know San Francisco. I know what it's like for newcomers here. Especially Black people. The gold rush is over, kid. It's been over for almost a half century. The jobs here go to Chinamen. And emigrants from Europe. That leaves you at the end of the employment line, doesn't it? So take it from me. If you're suffering the hardship of being Black, why not profit from a few of your assets? Why not use that big black pecker of yours to make a few extra bucks?'

Smoky's voice was thin, full of anger. 'Lady, now you let *me* tell *you* something. Maybe you peeked on me. Maybe you saw how I'm built. That's your business. This is your house. But let me tell you this.

'I'm not built big 'cause I'm Black. Understand? Black people aren't freaks. Understand? I got big hands, too. See these.' He held up one fist, opening and closing his fingers.

Nodding at Rob Johnson, he said, 'But then so does he have big hands and is he Black? No. And I also got big feet. Big size twelve feet!'

He held up one foot, twisting the lace-up brown boots his grandfather had given him as a going-away present from home. 'So don't you go around saying Niggers got big peckers just because they're Black. Niggers don't like that. You savvy, lady?'

Elizabeth glared up at him. 'Well, whatever the reason, you're hung, kid, you're still having a difficult time finding work, right?'

'Maybe, yes. Maybe no. But I won't be a whore in some whorehouse. Not for you. Not for nobody. I'd rather starve first.'

Elizabeth lowered her voice. 'Listen, why don't you take a walk and cool down. I'm offering you more than three hundred and fifty dollars per week. Think about it.'

Nodding, she turned and strode from the parlor.

Behind her, Smoky thundered, 'I said I won't be a whore!'

He looked to his right. Rob Johnson had disappeared from the room.

He shouted louder, *'I won't be a whore!'*

* * *

The morning rain slackened, the San Francisco sky lightening towards the west of Nob Hill and the adjoining peak, Russian Hill, a blue smear blurring through the dull overcast cloud of pewter grey. Alicia Fargo turned from the window in Petal's bedroom, a smile on her face, pleased not so much with the break in the morning downpour as with the sight of the young Black man slouching down Pleasant Street with a suitcase in one hand.

Crossing to the bed placed against the wall, Alicia pulled down the top sheet and brushed her lips against Petal's forehead, awakening her softly. 'Morning, baby.'

Petal, stretching, groaning pleasurably, emerged from a dream she was having about Smoky Summers making love to her, a dream in which he was covering her shoulders and breasts with kisses as he lay astride her, driving his salami-sized pecker between her legs, a feeling which seemed like a burning rod in her groin. Surfacing farther from her deep sleep, she blinked at Alicia's face bending over her, surprised that it was Alicia, not Smoky, greeting her for the day.

Folding her arms across the front of her orange-and-blue silk kimono, Alicia sat down on the edge of the bed, arching a thin eyebrow as she announced, 'He's gone.'

'Gone?' Petal raised herself from the mattress on one elbow. 'Who's gone?'

'The kid. The buck the old lady wanted to turn into the new stud around here. I just saw him go down the street with his suitcase.' Nodding toward the window, Alicia added, 'The old lady must have given him his walking papers.'

Petal rose higher in bed. 'Smoky's gone?'

'Smoky? That his name?' Alicia shrugged, her morning face looking older, harder than it did with cosmetics.

Sufficiently awake to suspect that Alicia might be testing her, trying to learn about any friendship she might have developed with Smoky in the past three days, Petal slumped back onto the mattress and curled into a ball. 'So what else is new?' she asked drowsily.

Alicia leaned over Petal nestled in the pillows. Stroking the hair from her forehead, she whispered, 'I love you, baby.'

Petal still felt the presence of Smoky's penis pressing between her legs, the dream which she so hoped to make a reality.

Alicia stroked Petal's high cheekbones. 'I love you more and more each day, sugar, and I'm going to get us out of here. You wait and see. I'm going to take us back home. Back to Georgia. I've got us a lot of money saved, honey.'

Petal kissed Alicia's hand. 'I love you too.' She knew that Alicia wanted them to leave San Francisco, to go back to Savannah and buy a small home, to live together as man and wife. The idea had also once appealed to Petal. But was it wrong to think about a future with a man? Smoky had made the idea clearer in her head – she *did* like being with men.

Reaching under the blanket, Alicia added in a stronger voice, 'I'm also horny as hell this morning, baby. I had that Finnegan cop for two hours last night. He kept pulling his dick while I had to make wisecracks about the dinky size of his meat.' Shuddering at the memory, she groaned, 'Oh, I do need to forget about Finnegan.'

The love affair between Alicia and Petal helped them both eradicate bad memories of work. But this morning Petal's only memory was of the dream of Smoky making love to her and, hungry for some release of her own sexual appetites, she groaned encouragingly as Alicia's hand moved under the sheet toward her breasts.

Squeezing Petal's bud into erectness, Alicia ran her fingers down the flatness of her stomach, towards the patch of wiry black hair curled into the delta between Petal's slim legs.

Petal slid back the covers, making room for Alicia to climb alongside her, pushing her midsection closer towards Alicia's hand.

Untying her kimono, Alicia knelt on the edge of the bed, letting the finger of her right hand drop to her own femininity. Pausing to admire Petal's writhing body, she whispered, 'Look at my little girl. Ripe and ready for picking. Ummm-uh.'

Petal knew what Alicia craved in the morning, especially after a night when she had had to be domineering and abusive with a customer.

Watching Alicia finger herself, Petal pushed harder against her, closing her eyes, imagining she was rubbing against Smoky, trying to move herself around the big, fleshy penis dangling between Smoky's muscled brown legs.

'That's a pussy,' praised Alicia, watching Petal work her midsection on her knee. 'Show Mama what you want. Show Mama what you need. That's a pussy.'

Petal rolled back on her buttocks, pumping her midsection in the air, squeezing, working, projecting her vaginal lips as she rested the flats of both feet on the mattress, pretending she was showing herself to Smoky.

Falling between Petal's thighs, Alicia knelt on the mattress, lowering her mouth to Petal's patch, her tongue darting in and out, the working vagina muffling her words.

'Who says I don't take care of my pretty baby girl . . . Who says I don't give you . . . what you need, baby . . . show me what you need . . .'

Alicia's words slowed as, more excitedly, she tongued Petal's thatch, saliva beading and stringing across Petal's wiry pubic hair, love juices soon spreading to Alicia's sucking lips, Alicia's fingers also working to satisfy her own hunger.

As waves of excitement coursed through Petal's body, she lifted herself higher from the mattress, straddling Alicia's knee as Alicia rose above her, lowering her mouth to one breast, then the other breast, squeezing both of Petal's erect nipples.

Petal still imagined Smoky was making love to her. She told herself that Alicia's knee was really the crown of Smoky's phallus. Her vagina was opening wider, ready, wanting only a man to make love to her. Smoky . . . Smoky . . . she kept seeing his penis in her brain . . . working into her – 'Screw my little pussy! Screw it!'

Alicia knelt satisfied above her.

* * *

Rob Johnson stood on a straight-back chair in the middle of a back bedroom. He wore nothing but a pair of black leather logging boots laced around his calves. The window shade was pulled against the morning light as the woman, June Myles, knelt unclothed on the floor in front of the chair kissing the toe of one boot, moving her mouth to the other boot as she stole a glance up Rob's naked legs, watching the full head of his penis poking through the skin forming its sheath.

Standing like a rugged, tousled-haired statue above her, Rob's mind drifted back to Smoky Summers, reflecting that he had been too embarrassed to admit to Smoky that he also worked as a whore, that he made extra money in the bordello by meeting love-starved ladies and letting them enjoy sexual fantasies with him.

It took more than a body to be a good prostitute. Rob had learnt that it often took a special kind of mind to give a woman what she wanted, a release of hidden thoughts as well as physical needs. Rob had found that a woman's desires ranged from a need to be loved and cherished, to a hunger for masculine domination. Rob had a theory why most women belonged to the latter category: they were disappointed with their husband's or boyfriend's lack of masculinity.

The touch of a hand on his thigh made him lower his eyes.

Pulling back his foot, he put the sole of the logging boot on June Myles's face, pushing her down to the floor, not hurting her, merely forcing her away from him, making her feel rejected, unwanted, unworthy of him.

The woman, beginning to crawl back for Rob, held her eyes on the boots, opening her mouth to begin kissing them again, to clean them with her tongue, to make love to the boots.

Watching her crawl closer to the chair, Rob began toying with his penis, slicking back its skin, letting it grow fatter over the bulk of his scrotum. His other hand rubbed the pectoral muscles of his hirsute chest, moving over his stomach as if he were soaping himself in a shower bath, rubbing the protruding cheek of one buttock, then the other, under his crotch, teasing June Myles with the sight of his body, but never letting her reach higher than the top of his black leather logging boots, keeping her a worshipper.

Chapter Three

THE BIJOU THEATER

On leaving Pleasant Street with his few possessions packed into his pasteboard suitcase, Smoky Summers turned right onto Taylor Street and walked slowly down the steep incline of cobblestones glistening from the morning rain.

Head bent forward, jacket slung over his shoulder, Smoky reached the bottom of Taylor Street and turned again onto Geary Street. He passed small grocery shops opened for the day, bushel baskets of fruit and vegetables pulled onto the boardwalk after the morning rain. He continued towards the green patch of Union Square at the end of the street.

Halfway down Geary Street, he paused under the awning of the Bijou Theater and glanced at the brightly painted billboards. 'Girls! Minstrels! Laughs!' – 'Madam Clara and her Dancing Bears' – 'The Amazing Wan Tong' – 'The Mississippi Belles and Beaux!'

Digging into his pocket, Smoky stepped towards the glass-fronted booth and bought a ticket for the day's first show. Moving towards the gilt and red lobby, he handed the ticket to the man at the door.

There was a climb of three flights of stairs to the top balcony. Smoky pushed through a pair of curtains and paused inside to adjust his eyes to the darkness, gradually making out only three or four people dotted around the balcony. Looking down beyond the railing, he saw gas footlights surrounding the stage far below him, a performer in a bright green suit.

The entertainer was the comedian, Sid Steen. He appeared on the bill before the 'Mississippi Belles and Beaux', the minstrel act in which Smoky's uncle – Jay Greene – was the lead dancer. Smoky had seen the Bijou's show more than a dozen times since he had come to San Francisco.

He moved down the aisle in the darkness and slumped onto a seat in the front row, setting his jacket and suitcase on the empty seat alongside him.

As Smoky sat staring blankly down at the stage, half-listening to Sid Steen bark his jokes to the roll of kettle drums and the clash of cymbals, his mind filled with questions.

What was happening? Was he doing the right thing by coming here to the theater? Spending the little money he had? He had to talk to Uncle Jay but the watchman at the stage door had stopped allowing him into the dressing room which Uncle Jay shared with fourteen other people. Besides, Smoky enjoyed watching the show. It was one of the few things he enjoyed in San Francisco.

This city of four hundred thousand people seemed busier, more crowded than New Orleans, and its inhabitants less friendly. San Francisco was a beautiful city, surrounded by water and low-lying hills, but Smoky had not felt happy since he had arrived.

Staring down at the stage lights, he thought about Lady Elizabeth's house on Pleasant Street. He remembered the fight he had had only a few hours ago with Rob Johnson, the invitation Lady Elizabeth had given him to work for her.

A whore. The idea revolted him. Angered and humiliated by the offer, he wondered what kind of men took money for making love to women.

In the past three days since moving onto Pleasant Street, he had thought that Lady Elizabeth was a refined and polite female. She had been generous with him, giving him a place to sleep, a chair at her table, three meals a day.

Ha! Now he understood the true reason for her generosity. She had been lying to him all along! She had never intended to hire him as a bartender at all. She had set a trap for him and he had walked straight into it. Since she had first peeked at him making love to Petal, she had only been interested in the size of his prick and how well he could use it.

Smoky knew he was built bigger than most men. But he became angry when he heard people say that the reason was because he was Black.

White people had strange ideas about Black people and sex. White people thought that all Black men were endowed like horses, that all Black women were blazing furnaces of love.

Smoky had gone swimming naked with enough Black friends to know the rumors about Negroes were not true. Smoky's friends kidded him about the size of his penis, saying that they wished they were hung as heavy as he was, wanting to do their part in spreading the 'Black Myth'. They had complained, too, that their wives or girlfriends were frigid in bed, cold as icebergs to them, not the blazing love furnaces which White men called Black women.

Black people laughed over the stories White people told about them, but they often suffered from them, too. White people wanted Blacks for nothing but sex. Not for work. Not for friends. Not to kneel alongside in Church and pray with. Not to go to school with. Not to laugh and be friends with. No. Only for sex.

Sitting in the darkness of the top balcony of the Bijou Theater, Smoky thought about being Black, about being descended from African slaves, about being hundreds of miles from the house where he had been raised. The only job he had been offered since arriving in California was what? Selling his body! Being a whore! Little better than a slave. But for three hundred and fifty dollars a week.

Smoky had never known his parents, but he knew that neither of them had been slaves. His mother and father had been born after Freedom Day; his grandparents, Gemma and Warren Rickers, had moved from Philadelphia to Louisiana the year after Freedom, 1866, coming to work the small farm in Longchamp Parish which they had inherited from the White family who had owned Smoky's great-grandfather, Longrow Rickers, before the Civil War.

Despite his comfortable, at times even pampered, boyhood, Smoky had been anxious to leave Longchamp Parish and make his way in the outside world. His grandparents had been stubborn about him not going to New Orleans. They kept making excuses why he could not go. When he reached his twenty-second birthday, he saw that his young days were coming to an end and he asked them one last time for their permission to go to the city. They finally consented, allowing him to find a temporary job in New Orleans before he settled down to farm life.

It had not been difficult for Smoky to find work in the city. He impressed people as being a happy-go-lucky young man and made many friends. He had moved from livery stables to vegetable wagons, doing one job after another, enjoying himself.

Smoky had met people his age who worked in the fine gaming houses and expensive bordellos of the French Quarter. He envied them their jobs of porters and waiters and bartenders, enabling them to mix with finely dressed people in swell surroundings. But when he had gone for jobs in the French Quarter, nobody hired him, always saying he was too young, too old, too friendly – always too something.

Having saved money from his odd jobs, Smoky had left New Orleans when the Yellow Fever epidemic had broken out in the French Quarter last summer. He had returned to Longchamp Parish and worked on his grandfather's farm, but he began to get restless again. After Christmas, he had asked his grandparents to let him go West, to visit his grandmother's brother – Uncle Jay – out in California. His grandparents had refused but, after he had helped with early planting, they finally relented. He left Longchamp Parish in March.

Travelling west on the Southern Pacific Railroad, Smoky had arrived in San Francisco almost a month ago. He had moved in with Uncle Jay and Uncle Jay's friend, Marc Bough, in their little apartment bordering Chinatown. He had immediately begun looking for work, any kind of work, as a dock hand, stevedore, janitor, garbage man, any job at any wage. But all the menial and odd jobs in San Francisco were going to Orientals. So deciding to try to get the kind of job he really wanted, he had purchased a guide-book to the city's bordellos – *The Gentleman's Guide to San Francisco's Pleasures* – and the first advertisement he saw was for Lady Elizabeth Raleigh's bordello on Pleasant Street.

A loud blast of trumpets broke Smoky's reminiscences. He looked down to the stage and saw two girls in bonnets changing large cards resting on an easel. The orchestra was breaking into a sprightly trot.

* * *

Leaning forward in his seat high above the stage, Smoky rested his chin on his crossed arms and watched Uncle Jay twirling a cane, high-kicking his way across the proscenium stage followed by a line of girls in white ruffled skirts, fluttering pink parasols.

Uncle Jay wore candy-striped trousers, an emerald satin jacket, white gloves, and had painted his face coal black. Sixty-four years old, Jay Greene danced better than men a third his age.

Watching his uncle tap his feet – clickety-clat, pitter pat, snap-snap – to a quick rhythm, Smoky recalled how proud his grandmother was that her younger brother had kept a job on showboats and in minstrel shows for the past forty-three years, a record even for White entertainers. Uncle Jay had always been a hero to Smoky, a man who had made a success of himself in the world away from a farm.

But, today, Smoky's despondent mood made him look at Uncle Jay in a new light. He thought of him not so much as a childhood hero but as another Black man overcoming obstacles made for him by White people.

Why did Uncle Jay paint his face? Wasn't his skin

already dark enough? Why did he redden his lips to look big? Why put on a spiky black wig?

Smoky knew that, yes, there was a demand for minstrel performers. White audiences loved minstrels and Jim Crows and Uncle Toms. But wasn't Uncle Jay exploiting his race by wearing a black face? Weren't minstrel shows one more form of yet another Black myth? Showing White people that Negroes were nothing but happy-go-lucky, big-lipped people who sang and danced and played banjos? Wasn't Uncle Jay making himself an object of mirth for White people? Wasn't darkening your face with cork the same as accepting a job for the size of your prick? Helping White people keep their narrow-minded beliefs that Black men were happy-go-lucky fools – or all hung like stallions?

The more that Smoky thought about the comparison between Uncle Jay's minstrel act in the Bijou Theater and the job which Lady Elizabeth had offered him on Pleasant Street, the more convinced he became about the similarity between minstrels and whores. Uncle Jay was making a living by dancing like a clown for White people. Why shouldn't Smoky do the same thing himself? Make a living because somebody wanted to sample his legendary Black pecker?

Grabbing his jacket and suitcase from the seat alongside him, Smoky climbed the sloping steps toward the curtain. He had made up his mind.

* * *

Smoky lay on a double bed, listening to the distant sound of laughter drifting upstairs from the main parlor, voices intermixed with the tinkle of piano music and the ring of crystal goblets. The only light in the back bedroom on the bordello's third floor came from a candle sitting on a bureau.

Naked except for a sheet pulled to his midsection, Smoky lay wondering if he had made the right decision about coming back to Pleasant Street. Alone in the small bedroom, waiting for his first customer, the decision to work as a prostitute seemed shameful, sinful, dirty, no longer comparable to the clean, harmless dancing which Uncle Jay did on a stage for an audience.

Thinking about Uncle Jay, Smoky wondered what his grandmother was doing at this hour. Supper would be over. Grandad was probably out milking the cows, giving a dish of cream to Butch and Tiger, the two yellow-striped barn cats. Grandma would be working by lamplight at the kitchen table, darning socks, mending Grandad's shirt or quilting some calico for the church ladies' bazaar, perhaps even writing a letter to Smoky and sending it to Uncle Jay's address.

Feeling guilty about waiting for a strange woman to pay him money to make love with her, Smoky looked around the shadowy room to distract his mind.

He caught his reflection in the mirror, his body greased to look shiny, darker than he was. His eyes moved quickly away from the mirror.

Hearing a creak in the hallway, he glanced at the door and, watching it open, he saw a White woman appear in the doorway, a slim woman with blonde hair, wearing a long, clinging burgundy dress.

Stepping into the dimly lit bedroom, she asked softly, 'May I come in?'

Remembering Lady Elizabeth's precise instructions about not being overly friendly with customers, Smoky kept one hand on the bed sheet covering his groin and moved his head to invite her into the room.

Closing the door behind her, the White woman kept her eyes on Smoky as she crossed the carpet.

Halfway between the bureau and bed, she glanced back toward the door, faltering, 'If my husband finds out I'm here with a nig . . .'

Smoky knew what she was going to say. 'Nigger'. He didn't care. He wanted to tell her that his grandparents would not be too pleased if they knew he was here with a

White woman, that his grandmother would probably give them both a piece of her sharp mind. Oh, why were White people always so worried about being caught in bed with Black people? Didn't White people think that Black people might not want to be with them? Did they think it was such an honor?

Stepping closer to the bed, the woman opened her mouth to speak but stopped as she studied Smoky's greased body.

Smoky thought about the seventy-five dollars she was paying for him to make love to her. He moved one hand down his chest, over the washboard muscles of his stomach, towards the sheet covering his crotch.

His penis was coming to life. The woman's attention must be exciting him. Or was it the fact that she was paying to be with him? Did that excite him? The money?

The White woman, spying the penis bobbing beneath the sheet, sank down on the bed alongside Smoky, her eyes on the shaft growing larger, more visible beneath the thin bed sheet.

Smoky gazed at her as he reached to begin unbuttoning her burgundy dress. Slipping his hand inside the bodice, he was surprised to find that she wore no corset or undergarment beneath the dress.

The woman closed her eyes, falling against Smoky, pressing her lips to his mouth.

Smoky froze at the action, surprised that a White woman would try to kiss him. But feeling her mouth press for a response, he turned his mouth towards hers, deciding to give her at least a little kiss, to brush his lips against hers.

The pressure of her lips gained force, and her tongue moved between his lips, plunging into his mouth.

Hesitantly, Smoky responded more firmly, his own tongue soon exploring her mouth as she opened her lips wider for him.

The woman, helping Smoky undress her, pressed her nakedness against his body, rubbing her groin against his crotch, pulling back the sheet to explore his masculinity.

Rolling her over onto her back, Smoky planted both knees on the mattress, spreading her legs as he decided to enjoy himself, to tease her with blunt jabs of his penis.

The woman, gripping Smoky around the neck, lay on her back and pumped more hungrily against him, lifting her furry patch towards him, whispering, 'I need you . . . I want you . . .'

Smoky continued teasing her, not entering her slit, only probing between her legs with the full head of his bobbing penis. He changed to the middle finger of his right hand, toying her moist vagina with his finger, alternating quickly back to his penis, to his finger, finally pressing his crown into her, but only doling out the first few inches of his greased hardness.

Feeling him thick and firm and persistent, the woman began kissing his face, chewing his chin, pumping her hips more wildly, begging, 'Talk to me . . . Please talk to me . . .'

Smoky knelt between her spread legs, deepening his plunges, working for a rhythm slickened by her excitement, not knowing what words to say to her.

'Please talk to me,' she pleaded. 'Call me . . . Barbara.'

Smoky answered by sinking a further two, three, four inches into her moisture, asking, 'Feel that . . . Barbara?'

The White woman, Barbara, lay on her back, legs spread, hands raised to smooth Smoky's muscle-capped shoulders, his bare chest, his strong biceps. 'You're beautiful . . . So beautiful . . . I don't deserve a man as beautiful, as handsome as you.'

Smoky stirred his penis, increasing the motion inside her walls, enjoying the sensation of his penis as much as her praise.

Tossing her head back and forth on the pillows, Barbara continued, 'You're so beautiful. And I'm nothing but a slut, aren't I? A cheap slut . . . Please say I'm nothing but a cheap White slut.'

Smoky paused. The request surprised him.

Tossing her head back and forth, she pleaded, 'Please say I'm a slut . . . Tell me. Please!'

'You're a . . . slut.'

'A cheap White slut,' she added. 'Your slut.'

Smoky felt his excitement growing. '*My* White slut. *My* cheap White slut.'

She thrust her midsection upwards with renewed heat. 'I'm a bitch, aren't I? Say so! Say I'm a . . . bitch.'

Smoky held her, his eyes on hers, driving deeper as he assured her, 'You're a bitch, Barbara. A real little White bitch.'

'I want to be *your* bitch.'

Smoky enjoyed her confession. Her request to be humiliated by him. He liked the feeling of dominating her, watching a White woman being so passive with him. Or was it any woman?

His voice steady, he said, 'You *are* my bitch, Barbara.'

'Thank you . . .'

Deepening his penis into the heat, he added, 'You like that big cock, don't you, Barbara?'

'I love it. And I love it being black . . . black and . . . so big.'

'You don't serve a Black cock, do you, bitch? Do you, you cheap White bitch?' Smoky's hips were driving more quickly, his buttocks squeezing as he dipped deeply between her spread thighs, feeling the sensation tingle his masculinity.

'No, I don't deserve a black cock. A black cock is too good for a White bitch like me.'

'Yeah, you're nothing but a dirty little White bitch, aren't you, Barbara?'

'Yes, I'm a bitch. But I'm *your* bitch. I'm yours to treat how you like. So punish me. Humiliate me. Hurt me for being such a cheap bitch.'

Smoky nodded, keeping his pace, becoming more excited as he listened to her requests. 'You need to be punished, Barbara.'

'Yes, I need to be punished. I want to be punished. I need to be hurt by you. Slapped by you. Dominated by you.'

Smoky, wrapping one hand around her waist, continued

dipping deeply into her slickened channel as he pulled back his other hand and slapped her face.

Gasping, Barbara's flesh broke into fine pinpoints of perspiration, and she began shaking with an orgasm.

Smoky slapped her again. He felt her squeeze for every inch of his working penis.

Looking down at her, he saw her staring at the mirror over the bureau, watching the candle reflecting his glistening Black body dominating her White softness.

Holding his eyes on the sight, he slapped her again, listening to her gasp, feeling her quiver from the abuse, enjoying the sensation himself.

His eyes on the mirror, he slapped her harder, and his enjoyment increased.

Chapter Four

A GOOD MAN

In the ten days since Smoky had been back on Pleasant Street, his first customer, Barbara Lowry, had returned four times to visit him and seven other females had begun requesting his services. Elizabeth saw that her hunch was paying off: word was obviously spreading around town about Smoky and there were enough women willing to pay for him, the color of his skin being no obstacle, perhaps even an incentive for a love-starved White woman.

As the days passed, Elizabeth began considering whether or not to assign Smoky to Judge Douglas's Thursday afternoon appointment. Rob Johnson usually performed for the Judge with the red-haired prostitute, Ava Wells. But Elizabeth was considering increasing the number of performers for Judge Douglas's pleasure.

In the past ten days, Elizabeth had witnessed Rob and Smoky patch up their differences and become friends. She saw them lolling together on the kitchen steps, basking in the warm April sun. This pleased her. She disliked enmity between employees.

During these bright days of April, Elizabeth began suspecting that Petal might be the spark of trouble.

Petal was smitten with Smoky. That much was obvious to Elizabeth. From questions Petal asked about Smoky. From the look in her eyes. It was clear she wanted to go to bed with Smoky.

It was also clear that Alicia was jealous.

Remembering how perfectly matched Smoky and Petal had looked making love in the upstairs parlor, Elizabeth could not resist the temptation to match them for Judge Douglas's Thursday appointment.

But would such a match only be fuelling Petal's crush on

Smoky? Worse, would it feed Alicia's jealousy over Petal?

Elizabeth considered what she should do. Judge Douglas was an important customer, not only spending a great deal of money on Pleasant Street but also a man who had a great influence in City Hall. On the other hand, however, Alicia was mean and vindictive, and Elizabeth did not underestimate her capabilities.

In the meantime, Elizabeth's main concerns during these quickly passing days were for Cory Roper. He had finally returned to San Francisco. But Elizabeth's worst fears had come true: Cory had been ambushed by thieves and shot on his way home from New Orleans.

Refusing to allow a doctor to examine him, Cory locked himself in Elizabeth's bedroom, insisting he only needed time to recover from his shoulder wound.

Exasperated by Cory's stubborness yet worried about his weak condition, Elizabeth decided to send word to Cory's daughter on Octavia Street, hoping that Caroline Roper could make her father see a doctor.

* * *

Smoky was pleased by his reconciliation with Rob. He did not enjoy quarrelling with people or bearing a grudge.

On Wednesday morning, Rob and Smoky lolled in the sunshine. Mrs Goodhew was washing the breakfast dishes in the kitchen as the two young men talked on the back stoop.

Boots crossed in front of him, Rob confessed, 'I was embarrassed to admit to you that I have a few customers myself. It's not easy for a guy to say he goes to bed with a lady for money.'

Smoky had recovered from his surprise. 'I used to see you disappearing upstairs now and then. I thought you were going to take a nap. Or maybe meeting one of the gals.'

'I started going upstairs with a woman for money a few years back.'

'Do you do it only for the money?' Smoky enjoyed his honest, straightforward visits with Rob.

Rob held his forearms folded across his chest. 'Some guys go fishing. Others go hunting. Me, I like the ladies. Everyone's different. Everyone's a whole new surprise to me.' He grinned, adding, 'And I like giving them a surprise now and then, too.'

The image of Barbara Lowry popped into Smoky's mind. He remembered how she had surprised him at first, by asking him to abuse her verbally, then to slap her. On her last visit to Pleasant Street, Smoky had put her across his knee and spanked her until her buttocks were bright red. When he had finished, she had fallen to the floor, taking his penis deep in her throat, sucking him until he gave her his explosion.

Considering Rob's remark about every woman being different, Smoky also thought of the peculiarities of the other women who had visited him in the past days. A Spanish beauty from La Jolla had asked him to pretend to be her husband as they were making love. Another woman enjoyed nothing but anal intercourse. A third woman wanted to suck Smoky's testicles, reaching her own orgasm as he masturbated onto her face, rubbing his seed into her face like some warm, thick lotion.

Smoky, stretched out beside Rob on the kitchen stoop, asked, 'Why do you think we get so many different requests? Why do so many women want to pay for so many strange things?'

'Because they can't get it at home.'

'Are you saying that if a gal wants her husband to bung her up the arse, he might refuse her? Say no to his own wife?'

'Absolutely, kid. Men can be more prudish than women. Also men get hooked on doing one thing in bed and never give their wife any variation. Love-making doesn't have to grow stale. People let it. And nine times out of ten, it's the man.'

Smoky's main concern at the moment was himself, his

guilt at being a prostitute. He asked, 'What would you say, Rob, is the worst thing about being in this business? For a man?'

Rob shrugged. 'Not being able to save money. The money seems good enough at first. But look at me. I thought I was going to be out of this game two years ago. I'm still here. No better off.'

'But folks still think you're a bartender. You're respectable. Me, I'm a whore. There's no getting round that fact.'

'A man can't worry about what other people think, Smoky. It's your life. Just worry about yourself.'

'But I feel like I'm leading a secret life here and that makes me feel kind of guilty.'

'Then quit. Because guilt will start eating away at you and you'll begin losing your self respect. That's a man's most important possession in the world. Even more important than his nuts. Self-respect.'

Smoky nodded. He knew he couldn't be a prostitute for too long. That fact was already clear to him. But what would he do? Where did he go from here?

* * *

Cora Prendergast, a middle-aged woman with alabaster skin and marcelled brown hair, lay on the divan in one of the bordello's front bedrooms, wearing a satin peach-colored robe which stretched against her plump figure.

Smoky opened the door, remembering what Elizabeth had told him to say when he presumably disturbed Mrs Prendergast in the bedroom.

'Oh, excuse me, mam. I didn't know someone was –'

He stopped, staring at the plain, chubby-faced woman lounging on the divan. Both of her ankles were exposed through the bottom of the peach robe, a satin slipper dangling from one little foot.

She demanded, 'Who are you, young man?'

Smoky's voice was polite. 'I was sent to fix the plumbing down the hall, mam. I thought this was the room. But I see I made a mistake.'

He looked at her more closely, adding, 'Excuse me for saying so, mam, but you're the most beautiful woman I've ever seen.'

She lifted her chin. 'Thank you.'

Smoky could not think of much more to say to the woman, only remembering Elizabeth telling him that she wanted to be praised.

'Yes, indeed. You are a very beautiful lady.'

Rubbing her hands over her thigh, she said, 'Thank you, young man, but I have to ask you to leave. I *am* a lady!'

'Yes, mam. Of course, mam.'

She demurred. 'But a compliment's always nice to hear.'

'Oh, I mean it!'

'My husband thinks I'm beautiful, too.'

'Your husband's a very lucky man.'

'Do you think so?' Her little brown eyes brightened.

Smoky nodded his head, hoping he was being a good actor. 'Yes, mam. Your husband's a very lucky man indeed to have such a beautiful wife as you to come home to.'

'Why, you're very polite. I suppose it won't hurt if you look at me here. Just a little bit longer.'

'Thank you, mam. I *am* honored, mam.' Smoky elaborated. 'A man doesn't get the chance to see many beautiful things in this world.'

She smirked, preening herself.

Watching her, Smoky felt for his cock.

'Please!' She sat forward on the divan. 'Please don't do anything . . . *rude*!'

Smoky lied, 'But you excite me!'

'I don't care,' she said petulantly. 'I won't have you doing anything rude. I told you you could look. But that's all. Don't take advantage of my hospitality.'

'I'm sorry, mam.'

She sniffed. 'I can't stand rudeness.'

'Can I tell you something, mam?'

She looked at him suspiciously. 'Is it rude?'

Smoky shook his head. 'No. Not really. Not how I mean it.'

She considered. 'Well, perhaps. If it's . . . sincere.'

Stepping closer, he lowered his voice. 'Mam, I'm going to think about you tonight.'

'Think about me? Tonight?'

Hoping he was not going too far to please her, Smoky nodded, saying, 'When I make love to my wife tonight, I'm going to think about you, to imagine that she's you.'

The woman gaped at him, genuine surprise in her eyes. She began, 'Why . . . why . . . why that's . . . that's . . . that's the nicest thing anybody's ever said to me!'

Blushing, lowering her eyes, she waved her hand at him, saying, 'You can go. Go away, you big rascal. Go on now.'

Smoky gently closed the door, smiling to himself at the woman's pleasure. Elizabeth had told him that Mrs Prendergast's husband had left her and run off with a younger woman two years ago. Mrs Prendergast visited the bordello every two weeks. She wanted nothing except for a young man to tell her that she was beautiful. Smoky felt that the good deed was hardly worth the seventy-five dollars she paid.

Chapter Five

SILVER BRACELETS

'Alicia, I want you to run an errand for me.' It was Thursday morning. Judge Douglas was arriving this afternoon and Elizabeth wanted Alicia out of the house when she mated Petal with Smoky for the occasion.

Sitting at a kidney-shaped writing desk in the upstairs parlor, Elizabeth held a white envelope in one hand, saying, 'I want you to take my carriage, Alicia, and deliver this note to Pacific Heights. The address is written on the front.'

'Yes, mam.' Alicia's nostrils dilated with fury, suspecting that Elizabeth was up to another scheme. But what?

'Alicia, you can have the rest of the afternoon and evening off. Go shopping. Have some supper. There's little reason for you to rush back to the house.'

Why was Elizabeth being so generous with her? Did it have to do with Petal? Alicia remembered that it had been in this very room that Petal had helped in Smoky's first interview.

Looking Elizabeth in the eye, Alicia said, 'Thank you, mam, but I will deliver your note and come straight back to Pleasant Street.'

'You stay cooped up in the house far too much, Alicia. It's time you took a break. Get out and mix with people.'

'I have appointments here, mam.'

'Who? Dan Charles?' Elizabeth shook her head. 'Mr Charles cancelled his seven o'clock engagement, Alicia. There's no reason for you to come back to the house.'

Alicia saw that it was futile to argue. 'Yes, mam.' She stepped forward to take the white envelope.

Holding the envelope towards her, Elizabeth asked, 'Alicia, are you happy?'

Alicia, tucking the envelope into a pocket, repeated, 'Happy, mam?'

'You seem rather tense and nervous lately. Have you had your check-up with Dr Coleridge?'

'Last week, mam. Don't you remember?'

'Of, yes. Of course.'

Elizabeth carefully weighed her next question. 'And things are fine between you and Petal?'

Alicia knew that Elizabeth had little concern about her and Petal's love affair except that it kept them from becoming involved with a client, from running off with someone, or moving to another house.

She answered, 'I'm fine as can be expected, mam.'

'I'm glad to hear that, Alicia.' Elizabeth added, 'You seem like a sensible woman.'

Alicia lowered her eyes to the cameo brooch pinned to Elizabeth's high-necked blouse. 'Why, what a lovely brooch, mam. But, then, you always wear such lovely brooches on your blouses, don't you? And scarves.'

Elizabeth's hand went quickly to her neck. 'Why . . . thank you, Alicia.'

Alicia smiled. 'I notice small things.'

Elizabeth rose abruptly from her chair. 'Fine, you can go now, Alicia.'

'Thank you, mam.'

Turning, Alicia walked quickly to the door, knowing that the time would come soon for a showdown between her and the fine so-called 'Lady Elizabeth Raleigh.'

* * *

Cory Roper lay in Elizabeth's tester bed, his eyelids heavy, his skin pale from loss of blood from his shoulder wound. Despite his fatigue, he saw Elizabeth was disturbed when she returned to the bedroom from the small parlor.

'What's the matter, Lizzie?' he asked in a weak voice.

Storming across the room, the heels of her button boots stamping quickly on the carpet, she fumed, 'Oh, that Black bitch is going to make trouble for me! I know it!'

'Who?'

'Alicia.'

'What can she do?'

Elizabeth stopped in front of the mirror, tucking a strand of hair back into the coiffure knotted on top of her head. 'I don't know yet but I can see it in her eyes. I can tell it from her voice.'

'What can she possibly do?'

'The worst wouldn't be bad enough for someone like her. She's a viper. I've got to get rid of her.'

'Does she know about –' Cory reached the tip of his fingers to his throat.

Elizabeth fingered the cameo brooch pinned to her blouse. She remembered Alicia's comment about the piece of jewellery, her remark that she always wore something pretty pinned to her neck.

As if thinking aloud, Elizabeth asked, 'How could she know?'

Turning to the tester bed, she added, 'I think she's worried about Smoky becoming too friendly with Petal. That's what I think.'

'What's he like, this new boy?'

Elizabeth crossed to the bed and began fluffing pillows for Cory. 'Oh, big. Broad-shouldered. Not too young. Not too old. A good kid.'

Slipping a fresh pillow under his head, she said more lightly, 'And he's got one of the biggest peckers I've ever seen.'

'You've sampled it?'

Elizabeth looked down at him with surprise. 'Why, you're jealous, Cory Roper!'

His voice sharpened, 'Have you?'

'No. But I watched him perform. But would it matter if I had tried it?' Her dark eyes twinkled. Jealousy was flattering to a woman.

'How could I object?' Cory asked, 'Love-making's your business.'

'You know perfectly well, Cory Roper, that I don't go to bed with anyone except you. Not any more.'

Leaning forward, she kissed his damp forehead. 'And talking about jealousy, sir, perhaps you will continue telling me about that woman who took *you* into *her* cabin.'

'Black Bess?' Cory laughed for the first time in the five days since he had returned to San Francisco. 'I pity the poor man who has to make love to that old harridan.'

Cory had told Elizabeth about the ranch where he had taken refuge after his gunshot wound. Ambushed by thieves outside Fort Worth, on the road called the Texas Cat Track, Cory had managed to fire a shot with his boot pistol as the robbers had been galloping away. Retrieving a saddlebag of bonds they had dropped, he took refuge in a nearby ranch. He did not learn until he was inside the small cabin that the ranch was the headquarters for a gang of hoodlums. The leader was an old Negress named Black Bess who put the bonds under her bed and kept Cory locked in her cabin. Waiting until she had fallen asleep, Cory had managed to escape, but he had had to leave the railroad bonds under her corncob mattress.

Elizabeth sat on a chair beside him, asking, 'Promise me you won't go back for those bonds.'

Cory squeezed her hand. 'Those railroad bonds are as good as money, Lizzie. They're better than stock certificates. With my name on only thirty-five per cent of them, I own the most and have the control of the entire Natchez-Pacific Line.'

'But the old witch will know by now that you have to endorse them to make them valuable. So if you go back, she'll make you sign them and kill you before the ink's dry. Oh, Cory, leave them there. Your life's more valuable.'

Cory closed his eyes. 'Those bonds were meant to provide for my daughter's security.'

Laying her head down on the bed alongside him,

Elizabeth said, 'I know you want to make certain that Caroline's provided for. But I don't want you pressing your luck with that dreadful old woman. You escaped her clutches once. The next time you might not be so lucky.'

'I can't send anyone else to get them. Not a Texas Ranger or Sheriff. The whole affair could be reported and that could jeopardize any great profit. These bonds are only worth a great fortune if they make a surprise monopoly at next month's board meeting.'

Elizabeth said excitedly, 'I have an idea! Hire Pinkerton's to go and get back the bonds. Their detectives go anywhere! Do anything.'

Cory shook his head. 'The Railroad Board has Pinkerton's trying to learn who bought the bonds. All my carefully laid plans could be ruined.'

Elizabeth saw that the situation was futile. She also saw Cory's eyes dulling with fatigue.

Rising from her chair, she said, 'You're tired. Get some rest. We can talk about this later.'

He clung to her hand. 'I love you, Lizzie.'

She squeezed his fingers, 'I love you too, darling.'

Tucking the sheet round him, Elizabeth crossed to the window, pulling the curtains shut to darken the room. Thinking of the note she had sent Alicia to deliver to Cory's daughter on Octavia Street, she hoped that Caroline would respond to her request to come here and make her father see a doctor. But Caroline Roper was a haughty, selfish little bitch. Elizabeth would not be surprised if she refused to set foot in the house to see her father. The only thing that might get Caroline Roper here was if she knew that her railroad stocks were in jeopardy.

* * *

Alicia sat on the buttoned black-leather seat of Elizabeth's brougham, listening to the clip-clop of the two horses moving at a neat pace through the traffic of other carriages, clanging streetcars, the few chugging motor cars beginning to appear in recent years in San Francisco.

Having left the envelope at the bow-fronted house on Octavia Street, Alicia thought of her own plans as she sat in the back of the carriage, wondering how she was to achieve peace of mind for herself. The jealousy over Petal had unsettled her.

Petal was love-sick over Smoky. Alicia's nerves tightened whenever she remembered the way Petal looked when Smoky was near her. She was acting like a young girl having a first crush.

Alicia reminded herself that Petal was little older than a schoolgirl. She could easily be swept off her feet. Prostitution to her was like some naughty game.

Alicia also reminded herself that Smoky Summers was probably the sort of boy whom Petal would have married had she stayed in Georgia. Smoky was a good-looking Southern boy, a fine catch for a simple farm girl.

Gripping the hand strap as the brougham tossed down Pacific Street, Alicia wondered what she would do without Petal. It was impossible to imagine life without her. What would happen to all their hopes and plans to get out of San Francisco? To buy a house? Have a little nest like a married couple?

Telling herself that Petal was too young to make her own decision, Alicia knew she was the one who had to decide what was best for them.

The carriage stopped in Van Ness Avenue, a bustling business district. Alicia opened the door, instructed the driver to wait for her, and crossed the boardwalk to a red brick building marked 'Police'.

Entering through the double glass doors, she approached a tall walnut desk, announcing to the uniformed officer, 'I'd like to see Sergeant Patrick Finnegan, please. I believe he's on day duty.'

The policeman studied Alicia, obviously surprised at seeing a Negress so well dressed, and with such an air of superiority.

In a thick Irish brogue, he asked, 'And who wants to be seeing him, lass?'

'*Miss* Alicia Fargo.'

The policeman studied Alicia's black hair piled high on her head with tortoiseshell combs, the expensive hat decorated with pheasant feathers, the finely tailored habit.

Nodding at the hallway behind her, he said, 'You'll be finding Sergeant Finnegan down that hall, Miss Fargo.'

'Thank you.'

Alicia's leather-soled boots echoed in the terrazzo-floored hallway, slowing when she saw a red-faced Irishman coming toward her. She knew luck was with her today. It was Finnegan.

Finnegan stopped abruptly when he saw Alicia. He grabbed her by the arm, whispering, 'What in God's name are you doing here, woman? Have you been arrested?'

Shaking off his hand, she hissed, 'Of course I haven't been arrested, you fool! I need to talk to you.'

'About what?'

'I need help.'

'If it's money, woman –'

'No, it's not money.'

'Do you have something? The pox?'

'No, I don't have the pox! Now listen – '

Leaning closer, she confided, 'I need manacles.'

Finnegan's laugh exploded in the hallway. 'What would you be needing manacles for?'

Alicia kept her voice low. 'That's my concern. Can you get them for me or not?'

Finnegan nodded his head toward a door. Standing back for Alicia to enter the room, he closed the door behind her and moved towards a wall cupboard.

Removing two pairs of iron manacles from the cupboard, he dangled them in front of her, teasing, 'Now what kind of wicked plan are you plotting with these silver bracelets, little woman?'

Alicia wanted none of Finnegan's games. But she knew

she might have to give him some satisfaction, a quick sample of what he paid for on Pleasant Street.

Her voice was thin with disgust as she arched one eyebrow, warning, 'Don't excite yourself, Irishman.'

Finnegan continued swinging the manacles back and forth, teasing, 'What would you be wanting these silver bracelets for?'

'Oh, don't excite that little red prick of yours!'

The smile disappeared from Finnegan's ruddy face.

Alicia stepped forward, demanding in a snide voice, 'What's the matter, Finnegan? Do manacles excite you? Do they make your miserable little cock get hard? Is this one thrill you haven't told me about?'

Finnegan glanced at the door. 'Shhh. Keep your voice down.'

'Why? Don't you want your freinds to know what a miserable little prick you have? Oh ho! I bet they already know. I bet everyone in the whole place laughs at your prick. Laughs behind your back, Finnegan. Laughs the way I laugh at you!'

Finnegan began to speak. He stopped. His throat had gone dry.

Moving to the door, he turned the key in the lock.

Alicia snatched the manacles from his quivering hand. Dropping them in her handbag, she ordered, 'Go on. Play with yourself, Finnegan. I've got a few minutes to waste on you.'

Finnegan hesitated.

'I said play with yourself!'

Finnegan's hand dropped to his side.

'Go on, Finnegan. Pull out that little red prick of yours.'

'Here?' His voice was weak. 'Now?'

'Yes, here, Finnegan. Now.'

Finnegan fumbled to unbutton his fly, finally pulling out his penis from his trousers.

'Now drop your hands to your sides!'

Surprised by the order, he raised his watery green eyes.

'Your hands.' Alicia commanded with military crispness. 'Drop them!'

Obediently, the big Irishman stood in front of Alicia, both hands dropped to his sides.

Looking scornfully at his penis protruding like a red acorn through the fly of his trousers, Alicia ridiculed, 'What a sad, disgusting example of manhood you are, Finnegan.'

Finnegan kept his eyes lowered, breathing more heavily.

'I don't know why I even waste my time with you, Finnegan. Just to look at your prick makes me sick. *Sick*!'

He nodded. 'Yes, mam.'

'Sick and disgusted.'

Alicia found it easy to mock Finnegan's penis. He reminded her of a White man back in Georgia, the foreman who had supervised the weigh-station on the plantation where her parents had been share-croppers. That man had had the same kind of penis as Finnegan's, Alicia remembered. Short. Red. Repulsive. Alicia also remembered how, when she had been eight years old, the foreman had forced himself on her, taking her virginity on a pile of dirty hemp sacks.

Chapter Six

THE THIEF OF TIME

'Procrastination is the thief of time', Smoky's grandmother had taught him, and on that bright Thursday afternoon he finally stopped procrastinating and wrote a letter home.

Sitting at the pine kitchen table, he began writing on the pad he had specially purchased – along with envelopes – for the dreaded task. Mrs Goodhew was busy making preparations for the evening meal.

Beginning the letter by apologizing to his grandparents for not writing sooner, Smoky reported that he was fine, hoped they were well, too, and told them how good Uncle Jay had been to him since his arrival in San Francisco. Smoky's penmanship was as matter-of-fact as his style.

Writing that he had found work, Smoky did not explain what the job was, nor where he was living, saying that he wanted to wait and make certain that he did not get fired before he boasted about the new job, implying he was going through some sort of trial period.

Digressing again to Uncle Jay, he described how popular the minstrel show was with the audience, how everybody loved Uncle Jay. He added the news that Uncle Jay was leaving town to tour up the Pacific Coast with his show and than San Francisco would be lonely without him.

Emma Goodhew interrupted Smoky as he was promising his grandparents that he would not let so much time pass before he wrote again, telling them to keep sending their letters care of Uncle Jay's address.

'Son, you said to say when it's three-thirty.'

Smoky glanced at the tin clock on the shelf. An hour-and-forty-five minutes had flown past.

'Thank you, mam,' he called, hurriedly scribbling a few more lines at the bottom of the seventh sheet. 'I'm just winding up the letter. I have the address to do and I'm finished.'

Hovering behind his chair, Emma Goodhew asked, 'How about a nice slice of the cake I've just frosted? There's some fresh milk to go with it.'

Fresh cake and cold milk tempted Smoky. But in less than a half hour he had to be upstairs with Judge Douglas.

'No thanks, mam. I'm running a little late.'

'It's my apple-sauce cake,' coaxed Emma Goodhew, reaching for a knife to cut it.

Emma Goodhew enjoyed having young men around the kitchen, especially a polite young man like Smoky Summers who ate second helpings of all her cooking and never failed to compliment her. In her opinion, Smoky wasn't like the other young men who had worked on Pleasant Street, not sullen and shifty-eyed and worthless. She had called his predecessors 'street trash'.

As Smoky licked the gummed flap of the envelope, Emma Goodhew wagged her knife at him. 'Don't you go wasting your good money on no postage stamps, hear? Leave that letter here in the kitchen and I'll pay the postman out of the sugar bowl.'

'No, mam. I couldn't.' Should he tell her about the cigar box of money he had managed to save from his short time at work here?

Snatching the sealed envelope from his hand, Mrs Goodhew looked at the address.

'My grandfolks,' Smoky said proudly, watching her read the name and address. 'They're more like folks to me really. They raised me.'

Propping the letter against a stoneware cookie jar on the shelf, she sniffed. 'And a good job they done, too.'

Leaving the kitchen, Smoky felt light, having accomplished a task he had been putting off for so long. He had not wanted to write lies home to his grandparents. But neither could he very well have told them the truth, that he had become a male prostitute.

Hoping they would stop worrying about him, Smoky

paused when he stepped out through the kitchen's swinging door. He saw a stranger sitting in the main hallway.

* * *

A young girl sat regally on the high-backed chair in the bordello's foyer, a young White girl wearing a full-skirted organdy dress and a wide-brimmed straw hat placed back on her long blonde hair. She looked to Smoky like an angel on White people's Christmas cards.

The same age as himself, the girl stared back at him with equal surprise, her large blue eyes dipping from Smoky's face down to the cotton shirt and trousers hugging his body.

Smoky nodded as he began climbing the stairs, glancing back over his shoulder.

The girl blushed, dropping her eyes to her lap.

On the first landing, Elizabeth emerged from her bedroom at the top of the stairs. She nodded at Smoky, stepping aside to allow him room to move down the hallway.

As Smoky hurried to his appointment, Elizabeth stepped to top of the stairs and, leaning over the banister, called, 'Caroline, your father's ready to see you.'

'Caroline?' 'Father?' Smoky looked back again over his shoulder. Who was 'Caroline'? Had Lady Elizabeth arranged an appointment for a customer who wanted to pretend that the pretty blonde girl was his daughter? Was 'Caroline' a prostitute who lived at some other house?

Smoky put the thought out of his head. He had his own business to attend to. He wondered what Judge Douglas's sexual quirk was to make him request two couples to satisfy him in bed.

* * *

Smoky lay naked on his right side, face-to-face with

Petal, their arms wrapped round one another, Petal's bare legs clenched around his thighs as he drove himself into her, making love on the same bed as Rob and Ava.

The bed creaked beneath the weight of the four people; Smoky and Rob lay back-to-back, Rob facing the opposite direction, Ava gripping her legs around him.

Smoky was not comfortable. His back and buttocks kept bumping into Rob; his feet became entangled with Rob's legs.

Judge Douglas, a short, wiry man, stood at the end of the bed scrutinizing the lovers. He had taken off his suit jacket, wearing only grey trousers, his waistcoat festooned with a gold watch chain, and a white shirt gripped at the elbows with sleeve garters.

He complimented, 'That's right, boys. Pump it to those wenches. Pump it to them, boys.'

Rob had warned Smoky that Judge Douglas was an odd man, like a meddling school teacher, an imperious professor coaching love matches. But Smoky had not anticipated that he would direct each and every action.

He called to the women, 'Now, girls, it's time for you to eat a little meat, hmmm?'

Ava moved away from Rob, sliding down the mattress, trailing her long veil of glossy red hair across Rob's chest, opening her mouth to take his penis between her carmined lips.

The Judge nodded approvingly at the way Ava licked the head of Rob's penis, pleased at the way she so enjoyably encircled its crown with the tip of her tongue. He gestured perfection with his thumb and forefinger at the way she took the first few inches of Rob's organ in her mouth, gripping the base with one hand, using the other hand to cradle the large sac of his testicles, savouring the taste and smell of his organ.

Turning from Ava, Judge Douglas frowned when he saw Petal still feverishly kissing Smoky, her arms wrapped around his shoulders, her thighs working.

One finger crooked, he scolded, 'If you don't do what I

tell you to do, young lady, I'm going to have to ask you to leave the room.'

Petal ignored the Judge's warning, enjoying Smoky's prowess, lost in making love with him after almost two weeks of having only dreamt and fantasized about him.

Judge Douglas, leaning farther over the foot of the bed, tapped Petal's bare shoulder. 'Miss? Do you hear me, miss?'

Petal jerked back. 'Don't touch me!'

The sharp words surprised him. He stood back astonished.

Smoky, hoping to avoid trouble, quickly withdrew himself from Petal's clutch, scrambling to his knees on the bed. Remembering the Judge's orders, he stood above Petal and jutted out his penis, nodding to her to take him in her mouth.

The Judge pushed Petal away. 'No, no, no, no! This young lady has disobeyed me. I'm afraid she'll have to leave the room.'

Petal put both hands on her hips. 'Who do you think you're talking to, mister? Some school kids?'

The Judge grabbed her. 'I'll have no bad apples!'

'Who *are* you?' she demanded.

Pulling Petal from the bed, the Judge ordered, 'Out with you! Out with you! Out!'

Petal looked from the Judge to Smoky; next, to Rob and Ava, seeing Ava busily satisfying Rob on the sagging mattress, obeying the Judge's instructions.

Judge Douglas tapped Ava's head. 'You there, miss. Stop. You have to take care of both my boys now. Do you think you can do a double order?'

Ava, glancing at Smoky's penis, looked back to Rob's manhood. Both organs were nearly matched in size.

Lying on her back, Ava beckoned Rob toward her, then gestured for Smoky to sink to his knees, to kneel on the opposite side of her shoulders from Rob.

'Yes! Yes!' approved the Judge at Ava's positioning on the mattress.

'A good spot. A fine spot. Excellent, girl. Excellent.'

Ava, oblivious of Petal lingering by the bedroom door, took Rob's penis in her mouth, moisturing it with saliva.

The sight of Smoky poking his penis closer to Rob's organ excited the Judge. The penises were almost identically proportioned in length and circumference, one being white, the other black.

'Excellent! Superlative! Bravo! Now, boys, play with her titties. Put your big willies together, boys, and play with her titties. Don't be afraid if you touch each other, boys. Don't be scared of touching each other's bodies. The game's all in good sport. So, let's relax and all have a good time. Come on, boys! Belly-up to that wench. Put your arms around each other's shoulders. Drive your big meat into her mouth. Drive your big meat together, boys. Drive it!'

Smoky tried to obey, hoping to please the Judge by prodding closer to Rob's manhood, using Ava's mouth for their target.

Ava, already having Rob's penis in her mouth, gave it a few more long sucks, and again beckoned for Smoky to move his penis alongside Rob's.

Smoky did not think she was going to be able to take both. But the saliva on Rob's organ smoothed the way for him to slide down alongside Rob's penis, the two crowns pressing tightly together in her mouth, her hands squeezing the fleshy organs tightly together.

The sensation was strange for Smoky, the warmth of the mouth, the pressure of Ava's hand against one side of his penis, the throbbing skin of Rob's penis bumping against the other side.

The Judge coached excitedly, 'That's the boys! That's the boys! Move closer together now, boys. Tight. Don't lose touch with each other. Go on, there. Put your arm around his shoulder there and bump those big willies together.'

Raising one arm over the back of Smoky's neck for support, Rob began moving his organ back and forth, back and forth, rubbing it snugly against Smoky's poking organ.

Smoky couldn't continue. Sinking back to his haunches, freeing his penis from Ava's hand and mouth, he frowned, apologizing, 'This isn't going to work.'

'What?' The Judge wrinkled his brow.

Smoky, sitting on his heels, flipped his penis with one hand, showing that his organ was going soft, losing its stand.

He repeated, 'This isn't going to work. Sorry.'

'But . . . But . . .' The Judge sputtered. 'But you boys look so good together. So . . .'

'Sorry.' Smoky shrugged. 'I can't.'

Stepping from the bed, he grabbed his clothes from a heap on the floor and nodded for Petal to lead the way from the room.

Outside in the hallway, Petal complimented, 'Good for you. The old coot's a fairy. Let's go to my room.'

Smoky was confused. Today was the first day he had not been able to perform for a client. He said, 'I just couldn't do what he wanted.'

Petal sidled against him. 'Don't worry. Let's go to my room. I'll get you boiling again.'

'No.' Smoky shook his head. 'Not now.'

'Come on. I've been waiting for you, dumpling. I'll show you a good time.'

Kissing her forehead, Smoky began pulling on his shirt, trousers, buttoning his fly. 'No. I just want to be alone. I'm going to my room. Thanks all the same.'

Moving down the steps, he carried his shoes in one hand.

Alicia, returning to Pleasant Street from the Van Ness Police House, entered the brothel through the front door as Smoky and Petal were emerging from the upstairs bedroom. They were both naked, arms around one another.

Her heart pounding with jealousy, Alicia stood in the shadow of the foyer, watching Smoky kiss Petal.

Watching him descend the wide mahogany staircase, Alicia heard him tell Petal he was going to his room.

Alicia remembered the manacles in her handbag. She thought about the gardener working by the front gate, the long pruning shears he had been using to trim the bay trees.

Turning, she opened the front door.

Chapter Seven

THE SECRET STAR

Cory Roper lay propped by pillows on Elizabeth's bed as his daughter, Caroline, sat primly on a chair placed beside the bed, furious with him for having lost the railroad bonds meant to give her financial stability.

'Daddy, people don't misplace a small fortune in bonds!'

Cory's voice was faint, his eyelids sagging with fatigue as he answered, 'People are robbed, Caroline. That's what happened to me.'

'But those bonds were for my future, Daddy. They were supposed to be my security. How could you have been so . . . careless?'

Elizabeth stepped forward from where she had been standing by the bedroom door. 'Caroline, there's no need to interrogate your father like a lawyer. Can't you see he's recovering from a wound. Minor as it may be, he should not be upset.'

Caroline replied without facing Elizabeth. 'You invited me here to speak to my father.'

'Why . . . yes. I called upon you, Caroline, to try and persuade your father to see a doctor. Not to harass him.'

'If Daddy needs a doctor, I'm certain he has the common sense to send for one. It's high time he knows how strongly I feel about my future. I'm no careless, frivolous child. I know the importance of money and investments. So, please. If you don't have anything constructive to add to the conversation, try not to interfere in matters which don't concern you.'

The rebuke stung Elizabeth. She replied coolly, 'Perhaps I had better leave you two alone, then.'

Cory raised himself in the bed. 'No, Lizzie. Stay. Please.'

Looking back to his daughter, Cory's voice sharpened,

'And you, young lady. I won't have you speaking to Elizabeth like that. You know I love her.'

Caroline was unimpressed. 'Your feelings are your own business, Daddy. Please respect mine, too. All I ask is to be given a fair chance to make sense of this life which you fobbed off onto me.'

' "Fobbed off" onto you?' Color rose in Cory's pallid cheeks. 'Why, you ungrateful little wretch!'

Caroline held her pert nose aloft. 'Let's stop calling each other names, Daddy, and get down to business. Are you or are you not going to tell me how you lost those railroad bonds?'

Cory shouted with anger, 'I was robbed, damn it! Held up at gunpoint!'

'Where? In New Orleans?' Caroline smirked at her father. 'At a gaming table?'

'No! If you must know, I was shot on the way *home* from New Orleans!'

'Where?'

Cory gripped both hands into angry fists. 'The Texas Cat Track, damn you, you inquisitive little brat!'

'The Texas Cat Track?' Caroline scoffed, 'What is that? Some disreputable saloon?'

'It's a road!' bellowed Cory, his eyes round with rage. 'I was held up at gunpoint on a road! Robbed! But I managed to get back the bonds. I lost them again when I took refuge – bleeding! – in a ranch!'

'You were robbed a second time?' Caroline frowned. 'Oh, Daddy. You do bungle up my life, don't you?'

'I had been shot! I was bleeding! I needed help! How was I to know the ranch was the headquarters of a gang?'

'Of a gang with masks tied around their faces, I suppose,' Caroline mocked.

'They didn't wear masks. But if you saw them, young lady, you would've wished they *did* cover their ugly faces, by God!'

Caroline added coolly, 'If you know who they are, Daddy, and where they live, why don't you take a Federal

Marshal back there and demand your rightful property? *My* rightful property?'

'Because I'm trying to corner controlling shares for you in the railroad before the board's election, you ungrateful little wretch.'

Caroline sat back in her chair, satisfied. 'That's the most sensible thing you've said in the last half-hour, Daddy.'

Elizabeth stepped up to the chair. 'Caroline, I think that's enough for the time being. Can't you see your father's not well? You're merely upsetting him.'

Caroline replied, 'If he tells me how to get back my bonds, I'll leave this house and not bother him again.'

Facing her father gasping on the pillows, she demanded, 'Tell me where the gang lives, Daddy, so I can go and get the bonds myself.'

Cory's face was flustered, his voice thundering. 'You'll do no such thing, young lady!'

'Why?' Her blue eyes danced with defiance. 'Because I'm a girl?'

'Yes. Indeed.' Cory nodded. 'Most precisely. Because you're a girl!'

She challenged, 'Well, I happen to have been a much smaller, much more helpless girl when you left me alone for the first time on Octavia Street, Daddy. When you left me alone in this town where there's probably far more hoodlums and gangsters and –' She glanced at Elizabeth. '– Whores than on this . . . Texas Cat Track.'

'Caroline!' Cory threw back the sheet, ready to leap at his daughter.

Elizabeth rushed forward. 'Cory, please. Calm yourself.'

Tucking the sheet back around him, she turned to Caroline, saying, 'I'd better leave the room before I do something I might regret.'

She moved towards the door as the angry words were resumed between father and daughter.

* * *

Elizabeth shut the bedroom door behind her, boiling with anger at Cory's daughter.

Caroline Roper was a monster. She had infuriated Elizabeth from the first day she had met her. Pampered, spoiled, indulged, Caroline needed a good, oldfashioned spanking. Elizabeth suspected that the main reason for her miserable behavior and her bad temper was having received too much money and not enough attention from her parents.

Caroline's mother had been Laura Harding, a golden-haired beauty whom Cory Roper had married after a brief courtship. When Caroline was only a four-year-old, Laura had run away to Europe with Daniel Atkinson, the youngest son of the San Francisco banking family, and never returned. Cory had brought the pretty little house on Octavia Street for young Caroline to live in with a governess. He visited her there when he was not travelling – or sleeping on Pleasant Street with Elizabeth.

Elizabeth was convinced she had done the right thing by leaving Cory and Caroline alone to settle their differences. She knew she was guilty sometimes of mothering Cory. Perhaps he was not as ill as she had thought. Obviously not. Deciding to try to follow her philosophy of worrying only about her own problems, she moved down the staircase towards the kitchen. She hadn't eaten all day and was starving. Mrs Goodhew could make her a pot of tea and a plate of toast.

'Afternoon, madam,' called Mrs Goodhew from the white porcelain sink where she stood dicing a colander of carrots.

'Afternoon, Mrs Goodhew. I don't mean to disturb your preparations for supper but –'

Elizabeth faltered, her eyes falling on an envelope propped against the cookie jar, the address written in broad strokes:

Mr and Mrs Warren Rickers

Nr Bossburg
Longchamp Parish
Louisiana

Mrs Goodhew, wiping her hands on her calico apron, crossed the kitchen, enthusing, 'Such a nice boy, that Smoky. He spent almost two hours writing to his grandparents.'

Elizabeth looked from the envelope to the red-cheeked cook. 'His . . . grandparents?'

'Yes.' Mrs Goodhew nodded. 'They raised him. Like parents, he said. His true folks died when he was only a tiny babe.'

Elizabeth was speechless. She felt winded, as if someone had slugged her in the stomach.

Looking back to the envelope, she asked, 'Gemma and Warren Rickers are Smoky's . . . grandparents?'

Mrs Goodhew saw the shock on her face. 'You know them, madam?'

Elizabeth wondered if she was in a dream, if she had gone from one nightmare to another, from the shock of feisty Caroline Roper being so disrespectful to Cory, to discovering that Smoky Summers was someone from her own background.

Mrs Goodhew said, 'Madam, you look like you've seen a ghost.'

Elizabeth nodded. 'I think I have.'

She began counting the years, realizing that, yes, it was possible for Gemma and Warren Rickers to be Smoky's grandparents. The name 'Summers' fit, too. The father of Emmaline Rickers' child had been called Alain Summers. How stupid of her not to have made this connection before!

Mrs Goodhew's voice seemed distant, faint to Elizabeth's ear as it asked, 'Madam, can I get you something? A glass of water? Tea? Maybe a little nip of brandy?'

'Where is he?' demanded Elizabeth, coming from her

trance, looking at Mrs Goodhew. 'Where's Smoky right now?'

'Why, in his room, madam.' She nodded to the door. 'He went to his room about twenty, thirty minutes ago.'

Elizabeth moved toward the door.

Mrs Goodhew called, 'Madam, excuse me for saying so, madam, but you look awful!'

Elizabeth did not reply. She had already passed through the back door, crossing the flagged garden towards the stables like a woman walking in a dream.

* * *

Holding the hem of her long skirt, Elizabeth mounted the steep, narrow wooden steps above the stables, the smell of hay and oats sweet to her nose as she wondered how she should tell Smoky that she not only knew his grandparents but that she had stood beside his mother on the day when he had been born into the world. That she was almost like his – oh, my God! – his godmother!

Hearing the sound of rattling from beyond the door at the top of the stairs, Elizabeth paused as she listened, wondering if she was disturbing Smoky.

The noise sounded like springs creaking. What was he doing?

She next heard the sound of a muffled call. And heard a voice speaking.

Intrigued, Elizabeth continued cautiously up the stairs, her heart beating as she reached for the door latch.

The voice speaking on the other side of the door belonged to a woman. To a very angry woman.

Elizabeth, straining to hear the words, recognized the voice, and a fury overtook her.

Flinging open the door, she saw Alicia standing next to Smoky's narrow cot, gripping a pair of long garden shears in one hand.

Alicia spun at the sound of the door.

Seeing Elizabeth, she ordered, 'You stay out of this!'

'What are you doing here?' Elizabeth saw that Smoky was tied – manacled – to the narrow bed, his mouth gagged, his pants pulled down to his thighs, his penis and testicles in full view.

Alicia waved the garden shears at Elizabeth, threatening, 'Stand back or I'll cut off something of yours too.'

Elizabeth, knowing she had to stall until she found a weapon, demanded, 'Alicia, what are you doing here with those . . . shears?'

Alicia's hair was dishevelled, her dress ripped as if she had been scuffling with Smoky. 'I'm going to cut off his nuts, that's what.' She snapped the shears loudly. 'He'll never touch Petal or any other woman again!'

'Alicia, put down those shears.' Elizabeth stepped forward.

'Stay where you are or I'll take a snap at you –' She pointed the shears at Elizabeth. ' – at your throat!'

Elizabeth's hand flew to her neck.

'Yes, I'll snip off that star!'

'Star?' Elizabeth stopped. 'What are you talking about?'

'That star you've got tattooed on your neck. I know from a customer back in Savannah what that little star stands for. A six-pointed star. I know from customers here in Frisco, too, that Jews ain't no more welcome here than in the south. That's why you hide it with high necks and scarves!'

'How could you know I've got a Star of David –' Elizabeth's hand gripped her neck.

'You believe me now, don't you?' Alicia snipped the shears in the air again, laughing. 'Your robe was open that morning you came to get Petal to help interview this –' She nodded at Smoky behind her on the bed. ' – this stud for a job.'

'You're mad,' Elizabeth gasped, her hand grasping her throat. 'You're stark raving mad.'

'Mad? Mad, am I? Well, you're nothing but a dirty, stinking Jewish bitch!'

Elizabeth's voice sharpened. 'What did you call me?'

'A dirty, cheap Jewish bitch!'

* * *

Mindless of Alicia's long, pointed garden shears, Elizabeth flew across the room, knocking her to the floor, sending the shears clattering against the bed.

Slapping Alicia's face, Elizabeth cursed, 'You little tramp! I'll pull out your tongue if you talk to me like that, do you hear?'

Alicia rallied from Elizabeth's attack. She gripped her by one arm, grabbing for a handful of hair.

Elizabeth kicked, freeing herself from Alicia's grasp, but forgot about the bed, and tripped on its leg.

Following Elizabeth to the floor, Alicia tore at her clothes, the two women rolling in a tangle of skirts, Elizabeth punching Alicia, Alicia tearing for hair.

Alicia reached under her long skirt and jerked a small knife from a garter scabbard. Holding Elizabeth to the floor with one hand, she sat on top of her, pressing the knife's small, thin silver blade towards her face, threatening, 'Jewish bitch, I'll cut you a six-pointed star right across your . . . face!'

Elizabeth, gripping Alicia's wrist, tried to toss her from her stomach.

Alicia grimaced as she pushed against Elizabeth's grip, straining to jab the knife lower.

Behind them, a hand grabbed Alicia's hand, twisting back the wrist, forcing her to drop the knife.

'What the hell's going on here?'

Rob Johnson stood above the two women, looking from Alicia to Elizabeth, to Smoky manacled to the narrow iron bed, his testicles and penis hanging across his bare thigh, the garden shears nearby on the plank floor.

Chapter Eight

A GIRL CALLED FRIDAY NIGHT

The night's sky glittered with stars as the Bay gently lapped the pilings of the Jackson Street Wharf. A man and woman sat side by side at the end of the Wharf, their feet dangling high above the slightly ruffled water. They had been sitting together for two hours and showed no signs of moving. They were talking about families and disappointments and early Franciscan missionaries who had settled in California and roughneck prospectors called 'Forty-Niners' who had become overnight millionaires in the middle of the last century. Their conversation flitted across decades, ranging from heartbreaks, to dreams, secrets to profanities, but always returning to the one subject they both had in common, the young woman who had died in the prime of her life, a girl called 'Friday Night'.

* * *

'What was Mom like?'

'Small. A little darker than you. Big eyes. Short, curly hair. Very, very pretty.'

'Did she laugh a lot?'

Elizabeth tried to remember. 'No. But she wasn't moody.'

Smoky's questions were difficult for Elizabeth to answer. Almost a quarter of a century had elapsed since she had known Emmaline Rickers in New Orleans. Nor did she want to say too much, to divulge facts which Smoky's grandparents might have kept a secret from him. Elizabeth gathered from his questions that he had no suspicions his mother had been a prostitute and she did not want to be the one to tell him. Events in her own life suddenly seemed upside-down, the last twelve hours having been a chaotic contrast of nightmare and bliss, so why make matters worse for somebody else?

'Where did Mom live when you knew her?'

The question jolted Elizabeth back to the present. 'Live?'

He nodded. 'In New Orleans?'

Elizabeth pictured the row of little shacks on Burgundy Street in the French Quarter – Smoky Row.

She answered, 'That was always your mother's biggest problem.'

'What was?'

'Where she lived.'

'How do you mean?'

'Your mom never could make it out of the wrong side of town.'

'What's the wrong side of town?'

'The wrong side of the tracks. Down-and-out neighborhoods. She never seemed able to better herself. Pull herself up in the world. I tried to tell her that it was important for a girl to have a good address, to live in a decent neighborhood. But she never seemed to understand.'

Smoky became defensive. 'Maybe that was because she was colored. Maybe because she didn't have any money to move into the Garden District. Or the Bayou St John. Or, or, or out here to . . . Nob Hill.'

'I was poor then, too, sweetheart. That's what brought your mom and me together. Both of us were poor as church mice. She was colored. Me, a Jew.'

Smoky was sorry that he had snapped at Elizabeth. He had forgotten that she had not always been rich, that there had been long hard days before she had become 'Lady Elizabeth Raleigh'.

He asked, 'Is it true you're tattooed to show you're a Jew?'

Reaching for her blouse, she asked, 'Do you want to see?'

Smoky shook his head. 'No. I saw it back in the room. I

just wondered if what Alicia said was true. About the six-pointed star. Why it's there.'

'My parents had me tattooed when I was a little girl. We lived in New York. The East Side of New York. The *lower* East Side. Definitely the wrong side of town.

'It was a Saturday morning. A man with long black curls hanging over each ear came to the one little room where we lived on Ludlow Street. My father told me what the man was going to do to me was for my own good. I remember my father holding me by both arms as the man heated a bottle of blue ink and pricked needles into my –' She flinched. ' – skin.'

'Why does the star have six points?'

'It's the ancient Star of David.'

'Do all Jews put the Star of David on their children?'

Elizabeth stared at the Bay's water white-capping in the night. 'None that I heard of.'

'Why did your folks?'

'To keep me from going astray. So they said. To keep me from forgetting my faith.'

'Did it hurt?'

'Of course it hurt. It hurt like hell! But I cried more for how it looked than how it felt. I ran away from home the next day. My father found me hiding behind a pushcart on Orchard Street. He brought me home but I kept running away. He kept finding me and bringing me back home and beating my little arse black and blue.

'Then I met a man who took me on a ferry ride. He bought me lunch. Lox and stuffed cabbage and apple strudel in syrup. He took me to a house in Williamsborough where he lived and let me play with his prick. He gave me a quarter to diddle him and fifty cents not to tell his neighbors.

'Sweetheart, I was no dummy. I got paid for my first lessons in sex! Later he taught me more things. His name was Arnold. Arnold Feldman. He may have molested me and taken my little cherry but he didn't hurt me as much as my parents did by marking me with –'

Elizabeth rubbed her neck, staring out into the night. 'Don't stay here in San Francisco. Go home, Smoky.'

'Why? You never went back to your family.'

'No. But it sounds to me as if your grandparents give you all the love and understanding and support that you need.'

'I want to make my own way in the world.'

'Nobody understands that better than me. But let me tell you this. If you decide to stay in this town, don't expect to keep your job at my place. No. That stops. As of tonight. Right now.'

'Why? I haven't changed.'

'What's this "I haven't changed" talk? A few weeks ago you swore up and down you'd never be a whore. That you'd never be exploited by White people for the size of your prick. Now you're begging to stay in a cathouse. You call that not changing?'

'Yeah. But –'

Smoky swung his legs back and forth from the wharf, looking down at the water. 'I had a little think about all that.'

'And how, Mr Summers, did you arrive at this new conclusion?'

'I did like you said to do. After our argument, I took a walk. I went to the theater. I sat in the dark and thought about everything you'd said to me. I thought about Black people having to make their way in the world. I thought about nobody else hiring me in San Francisco. I thought about the money I could make at your house –'

'Oh, honey, there's better ways to make a living than being a whore. The money might seem good at first. Sure. But prostitutes have a hard row to hoe. It leads nowhere except an early grave. Go home, Smoky. Take the first train back to Louisiana and count your blessings.'

Smoky spoke as if he had not heard her, staring down at his swinging feet, saying, 'Besides, there's been a change in the last couple of weeks, hasn't there?'

'Change?' She looked at him. 'What change?'

'I know you now. You know me.'

Elizabeth laughed. 'What does that have to do with the price of spuds?'

He looked out over the Bay, the wind blowing against his cheek. 'A lot. You knew my mother.'

'So did your grandparents know your mother. And one hell of a lot better than I did!' She playfully slugged his forearm. 'That's no argument to keep peddling your dick!'

'But when Grandma and Grandad talk about Mom, it's like she's still their little girl. They call her nicknames like . . . "Peaches" . . . and "Sugar" . . . and "Friday Night" . . . and "Fried Eggs".'

Friday Night!

Elizabeth took a deep breath as more memories about Emmaline Rickers flooded through her brain, the girl whose parents had called her Friday Night.

Smoky noticed the silence. 'What's the matter? Did I say something wrong?'

A fog horn sounded in the hazy distance.

Elizabeth, looking down at her skirt blowing beneath the edge of the wharf, asked, 'Do they ever talk about your father?'

Smoky's voice brightened. 'You knew my dad?'

'Not very well. Alain Summers was never too fond of me.'

'Was he handsome?'

'Very.'

'Were they in love?'

Elizabeth remembered the strange way Alain Summers had chosen to show his love for Emmaline. He had been a handsome but very selfish, perverted man who had put her on the street as a whore, and Emmaline had obeyed him like some beaten-down slave.

'What do your grandparents say about your father?' asked Elizabeth.

'They never talk about him. Except that he was connected in some way to an old White lady who lives over the hill from us in a tumbledown house.'

Elizabeth seized the chance to change the subject. 'Talking about neighbors, whatever happened to the Crowleys?'

'Sabrine and Cramer Crowley? You knew them too?'

'I met them. Are they still close friends of your grandparents?'

'They're both dead. Cramer died first. Then Sabrine. Poor Grandma, she mourned Sabrine Crowley like a sister. In a way, they were.'

Elizabeth's mind travelled back to the St Louis Hotel on Royal Street in New Orleans, to the afternoon she had surrendered Smoky to his grandmother. The Cramer Crowleys had brought Mrs Rickers to town from Longchamp Parish. Smoky had been little more than a week old, a beautiful little baby with chubby brown cheeks, small soft fists, already a twinkle in his large hazel eyes.

'What about Sabrine's brother?' Smoky asked. 'Do you know Junior Dehasset, too?'

'I remember your mother talking about somebody named Junior Dehasset, being involved with the Ku Klux Klan.'

Smoky nodded glumly. 'He still is, we think. Junior Dehasset's a bad person. He went to jail a long time ago for killing a woman. He's out now. He's the one who runs Belrose Plantation.'

Leaning back on his elbows on the wharf, Smoky looked overhead at the dome of bright stars. 'I can't believe I'm having this conversation with you. All the way across the country from home. Talking with you about the Crowleys. Junior Dehasset. And my own mom and dad. I just can't believe it.'

'Smoky, what are you going to do if you stay in San Francisco?'

He lay on the wharf, both hands locked behind his head, staring up at the stars. 'My uncle's going on tour with his vaudeville show. In fact, I'm supposed to pick up the keys to his apartment tonight. Uncle Jay says I can stay at his place while he and his room-mate are away. But I think I'd rather keep staying on Pleasant Street . . . if you don't mind.'

'You're serious about working on Pleasant Street, aren't you?'

'Why not? I've got friends there. Rob and Mrs Goodhew and –'

'You've also got enemies. Alicia.'

'I thought you fired Alicia. Told her to pack up her things and get out.'

'I did. But I think Alicia Fargo's going to be more difficult to get rid of than that.'

Elizabeth turned to Smoky. 'Say, you never told me if that little incident frightened you? Having someone threaten to cut off your –' She nodded at his crotch. ' – all your stuff.'

'Heck, I'm not brave. I never pretend to be. I'm surprised I didn't shit the bed!'

They both laughed. Elizabeth liked that quality about Smoky: one minute he would be serious, very intelligent; the next moment, crude and earthy.

A sober tone returning to his voice, Smoky asked, 'Do you think I'm going to be difficult to get rid of too, Elizabeth?'

'Smoky! Don't say that!'

'No. I'm serious. Do you think I'm going to be as difficult to get rid of as Alicia?'

'Most definitely not. Because I'm going to tell you to do exactly what I said the last time. Go take a walk and think things over. Then you can come back to Pleasant Street and we'll have a talk.'

Smoky did not look at her as he asked, 'What other work have you done in your life, Elizabeth? Besides being a madam? Owning a house?'

'Lots of jobs.' Elizabeth was surprised that Smoky had not asked this question before now. She had wondered when he was going to start hinting about where – and how – she had met his mother, if they had been prostitutes together in New Orleans.

Gathering her skirt, Elizabeth rose from the pier. She looked for her carriage in the distance, changing the subject. 'Can I give you a ride to your uncle's place?'

'No thanks. He doesn't live far from here. Over on Jackson Street.'

'Be careful. This is a rough neighborhood.'

'The wrong side of town?'

'About as wrong as you can get.'

'Worse than where my mom lived in New Orleans?'

Elizabeth pretended not to hear Smoky. She moved towards her carriage, tossing her hair in the breeze.

* * *

It was past midnight when Elizabeth returned to Nob Hill. She moved quickly up the staircase to the bedroom, avoiding the customers laughing and drinking with the girls in the downstairs parlor. The past few hours with Smoky on the wharf had been tranquil, so refreshing that she did not want to be hurled immediately back into the reality of Pleasant Street.

Cory was awake and sitting up in bed reading a book when Elizabeth locked the bedroom door behind her. She was surprised not only that he was awake but by how much healthier he looked than when she had left him late this afternoon.

Making room for Elizabeth to sit beside him on the bed, he squeezed her hand, saying, 'I was beginning to worry about you, Lizzie. Did everything go okay with the boy?'

'Can we not talk about the day, Cory? None of it?'

'Of course. I understand.' He pulled her towards him, confessing, 'You were right. I needed rest. I feel much, much better. But you were wrong about the doctor. I think the sleep cured me.'

Snuggling against his bare chest, she agreed, 'You *do* seem better.'

'I'm sorry I haven't been more attentive to you since I've been back.'

Elizabeth moved to begin pulling pins from her hair, letting it fall to her shoulders as she said, 'Darling, you may not have been as ill as I thought but don't deny it. Somebody did take a shot at you and –'

Cory put one finger to her lips. 'Shhh. Let's not talk about me. Let's talk only about you. How beautiful you look. How sensual you feel. How –'

'Oh, you *are* much better!'

He pulled her towards him and, nibbling at her ear, whispered, 'You taste quite delicious.'

Elizabeth warmed to his attention, soft words and gentle caresses, letting him undress her, returning his prolonged kisses, gripping him lovingly as he moved to lie between her open legs.

Cory, realizing that too much time had passed since they had made love, decided to spend his rallying energy on satisfying Elizabeth's lusty appetite.

Kissing and fondling her gently, he moved to kneel on the mattress behind her, gripping her by the buttocks, driving his penis into her vagina from behind, probing her sensitive spots as he drove into her pinkness, stirring himself inside her, making her gasp, squirm, tense, relax, cry out her love for him.

Prolonging his own explosion, thinking only about Elizabeth's satisfaction, Cory took her to repeated sexual heights, coaxing her orgasms with loving firmness, forgetting about time as he plunged and embraced, stroked and caressed.

Elizabeth finally pulled away for a lull; Cory lit a cigarette and lay back against the pillows heaped on the bed, holding Elizabeth in the crook of his arm.

Snuggling close to his chest, she murmured, 'I should invite your daughter around to Pleasant Street more often.

A family argument seems to be the best medicine in the world for you.'

Cory smoothed his hand against Elizabeth's shoulder. 'Sorry about Caroline's behavior.'

'It's not your fault, darling.' She kissed his chest.

'I haven't been a very attentive father. I've been thinking about that all evening.'

'Is she serious about going to Texas and getting back those railroad bonds?'

'Absolutely.'

'Doesn't the prospect of meeting Black Bess frighten her?'

'I tried to explain to her that the world's not so genteel beyond Pacific Heights. But you know Caroline. She won't listen.'

'What's her plan?'

Cory exhaled a shaft of blue smoke. 'To buy a gun to protect herself and leave town.'

'Silly girl. She'd be better gathering a small army to meet Bess.'

Inhaling the rich Turkish tobacco, Cory admitted, 'I don't relish the idea of going back to that ranch with her. But I don't have much of an alternative. She's absolutely right about me jeopardizing her security by losing those bonds.'

Elizabeth bolted upright. 'Oh, Cory! You can't go back to Texas! If Bess sees you, she'll force you to endorse those bonds and shoot you in cold blood.'

'I know. I know. You're right. But –'

Elizabeth curled back against him, 'Caroline's not authorized to endorse the bonds. She can get them away *if* she can lay her hands on them.'

'That's part of her argument for going.'

'Then it's absurd for you even to *think* about travelling with her, Cory Roper!'

'I wish I could find her a suitable escort. Somebody who wouldn't jeopardize the security we need to obtain the controlling votes. Some civilian, disinterested guard.'

Elizabeth had an idea but quickly rejected it. The prospect of sending Smoky Summers as a travelling companion for Caroline Roper was not only too risky for Smoky but Elizabeth also doubted if Caroline would ever travel with a Negro.

Reaching for Cory's hand, Elizabeth took the cigarette and inhaled deeply, enjoying the smoke.

'Shameful woman!' He kissed her forehead. 'Cigarettes! What will you be doing next?'

'Want to see?' Her brown eyes danced with mischief.

'Hmmm.'

Handing back the cigarette to him, Elizabeth lifted the sheet and slid down over his naked legs.

Grabbing his softened penis in her mouth, she began sucking, chewing it into hardness.

Moving the organ to one hand, she kept stroking it with curled fingers as she began licking his scrotum, sucking one testicle, then the other, putting the entire sac into her mouth.

Moving her mouth back onto the stiffening penis, Elizabeth began covering it with saliva, rubbing it across her face.

Elizabeth was revelling in the organ's feel, touch, smell when she felt the house give its first lurch.

* * *

Petal had been trying to forget for the past hours the events of yesterday afternoon on Pleasant Street. The time was near four o'clock in the morning and Petal had a customer in her bedroom.

The man's name was Jeff Garnet, fat-bellied, red-haired, with whisky on his breath. Petal tried to pay attention to him as he lay on top of her but her mind kept wandering back to Alicia and her problems.

Alicia had told Petal how she and Lady Elizabeth had fought and how Lady Elizabeth had ordered her to leave

Pleasant Street. Alicia had also told Petal that Lady Elizabeth was neither a 'Lady' nor a White woman. That she was a Jew.

Petal did not know what a Jew was. Neither did she care if someone wanted to call themselves 'Lady' and say they were English. What did a name mean? Nothing. But Petal knew that she had to make up her mind whether or not she was going with Alicia. Alicia was taking the money they had saved and moving back to Georgia. She had given Petal the choice of going back to Georgia and settling down with her, or to stay here on Pleasant Street and forgetting about her forever.

Petal did not know if she wanted to spend the rest of her life with a woman. She also did not like making decisions. She wanted to forget about all the sudden problems, bury her head in a hole and pretend life was going on as usual.

But in the darkness of the new day, Petal worried about Alicia's ultimatum. She thought how the answer might be to marry a man. She did not care who he was. But where would she find him? Should she start looking for a man here? She did not think that Smoky was going to give her a home. So perhaps she should look for another man.

Trying not to worry, Petal listened to her customer whispering how good she felt to him, saying in his whisky-slurred voice, 'You've got one hot little box, honey. One hot little box for a good man to plug.'

Petal knew that Garnet was already married. He would not give her a home. She also knew he was not praising her as much as trying to awaken his alcohol-dulled sexuality, to make himself hard.

Ignoring his words, Petal lay beneath his perspiration-wet body, praying for some kind of sign from God to tell her what she should do with her future, where she should settle down.

Her aunt back in Georgia, Millie Bluegrass, had taught the children at home how to look for signs from God, how to keep their ears open and eyes peeled for signs from Heaven.

Swallows flying in flocks. Crows alighting on a window ledge. Cats running across your path. Doors creaking in the night. There were hundreds of signs from the Lord telling you what to do.

Ignoring Jeff Garnet whispering crude words into her ear, Petal finally thought of a sign she could look for from God.

If a pane rattled in the frame of her bedroom window tonight, she would go back to Georgia with Alicia.

But if the floor creaked in the next few minutes, she would stay here in Pleasant Street and forget about Alicia and look for somebody else to give her a home.

Petal thought she was imagining it when the entire house – windows, floors, ceiling, walls – began shaking, rattling, moving, all at the same time.

* * *

Chickie Ling did not know how late it was – or how early in the morning – but Canwell Mathis had said he was going to spend the night with her and, as that meant she would get one-hundred-and-twenty-five dollars, she could afford to forget about time.

Canwell Mathis, the size of a grizzly bear and covered with black body hair, liked small women. But fearing he could rip Chickie's vagina with a few forceful thrusts of his penis, he urged her to plant both feet on the side of his hips, to ease herself up and down on him.

Holding his eyes shut as he enjoyed the sensation on his phallus, he heard the bed rattle and cautioned Chickie to slow her actions. Chickie began to protest, saying it was not her rattling the bed, but the room began to shake, and the bed collapsed onto the floor.

* * *

In the room next to Chickie's, Ellen Carlson held her left leg in the air, coaxing her visitor, Jim Baker, to look at himself in the mirror on the door of the walnut armoire as they copulated. A bashful man, Baker refused, pleading that he was ugly and would break the mirror. But Ellen insisted and, as Baker reluctantly moved his eyes towards the armoire, it tipped towards the bed, the mirror crashing to the floor, shattering into hundreds of small pieces.

* * *

Lillian Benoit, the self-proclaimed French queen of the sexual act, known as *soixante-neuf* on Pleasant Street, lay on her side, positioned in the opposite direction from sinewy Robert Mern. She was holding Mern's flaccid penis in her mouth, and he was chewing, tonguing, sucking the silky tissues of her vagina when a great force flung them off opposite sides of the bed.

* * *

Gus Dawson, a lawyer with wheat-colored hair and a ruddy complexion, frequently stopped by Pleasant Street after midnight, when the girls and customers had thinned from the parlor – and Rob was working alone behind the bar. Dawson paid Rob to tell him stories about making love to his wife, Eileen Dawson. He leaned across the bar, dabbing nervous perspiration from his forehead, listening to hear what his wife enjoyed doing with Rob after sucking his penis. Before Rob could share the latest secret about Dawson's wife's sexual quirks, the bar began to shift on the floor, the chandelier swinging from the center of the ceiling, and Rob shouted to Ava Wells sitting across the room with a bald-headed customer, 'Outside, everybody! It's an earthquake!'

Chapter Nine

THE BARBARY COAST

Six hours before the earthquake struck San Francisco, Smoky had refused Elizabeth's offer of a ride in her carriage and had instead walked to his uncle's apartment on Jackson Street where he had found a pile of boxes, bags, and suitcases heaped inside the front door.

Jay Greene, a small-boned man with flecks of white color in his short black hair, wore a long astrakhan-collared coat over the shoulders of his dark suit, ready to go to the Southern Pacific Terminal.

Smoky complimented, 'Uncle Jay, you look more like some bigshot vaudeville producer than a dancer.'

Jay's room-mate, Marc Bough, lanky with cocoa-colored skin and a thin beard tracing his jawline, drawled, 'Your uncle's the big star of his act, boy, so he's got to look like a star.'

Jay frowned. 'I'm also going to be late if we don't shake a leg, boys.'

Nodding at the luggage, he asked, 'Marc, can you start loading things into the cab? I'll make one last check around the place. And keep my hat box away from the front. I don't want the horse shitting on my fedora!'

As Marc began carrying valises and bags down the steps to the street, Jay turned to Smoky. 'Are you sure you're not going to accept our invitation and stay here while we're away?'

Smoky hedged, 'I don't know yet, Uncle Jay. But I'll keep an eye on things whether I stay here or not.'

Jay, a nervous, excitable man, moved quickly around the cluttered apartment, checking locks, closing curtains, shutting doors.

He called as he fussed, 'You still haven't told me about that mysterious new job of yours.'

Smoky stood against the wall, safely out of Jay's way. 'I might be quitting.'

'Quitting?' Jay stopped in front of a bookcase lined with china figurines. 'Child!'

'I might be going back home.'

Jay slapped one hand against his cheek. 'Home! I forgot! Two letters came from your grandmother. One for you. One for me. I opened mine. But –'

Glancing around the room, he asked himself, 'Now what did I do with yours . . .?'

'Uncle Jay!' Smoky protested. 'You don't have time to stop and look for letters. Grandma always writes us the same news. Just tell me what your letter said.'

Jay stopped digging through a knitting basket on the floor and lifted his head, eyes narrowing suspiciously.

'What's the matter, Uncle Jay?'

Jay pursed his lips, arching one eyebrow, shaking his head.

Alarmed, Smoky repeated, 'What's the matter, Uncle Jay? Was the news bad?'

Jay's voice was low, thin, almost a hiss, as he rose from the floor. 'You know that White trash neighbor of yours?'

'Who?'

'Dehasset.' The name sounded like venom on his tongue.

Smoky nodded. He had mentioned Junior Dehasset's name to Elizabeth only an hour or so ago, telling her how Dehasset had been jailed for murder but had been paroled and was now running Belrose Plantation.

Jay planted one hand on his hips. 'Well, the bastard's doing it again. Causing trouble.'

Marc called from the foot of the stairs. 'Cab's loaded, boys. The driver's already charging us.'

Jay's hands flew into the air. 'We're coming! We're coming!'

Pulling Smoky out into the hall, he slammed the door, turned the key in the lock, and shoved it into Smoky's chest. 'If you decide to leave town, just drop the key through the letter box.'

Marc called a second time from the bottom of the stairs. 'You're going to miss your train.'

'I'm coming, lover! I'm coming!'

Jay clattered down the narrow wooden stairs, the long top coat flapping behind him like a cape.

Smoky followed, momentarily forgetting about Junior Dehasset causing trouble in Longchamp Parish, thinking instead about the name which Jay had just called his room-mate – 'Lover'.

Were they? Lovers?

* * *

In the grey light of the first dawn, Smoky ambled between the old weather-beaten buildings lining Clay Street, hands tucked into his trouser pockets, his brain sorting out thoughts about his mother, Uncle Jay, his grandparents, what he should do with his future. He had not been to sleep for almost twenty-four hours yet he did not feel tired. Too many things were happening.

Five hours had passed since Smoky had bade farewell to Jay and Marc at the Southern Pacific Terminal. The platform had been crowded with actors and dancers and trapeze artists and animal trainers travelling with the show. Everyone seemed to be kissing someone good-bye – or shouting about a lost suitcase. Smoky had realized that his uncle's world was far, far removed from anything he had ever seen, or could begin to understand.

Suspecting that Uncle Jay and Marc might be lovers, he felt strangely relieved that Uncle Jay had someone close to him.

Since childhood, Smoky remembered his grandmother wishing that Jay would get married and raise a family. She didn't want her brother to spend his old age in loneliness, having no family to take care of him.

Marc Bough seemed to be a kind man. Calm and

well-organized, a totally different kind of person from flighty, dramatic Uncle Jay. Smoky decided that, yes, if they were lovers, they were a good match. He hoped they were equally well matched in bed. Somehow he guessed they were.

Walking down Clay Street, Smoky raised his eyes toward the dawn bleaching the sky in the east as fog horns cut the bay's misty distance. Remembering that this was the Barbary Coast, he kept a safe distance from the shadowy buildings, walking down the middle of the street.

The tumbledown district of the Barbary Coast ran from Clay Street to Broadway, bordered on one side by the ghetto called Chinatown, on the other side by San Francisco Bay.

Jay had explained to Smoky how the Barbary Coast had been named after Africa's infamous north coast, the long-ago home of pirates and privateers. The name had been tagged to this harborside district when sailors off ships from around the world had first begun streaming into San Francisco.

A neighborhood of tough saloons, flea-infested flop-houses, cheap hotels where street-walkers took customers, the Barbary Coast had become a mecca for pickpockets, cut-throats, every conceivable kind of murderer and thief.

A jungle of dark alleyways and rickety old buildings, the Barbary Coast contrasted sharply with millionaires' new turreted homes, the fine hotels fronted with awnings, the limestone libraries and the pristine churches which covered the surrounding hills.

His footsteps echoing in the stillness of early morning, Smoky thought about the vast difference between the Barbary Coast and Nob Hill, and he remembered Elizabeth's words about his mother living on the wrong side of town.

Smoky had not told his uncle about Elizabeth. He suspected that Uncle Jay might have heard stories about the notorious Nob Hill madam and he would naturally have wondered how his nephew knew such a woman.

Neither had Smoky told him that he had met someone who had known his mother in New Orleans. There were too many facts that he still had to glean about his mother's past, questions which troubled him.

What had Elizabeth been doing for a living when she had known his mother? Had she owned a whorehouse? Been a prostitute? What was the name of the section of New Orleans that Elizabeth had dubbed 'the wrong side of town?' The section where his mother had supposedly lived?

Smoky's grandparents had always told him that his mother had gone to New Orleans to work as a maid for a White family in a fine, big house. But had that story been a lie? Had his mother been a whore? Was that why nobody ever talked about her at home? Or if they did, was that why her name was always mentioned in hushed tones?

And what about his father?

Smoky had noticed that Elizabeth had actually side-stepped certain questions about his father. Why? Had his father been a scoundrel? Been cruel to his mother? Perhaps hadn't even married her?

Walking down Clay Street, hands in his pockets, shoulders slumped forward, Smoky wondered if he was illegitimate.

Hearing a deep growl which he at first thought might be the blast of a fog horn, he glanced over his shoulder.

As he turned his head, he felt the street shift beneath his feet.

The rumble grew louder, coming from the center of the earth, making the ground feel as if it were being pulled from beneath him.

'*My God!*' he thought. '*An earthquake!*'

* * *

The roar became louder, joined by the sound of wooden beams crashing in nearby buildings, brick walls collapsing, window panes popping in their frames like paper bags exploding in fast succession.

Looking around him, Smoky saw buildings shake, twist on their foundations, regain their original position and repeat the same wild movement.

Smoky's first instinct was to run. But he could not move. The earth felt as if it had become glue and his feet stuck to it.

Another quick jolt shot beneath his feet, the roar sounding louder than the last, throwing Smoky face forward to the ground.

Raising himself to his hands and knees, slowly managing to stand, he wondered what he should do, where he should go.

Suspecting he was closer to Uncle Jay's apartment on Jackson Street than to Elizabeth's house on Nob Hill, he remembered the flimsy wooden tenement building where Jay lived and decided to take his chance by going to Pleasant Street.

Nob Hill lay directly ahead. He knew that if he went toward Kearny, Grant, Stockton, Powell Streets, he could climb the hill toward Mason, then Taylor and Pleasant Street.

No longer feeling as if his feet were glued to the earth, Smoky began to run, looking to the left and right as he followed Clay Street.

Crowds of people were gathering on the side streets, women carrying children, families clutching each other. Few people were speaking, though, behaving instead as if they were dazed, as if sleep-walking in some awful nightmare.

All around him clouds of smoke were belching from buildings, and church bells rang in the distance; not the steady peal of a call to Sunday services but short, erratic jangles caused by the earthquake shaking bell towers and steeples.

Along the street, gas hissed as it escaped from the earth, and water mains gurgled like artesian wells.

Smoky stopped when he saw a smoldering heap blocking the street. He realized with a start that it was Fisher's Department Store – a four storey building collapsed into a mountain of smoking rubble.

Dashing to his left, hoping to be able to escape up Sacramento Street, he saw more people filling the street, their faces blank of expression, carrying an odd variety of possessions: over-stuffed chairs, bed pillows, china dishes, a bird cage, victrolas.

He heard a whistling sound and jerked his head; a column of fire was falling towards him. He jumped as a telegraph pole careered to the ground.

His heart pounding, Smoky told himself to keep calm, not to panic.

As he looked around him, trying to regain his bearings, he saw that the trolley car tracks had been twisted from the street, that their wires had fallen and were sparking on their connectors.

Stopping at another rubble heap, he spotted a human arm extending from the pile of bricks, a hand twisting, turning as if beckoning for help. Smoky fell to his knees and dug in the bricks, burrowing his way down to the man's shoulders, freeing the trapped victim's head and then moving down to his body.

Surprised that the man's face was only scratched and bruised, Smoky helped him to climb from the rubble, asking, 'Are you alone? Where's your family?'

Stupefied, the man looked around him in the smoke.

Grabbing his arm, Smoky repeated, 'Are you alone?'

The man brushed off Smoky's arm and, turning, disappeared into the clouds of dust and smoke.

Deciding there was nothing he could do here, Smoky

decided to continue towards Nob Hill. The ground no longer rumbled. He guessed that the earthquake was over. His problem now was to find a way through the fire.

* * *

Pleasant Street had been transformed from a short, tranquil stretch of vanilla-washed houses to a smoke-filled inferno of lapping flames, bolting horses, people fighting to salvage what they could from their homes.

Yellow tongues of fire licked from the upper windows of Elizabeth's bordello; the mansard roof was enveloped in smoke; the heat drove back the group standing in the forecourt – Mrs Goodhew clutching Rob Johnson's arm, Ava Wells hovering between Petal and a woman wrapped in a blanket who Smoky realized was Elizabeth, her hair a wild tangle around her soiled face.

Seeing Smoky, Elizabeth ran to him. 'Thank God you're safe.'

Smoky stood gulping for air after the long run.

Elizabeth gripped the blanket around her like a shawl. 'We thought you were trapped inside the stables.'

'I was with Uncle Jay. I took him to the railroad station.'

'Is the rest of town bad?'

Smoky pointed behind him. 'The fire goes all the way down to the Bay.'

'To Broadway?'

'As far as you can see.'

Elizabeth brushed shanks of hair from her face. 'That explains why there's no firemen. The whole town must have been hit.'

Smoky added, 'You can hear gas hissing from underground.'

'Kerosene lamps and candles don't help it. Especially in those wooden frame houses. They're as dry as kindling wood. Let's just hope most of the people get out.'

'Were you asleep when it hit?'

Elizabeth repressed a smile, remembering how she had

been in bed with Cory when the earthquake had almost rammed his penis down her throat.

She said, 'Some of us were lucky we weren't hurt worse than we were!'

'Everybody got out?'

'Yes. Cory went to find his daughter on Octavia Street and told me to stay in charge here –'

The sound of collapsing timber attracted their attention. Looking at the house, they saw a blanket of flames shoot from the second-storey windows.

In front of the fire, Eva and Chickie were fighting to keep Petal from running towards the lapping flames.

'Alicia!' Petal screamed, struggling to escape, '*Alicia!*'

Elizabeth dashed to Petal, grabbing her by both shoulders. 'Where's Alicia?'

'Inside! She went inside to get our money!'

Elizabeth looked back towards the house as a second crash cut the air; sparks flew; smoke billowed; the heat drove them further back from the flames, and, with a loud *swooosh*, the entire house collapsed in an explosion of fire, smoke and sparks.

Centre had seen Clare when she [illegible] [illegible] over her.

She said, 'Some of us were lucky, we were [illegible] than we [illegible].'

[illegible]

[illegible]

[illegible]

[illegible]

[illegible]

[illegible]

[illegible]

Chapter Ten

THE FIREFIGHTERS

San Francisco burned for three days, the largest fire the city had ever known, levelling the Barbary Coast and three adjoining square miles. The damage extended from the new homes built along Van Ness Avenue down to the squalid dockyard buildings of the Bay.

An exodus began from the city, people taking possessions they had managed to salvage, crossing to the safety of hostels constructed in neighboring communities.

People also poured into San Francisco. Doctors. Nurses. Troops. Firefighters. Looters.

Smoky listened to all these reports as he remained with Elizabeth and Cory on Nob Hill, learning how the damage had not been restricted to the city but spread north beyond Humboldt County.

The earthquake had followed a weak line beneath the ground and the sea, a crack called the San Andreas Fault which ripped when pressure had built up within the earth.

Travelling at two miles an hour, the quake had tossed ships at sea, over-turning large, new steel ships as easily as smaller, older wooden vessels.

On land, the quake had caused landslides along the coastline, levelling centuries-old redwood forests, toppling villages, moving train tracks more than fifteen feet from their original position.

The most terrifying report heard about the quake, however, was that it had left large gaps in the earth, deep chasms into which buildings, trees, and animals had disappeared forever beneath the ground.

Farms. Hotels. Hospitals. Insane asylums. Nothing built along the fault line was spared. The only consolation was that the quake had not struck at an hour when most people were awake and gathered in the streets or other public places.

Because of the city's size, San Francisco seemed to be the worst hit, and the people who did not flee were asked to stay in their own neighborhoods.

Tents had been pitched on Taylor Street at the foot of Pleasant Street. A communal kitchen was started as crews began digging through ashes, sifting through smoking debris.

No remains of Alicia's body was found, only tokens of what had been Elizabeth's once fine house – a monogrammed fork, the hinge of a French armoire, the iron headboard of a double bed.

Petal and Ava chose to stay with Elizabeth. But Ellen, Chickie and Lillian caught boats to Oakland on their way east, hoping to find new homes and work in other cities.

Explosions sounded throughout the city day and night, firefighters setting dynamite charges to stop the fire spreading and, later, to clear way for crews beginning to burrow through the rubble.

All services were shut. Water. Sanitation. Postal. The banking district had been one of the city's worst-hit areas, its safes and vaults buried beneath the buildings, some even melted in the intense heat, paralysing the banking community.

With no effective police force to protect them, people resorted to vigilante rule. Cory Roper armed himself and Elizabeth with firearms he brought from Octavia Street. Caroline Roper's house in Pacific Heights had been spared, frame structures proving to be more durable in the earthquake than brick buildings, and its location had been safely outside the fire area.

From Octavia Street, Cory supplied food, drinking water, and medicine to Pleasant Street. Elizabeth was left with only the clothes – and the blanket – on her back. But she had managed to empty one jewel box into a pillowcase before fleeing the fire, the pillowcase dangling beneath her long skirt, a fortune of diamonds, emeralds, pearls, rubies, gold, and six large rolls of cash hanging like a spider's poison sac between her legs.

Smoky's quickly-acquired savings of two hundred and fifteen dollars had burned in the cigar box he had hidden beneath a floorboard of the stables. Trying to be philosophical, he thought, 'Easy got, easy lost,' and told himself he had more important things to worry about than money.

Somehow he had to get word to his grandparents that Jay had left San Francisco safely before the earthquake had struck, that he himself had been spared any harm.

He also worried about Petal wandering through the ashes, calling for Alicia, mumbling about a sign from God telling her what she should do.

Petal's mind seemed to have blocked out the world. Smoky did not think she had gone insane, only that she was refusing to face the problems of being homeless and of losing Alicia. She tagged behind Smoky during the day, sometimes not saying a word, sometimes muttering, 'Marry me . . . Please be the man to marry me.'

At night, Petal crawled into Smoky's tent and slid into the cot with him. Her body felt deliciously warm against his nakedness. But when she began whispering for him to marry her, please to marry her, Smoky hesitated about making love to her. She was looking for a husband. It would be selfish and wrong to give any false hopes to such a troubled mind.

* * *

The fourth morning after the earthquake, officials began travelling through the city to begin taking a census of survivors. Smoky was piling bricks in the area which had once been Elizabeth's front garden when he heard a disturbance at the bottom of Pleasant Street.

Moving down the hill to see whether anyone was in trouble, Smoky recognized Caroline Roper berating a stranger, a big White man with a bushy red beard and a green band pinned around his upper left arm.

Smoky had not spoken to Caroline Roper since seeing her last week waiting to speak to her father in the hallway of the bordello. But he had noticed her walking back and forth from Pleasant Street to Octavia Street in the past seventy-two hours, a small, trim young lady dressed in impeccable clothes, an incongruous figure among the ruins of earthquake and fire.

He called, 'Morning, Miss Roper.'

The stranger frowned at Smoky for intruding. 'What do you want, nigger?'

Smoky forced himself to be civil, offering his hand to the census-taker. 'My name's Summers.'

The official ignored Smoky's hand. 'I'll call you "boy." '

Cory and Elizabeth had warned Smoky about the men assigned to take the census, many of them being recruited from the drifters who had come here to fight the fire but spent most of their time looting, plundering, profiting from the catastrophe. They were a dangerous lot.

The man turned back to Caroline. 'I know there used to be a big fancy house here on this hill. By the fine looks of your trapping, honey, I'd say you were one of the gals who worked there.'

Caroline flared. 'How dare you.'

'You're a feisty one, ain't you?' The stranger stroked his red beard, considering, 'Well, let me see. Pussy probably goes pretty high in the good days. But in these times, a gal's got to take what she can get, right?'

'I'll have your tongue for this!' Caroline shrilled.

Smoky's mind was working quickly. He knew that if he attacked the man, he would have to hit him hard because other men would come to the rescue, arresting him for striking an official.

The census-taker, digging in his pocket, pulled out a shiny silver dollar. He held it in front of Caroline, asking, 'How much loving can this buy, honey?'

Smoky's fist flew, hitting its target squarely on the nose. His second aim thudded the big man's stomach, doubling him over. He pulled back his left fist, clipping the man on the chin, using his right fist to send him toppling back onto the ground.

As the man lay sprawled in the dirt, Caroline accused, 'You killed him!'

Smoky rubbed his fist, wondering if he had broken it as he looked down Taylor Street for other fire-fighters. 'I don't think I killed him, mam. But I do think he could have harmed you.'

She sniffed. 'The rude boor.'

'Miss Roper, why don't you let me take you back to Octavia Street before any more snoopers start asking questions?'

'What kind of questions?'

'He's a Government man, Miss. A census-taker. See that arm band he's wearing.'

'Oh, dear.' Caroline bit her lower lip.

'Don't worry,' Smoky assured her, seeing her fidget. 'You won't get into trouble.'

'What about you?' Caroline studied Smoky, asking in a more serious tone, 'Do you want a job, Mr Summers?'

'Job?'

'I'm catching a train from Oakland continuing on to New Orleans. Do you want a job travelling as a bodyguard?'

'Bodyguard? To whom?'

'Me. I will be visiting a ranch in Texas for a few days. I don't foresee any danger but my father thinks I should have protection.'

Caroline looked back to the big man lying unconscious at her feet. 'And I think you're exactly the kind of protection Daddy means.'

The idea of going to New Orleans tempted Smoky. It was also a chance to return to Longchamp Parish with money in his pocket, not to return home broke. But he knew he had to be level-headed and not jump at the first offer of work.

He began, 'Mam, I appreciate your offer but I think you

should know that it might be dangerous for you to travel with a Black man. Especially through Southern states.'

Caroline dismissed the idea with the wave of a hand. 'Oh, don't worry about a little thing like that, Mr Summers. We won't be travelling alone. There'll be another man with us. In fact, I believe you know him. Rob Johnson.'

'Rob's going with you to New Orleans?'

'He agreed this morning.'

Smoky reconsidered the proposition. There was no need to stay here. In fact, it might be wise to leave San Francisco. Also, he could telegraph word to his grandparents to keep them from worrying about him and Jay.

'I'll go, Miss Roper. But only on one conditon.'

'Which is?'

'There's a girl here named Petal. I take Petal with me or I don't go.'

Caroline had seen Petal wandering aimlessly through the debris in recent days. Her father had explained how Petal had lost a friend – her best friend – in the fire and how the loss had seemingly affected her brain.

Smoky elaborated, 'Somehow I've got to get Petal back to her people in Georgia.'

'Mr Summers, if she can be ready to go this afternoon, she can leave with us from Octavia Street. Oh, and don't worry about clothes. We'll buy new things in Oakland before boarding the train east. Now if you will excuse me, I have a million and one things to attend to.'

Gathering the hem of her white skirt, she stepped gingerly through the rubbish as she pointed to the man still lying on the ground, calling, 'If you're wise, Mr Summers, you also will get away from here as soon as possible.'

* * *

'EARTHQUAKE DESTROYS SAN FRANCISCO!' blared the headlines of the *Louisiana Picayune* which

Junior Dehasset had brought back from New Orleans to Belrose Plantation.

Dehasset, a barrel-chested White man with thick, steely hair and a grey moustache, sat with his black leather boots firmly planted on the floor of the upper gallery of the big house of Belrose Plantation as he held the newspaper open in front of him.

At his feet curled Sophie French, a pretty Black girl with skin the color of milky coffee, and black hair soft and curling around her small face. As Junior read the newspaper, Sophie gazed blankly down at the driveway dipping towards the Parish road from the large, white-pillared house.

Across the gallery moved the Black houseboy, Davey, carrying a silver tray on which rested one tall glass of whisky and water. Setting down the glass on the wicker table next to Junior's chair, Davey glanced at the newspaper's headline.

'Earthquake!' Davey shook his head. 'I wonder if old man Rickers' grandson got caught in all that big trouble? My, my, my my!'

Dehasset lowered the paper. 'Who?'

'Warren Rickers' grandson.'

Sophie offered, 'That boy named Smoky. He's gone out to California.'

Dehasset chastised Davey, 'Don't go showing off you can read, nigger.'

Looking down at Sophie on the floor, he demanded, 'And how do you know about some nigger's comings and goings when you're supposed to be living here, taking care of me?'

She shrugged. 'Talk.'

'You'd do better minding your own business and listening to less nigger talk.'

He looked back to Davey, nodding his head at the door. 'Get going.'

'Yes, Mr Dehasset, sir.' Davey, the silver tray under one

arm, moved towards the gallery door.

Alone, Dehasset studied Sophie: the thin cotton shift covering her high-riding breasts, the tempting curve of thighs and knees.

Lowering his voice, he asked, 'Did you have Billy make us that love dolly when I was away in New Orleans?'

She nodded, bored.

'Answer me.'

'Yes, I did!' She was unable to hide her disgust. 'But it ain't easy asking Billy to make such a crazy thing in the workshop. He's no dummy. He knows what it's for.'

'What do I care what some nigger knows?'

'But *I* care!'

He glared at her. 'Who are you?'

'What?'

'Who, I ask, are you? Just some two-bit slut who should be in prison if I hadn't come to your rescue.'

'I would *not* be in prison!' she protested. 'I did nothing wrong.'

He smiled. 'Stealing ain't wrong?'

Sophie thought back to the day when three White men had stood in Fowler's General Store in Bossburg watching her examine the new bolts of cotton yardage. Sophie knew they were looking at her, admiring her, commenting among themselves about her body. Attention always flattered her, making her feel pretty, desirable to men, no matter how poor and ragged her clothes were. She had little else in the world to make her feel important.

Junior Dehasset had been part of the group. He had approached her, announcing that he and the other two men had seen her take money off the counter top. He had said that he might help her by asking the two men, Sheriff Laird and Mr Fowler, not to arrest and prosecute her for stealing if she went home with him. Sophie had protested that she had stolen nothing. But Junior had produced a roll of money, saying she would have difficulty proving her innocence to a judge against the word of three White men. Sophie had realized she was trapped, that there was no way to argue against the word of White men, especially three of the most important men in Longchamp Parish. That incident had happened two years ago and Junior Dehasset still kept an iron hold on her, treating her no better than a slave inside his house. She had no place to run to. No one to tell. No one to ask for help.

'Come here, bitch. Suck my dick.'

Sophie glared at Junior sitting in the rocking chair, newspaper crumpled to his lap.

'Suck my meat,' he ordered, nodding to his crotch.

The order did not surprise Sophie. Junior Dehasset liked being satisfied at this time of day, when he was enjoying his first evening whisky, when the sun was setting behind the hills.

As the Louisiana sunset glowed orange on Sophie crouched between Junior's tall black leather boots, she held his small organ in her mouth, obediently satisfying him.

'That's my good little slave bitch,' he praised, watching Sophie working between his legs. 'Take that dick deep down in your throat.'

Sophie's mouth worked on the small penis.

'Suck that big dick. Nice and easy. Nice and easy. You hear, slave girl?'

Slave girl? Junior acted as if slave days were not over. And they were not. Not here on Belrose Plantation, Sophie thought. Not in Longchamp Plantation, or in many other places in the south. White men like Junior Dehasset and his cronies still kept a hold over Black people. They rode at night wearing hoods, terrorizing Black families who did not obey them. Sophie considered herself lucky that at least she had the comfort of Belrose. Many Blacks had nothing. They were still little better than slaves. Slaves with no masters. No money. No food for their chuldren. No jobs. No medicine. The Civil War had abolished slavery, freeing four million Black people. But in the last forty years since the war, no one had done anything to find a place in the world for many of those Black people, letting them wander aimlessly, going hungry and without jobs.

'Worship that dick, slave woman . . . Don't be afraid of that big dick . . .'

Sophie hated Junior Dehasset. She hated all his White friends, all the men who met here at Belrose and called themselves the Ku Klux Klan. They tried to control the world, doing everything to keep Black people from working, from living like decent people.

'Bitch, don't be scared of choking on that big meat.'

Junior Dehasset had the smallest penis Sophie had ever seen. But he talked as if he were hung like a stallion. And he had made up for its size by having the plantation worker, Billy, make a wooden and leather penis which he called his 'lovedolly'. Sophie feared the day when he would start using the lovedolly on her.

Wanting to forget about Junior Dehasset's crude ways, his threat of the love dolly, she tried to think of another man, somebody nice, gentler, an image which would not make her work quite so repellent.

She remembered Davey mentioning Warren Rickers' grandson, Smoky Summers, going to California.

Had Smoky been in that earthquake? Would he ever come home? If so, would she see him?

Oh, wouldn't life be wonderful, Sophie thought, if she could marry sombody like Smoky Summers! But escaping Junior Dehasset and Belrose Plantation would be harder than escaping any earthquake.

PART TWO

THE TEXAS CAT TRACK

Chapter Eleven

AMARILLO-FORT WORTH

The coal engine of the *Amarillo-Fort Worth* chugged southeast across the dusty Texas panhandle, trailing a cloud of smoke in the turquoise blue sky.

In the front passenger carriage, Smoky swayed back and forth to the toss of the five-car train, a suitcase balanced on his lap for playing Solitaire with the pack of cards Cory Roper had given him as a farewell gift in San Francisco. Periodically, he raised his eyes to look at Petal staring out of the window at the flatlands dotted with sagebrush. Rob slouched beside her on the rough bench, reading a dog-eared copy of the *Police Gazette*. Two cars away Caroline Roper rode in the comfort of the train's First Class carriage.

Caroline had talked little to Smoky, Rob, and Petal in the five days since leaving San Francisco. She had promised to disclose details of her plan when they got closer to their destination in Texas. During meal times, she ate in the dining-car while Smoky, Rob and Petal gobbled food from boxes purchased at the train's watering stops. At night, she slept in a comfortable First Class berth while the others tried to sleep on improvised beds spread across benches or on the floor.

The *Amarillo-Fort Worth* train was less than half full on the run between Amarillo and Fort Worth, only a few passengers sharing the pineboard carriage with Smoky, Rob, and Petal. Three men with drooping moustaches and wide-brimmed hats. Two farm women wearing old-fashioned poke bonnets, with eyes as pale as blue milkglass. A Tawakoni chief with a brightly woven blanket around his thick chest. A tall hawk-nosed man wearing a rusty black suit, who kept raising his eyes from the Bible he was reading to watch Petal staring out of the window.

Smoky had seen the last refugees from San Francisco this morning in Amarillo, when they had transferred from the *Southern Pacific* to the *Amarillo-Fort Worth*. The farther east they had travelled the fewer people he had heard talking about earthquakes and fires. Ranchers and small town people preferred discussing their own problems: droughts, cattle epidemics, sheep ruining grazing land.

Although Smoky was pleased to be going home, he had been sorry to say good-bye to Elizabeth. In the last few days in San Francisco she had been kind and considerate to him, so different from the cold, formal façade she had shown him at their first interview, so unlike the cruel, calculating person people said she was.

Kissing him good-bye by the iron spear fence on Octavia Street, Elizabeth had whispered, 'This is for you,' and had pressed a fat roll of paper money into his hand.

'Thank you, but I don't need it.'

She looked astonished. 'But you can't go home without money in your pocket.'

'I get paid in full when we reach New Orleans.'

She pressed a second object into his hand, 'At least take this. For an emergency.'

Smoky looked down at a folded piece of paper.

Elizabeth explained, 'It's a letter to an old friend of mine on Basin Street. She'll give you work if you need it.'

Smoky remembered the opulent bordellos on Basin Street – the stretch of palm-swagged houses called 'The Line' in New Orleans – and how he had tried to find work there before coming to California. He also remembered Elizabeth's advice to forget about being a prostitute.

As if reading his thoughts, she added quickly, 'I know, I know, I told you this life leads nowhere but to an early grave. I still say so. But the kind of work Mattie Hayes will give you is different from what you've been doing on Pleasant Street. Go and see her if you need a little loose change jangling in your pocket when you go home.'

Smoky tucked the letter into his shirt. 'Is there any message I can give anyone from you?'

They had not spoken about Smoky's grandparents – nor reminisced about his mother and father – since talking on the wharf the night before the earthquake. There were many questions Smoky still wanted to ask Elizabeth: about his mother, details about his father, and their marriage. But there had also been a great deal of work to do on Pleasant Street, and so many people milling around Nob Hill after the fire; a private conversation had been impossible.

Kissing Smoky on the cheek, Elizabeth said, 'The only advice I can give you is to watch out for Caroline Roper. She's a selfish little bitch.'

'I'm not worried.'

'How much has she told you about the Texas Cat Track?'

'That some people have a ranch there. They're holding papers which rightfully belong to her. She hasn't told us what those papers are yet but she says she has a plan to get them back without any trouble.'

'Oh, Smoky, be careful of Caroline Roper's plans.'

'Why are you so worried?'

'Because she's spoiled and pampered and has always been so sheltered from the world. For all her sophisticated airs and graces, she's as innocent as a parson's wife.'

Smoky's warm thoughts about Elizabeth were distracted by a flurry of white out of the corner of his eye. Raising his head, he saw Caroline Roper approaching from the far end of the railroad carriage, holding the full skirt of her white dress as she edged her way between the rough wooden benches, a look of displeasure on her pretty oval-shaped face.

* * *

Caroline Roper perched next to Smoky on the wooden bench, explaining to him and Rob that they would be arriving at Fort Worth tomorrow afternoon. They would leave the following morning for the small town of Lead Springs, Texas.

'We'll spend tomorrow night at the Indian Wells Hotel in Fort Worth. When we arrive at the hotel, Mr Johnson, you and Mr Summers will make arrangements to hire a buckboard from their livery stables. I want to leave Fort Worth bright and early the next morning.'

Rob pushed back his new tan wide-brimmed hat with one finger. 'Mam, can we settle one thing right now?'

'What's that, Mr Johnson?' Caroline's eyes were blue, sharp, ready to meet criticism.

'I'm not "Mr Johnson", mam. I'm "Rob".'

Smoky chorused, 'Same goes for me, mam. When I hear somebody call "Mr Summers" I got to look and see who they're talking to.'

Caroline nodded 'Fine. Mr Johnson, you shall be . . . "Rob". And Mr Summers . . . "Smoky". In the meantime, I'm content for you both to continue addressing me as you have been doing. That is, until we reach our destination when, for reasons of security, you shall both address me by another name to protect my true identity. I shall give you that name and the reason for my disguise in due course.'

The mystery surrounding Caroline's plans piqued Rob and Smoky but they still resisted questioning her.

Smoky's concern at the moment was Petal. Still not sleeping with her, not wanting to mislead her into thinking he was going to marry her, he nevertheless did not want to leave her alone where other men might take advantage of her. She obviously needed to be cared for.

He asked, 'What do we do with Petal when we leave the hotel?'

Caroline clasped both hands primly on her lap, a yellow silk drawstring purse dangling from one wrist. 'Your friend will stay at the hotel until we conclude my business. When we return to Fort Worth, we shall collect her along with our luggage and continue by rail to New Orleans.'

'Miss Roper,' Rob drawled, 'how long do you expect to take settling this "business" of yours?'

'A few days. No more than a week.'

'Is it too much to inquire where Smoky and me will be sleeping and eating during that time?'

'That's all part of my plan, Mr Johnson – Rob. You must have patience. As I said, I'll explain everything in due course.'

Smoky was still concerned about Petal. 'Mam, you expect Petal to stay all by herself in some big hotel while the rest of us go off someplace? Maybe leaving her alone for a whole week?'

Caroline answered indignantly. 'She'll have a very comfortable room, Mr Sum – Smoky. Full access to the hotel's accommodation. As I shall be paying for it, I can't imagine what else she could ask for.'

'I appreciate you paying for her, Miss Roper. But leaving her all alone in a big hotel could be dangerous.'

Smoky lowered his voice, explaining, 'Most folks in this part of the country's never seen a Black gal, mam. Ranchers and farmers hereabouts are all White folks and –'

'Oh, are they?' Caroline smirked. 'That shows how much you know about Texas!'

Smoky and Rob exchanged quick glances.

Rising from the bench, Caroline held herself erect, concluding, 'The important fact to concentrate on at the moment, gentlemen, is that we arrive tomorrow at Fort Worth. We spend the night there before beginning our tour.'

Smoky asked, 'Can I ask the name of the first town we drive to?'

'Lead Springs.'

Rob asked, 'Does the ranch we're going to have a name?'

'Rattler Gulch.' Caroline held up both hands, insisting, 'Now, that's all I'm going to say. You're going to have to wait.'

Nodding farewell, she lifted the hem of her white dress

and moved back towards the door leading to the First Class carriage.

Rob glanced over his shoulder to make certain she had departed. 'You know what I think, don't you?'

Smoky shook his head, remembering Elizabeth's warning about being cautious of Caroline's plans.

Rob said, 'I don't think she's got the foggiest notion where we're going or what she's going to do once we get there.'

'That's her business, I guess. It's her money.'

'You're too trusting.'

Smoky looked at him.

Rob lowered his eyes to the *Police Gazette*. 'It's our lives!'

* * *

It was night time, and Caroline Roper cursed her father, damning him for frightening her with stories about Black Bess, for telling her how the old Negress kidnapped people from the Texas Cat Track and staked them to the ground, branding them on the thigh like cattle.

But Caroline also knew she had little choice but to face the old harridan and somehow get back the railroad bonds. A future without financial security was unthinkable.

Lying in the walnut panelled First Class compartment of the *Amarillo-Fort Worth*, Caroline thought about Rob and Smoky questioning her this afternoon, and she realized how badly prepared she was for the venture.

Rattler Gulch was located near the town of Lead Springs but Caroline did not know exactly in what direction the ranch lay. Her father had been delirious with fever when he had taken refuge there and had been unable later to draw a detailed map.

Caroline rolled over on the thin mattress, trying to convince herself that she would have no difficulty in finding Rattler Gulch, telling herself that there could not be too many Black women who owned ranches in Texas.

Listening to the click-click-clickety-click of the little train chugging over the tracks, Caroline's mind drifted back to Rob and Smoky.

Smoky intrigued her more than Rob. Why? Because he was Black? Closer to her ideal of the perfect man – someone dark and handsome?

For as long as Caroline could remember, she had weighed men in parts rather than as a whole. She had never yet met a man whom she found totally desirable.

At Miss Baldwin's Seminary in Virginia, she had lost her virginity to Wayne Everett, a young literature teacher. Everett had had a pretty face and dark eyes, but when he had taken his clothes off, Caroline had discovered he had no waist and a sunken chest.

Since that time, Caroline had judged men like a child playing with scissors and paste, making paper dolls, choosing curly black hair, broad shoulders, narrow waist . . .

Lying in the narrow berth, she crooked her finger and reached down between her thighs. Moving her finger in and out between her cleft, she tried to imagine her ideal man.

He was tall. He had dark hair. He was forceful. He stood up to her yet he was respectful. He had polite manners. He had a deep voice. And he smiled –

Working her finger faster, Caroline imagined her make-believe lover smiling at her as he lay beside her on the berth, his voice whispering softly in her ear as . . .

She stopped.

She was imagining she was listening to Smoky's deep-chested voice.

And yes! It had been Smoky's smile – that boyish grin – she had also been picturing in her brain!

Squinting her eyes shut, Caroline tried to eradicate him from her brain, to imagine another man making love to her. She could not have a Negro for her ideal man. No, no, not ever!

* * *

The whispering disturbed Smoky. He sat up on the floor of the rumbling carriage and looked at the other people sprawled around the floor or on the benches in the night's darkness.

Smoky listened closely and heard the whispering again. He was sure it was Petal.

'Will you marry me?'

Smoky's heart began to pound. The whispering had come from across the aisle.

'Do you love me?'

Smoky knew who she was with even before the man answered.

'Sure I love you, Black gal. Just open those legs wider and keep hushed.'

Smoky's first instinct was to pull the Bible-reading man from Petal, to tell him that Petal was unwell. But Smoky checked the impulse. Did he have the right to chaperone Petal? Had she not been a whore in a bordello? Was she not legally an adult? Did he have any right to interfere in her life?

Smoky slumped back to the floor, deciding that the best he could do was to insist to Caroline that Petal did not stay alone in the Fort Worth hotel.

* * *

The public wagon had stopped running between New Orleans and Longchamp Parish. At least temporarily. Sophie French stood outside the closed library doors of the big house at Belrose Plantation, listening to Junior Dehasset discussing with his friends how the wagoner, a young Black man, Robinson, had been killed with a lead pipe and his body disposed of. As soon as the gossip had died down in the Parish about the Klan killing Robinson, they would give the job to Ray Joe McNally, a White man who had joined the Klan and needed work.

Listening to the White men, Sophie French realized more than ever that she was trapped like a slave at Belrose, deprived of a decent life by these men who lived by the standards of old slavery.

Another voice spoke behind the closed doors.

'We got to keep White folks from speaking out against the Klan. Maybe we done wrong by leaving one of our hoods at the murder as a sign. Lots of people around here – even Whites – liked young Robinson.'

It was Junior Dehasset's voice which answered. 'We'll solve the problem of nigger lovers by making an example of one of them.'

There was silence.

Dehasset explained. 'Like Marisse Summers up at High Hill. We can burn her out.'

'She's an old lady!' protested one man.

A second voice argued, 'She don't bother nobody.'

Junior disagreed. 'Marisse Summers has been treating niggers like human beings for years. We'll burn her out. Other nigger lovers will soon get the message.'

Inside the closed room, the White men's voices began arguing, insisting that burning High Hill would not distract attention from the Klan, but merely increase it.

Junior Dehasset held firmly that they should put a torch to the old White woman's home.

'Good shit!' he bellowed. 'She gave birth to a nigger kid! What kind of decent woman would do a thing like that? She should've been burnt out years ago!'

In the hallway, a man appeared beside Sophie and warned, 'Don't listen at doors, girl.'

Jumping, Sophie saw Davey, the houseboy.

Davey shook his head woefully. 'It don't do Black people no good listening to plans if we don't aim to do something about it. And are you planning to be some kind of hero, honey?'

Sophie lowered her head. Ashamed, she knew Davey was right. Junior Dehasset had too much hold over her. If word leaked out from Belrose about the Klan's action, Junior would know where it had come from. She shuddered to think what Junior would do to her. But worse, she hated what had become of herself. Everybody saw her as Junior Dehasset's fancy wench. She felt humiliated being connected to him in any way. But what could she do?

Chapter Twelve

RATTLER GULCH RANCH

Caroline Roper stepped down from the hired buckboard and, holding one hand over her eyes to block the midday sun, looked up and down the dusty main street of Lead Springs, Texas. Smoky sat beside Petal on the rear seat of the open wagon, and Rob sat in front, the reins to a pair of dappled mares loose in his hands.

'Everything's so quiet,' Caroline whispered, surveying the empty street and rickety boardwalks.

'You been here before?' asked Rob, looking at eight horses tied to a hitching post in front of a saloon marked 'Buck's Place'.

'No. But I know the ranch isn't far.'

'How far?' Rob saw six more horses across the street but no one standing in the doorways or moving along the boardwalks.

'A few miles.' Caroline was not pleased with Rob interrogating her.

During breakfast this morning at the Indian Wells Hotel in Forth Worth, Caroline had finally explained the first details of her plan to Rob and Smoky. They would drive to Rattler Gulch Ranch and introduce themselves as refugees from San Francisco's earthquake, saying that they were looking to buy a new home in Texas. So far, though, Caroline had not confided to Rob and Smoky anything about her personal property which the ranch-owner was presumably holding.

Rob moved the reins to one hand and swatted at a buzzing fly. 'You still think it's the best idea to drive straight into the ranch, Miss Roper?'

'I told you the time's come to stop calling me "Miss Roper". I'm Caroline Winfield until we get back to Fort

Worth. Mrs Abner Winfield of San Francisco, California.'

Smoky sat forward on the rear seat. 'Mam, if you're making up stories, who are we supposed to be if somebody asks us?'

Caroline replied icily without turning to Smoky. 'Yourselves, of course.' She was still angry at Smoky for insisting they bring Petal with them in the buckboard. The girl looked perfectly fine to her. Very content to be travelling alongside Smoky. Caroline suspected they were lovers.

Smoky believed he detected twinges of jealousy in Caroline's behavior. But why would a rich young White lady, who had everything in the world, be jealous of a poor girl like Petal? Somebody with a weak mind and very little to look forward to in the future?

'What about me?' Rob asked. 'Who do I say I am if somebody asks me?'

'My foreman. My husband sent you along with me to help choose land.'

'Why didn't your husband come?'

'He's home working!'

Looking one last time down the dirt streets, she added with exasperation, 'Gentlemen, please. You must start using your imagination.'

Rob corrected, 'We've also got to get our stories straight if you're going to be making up lies.'

'They're not lies, Rob. They're prevarications. Little fibs to get back my rightful property.'

He said, 'You still haven't told us what that property is.'

'You'll find out in due course.'

Stepping back up into the wagon, she opened her parasol and pointed to the far end of the wide street. 'Head down that way. Rattler Gulch lies to the south-east.'

'Yes, mam.' Rob snapped the reins and the pair of dappled mares moved off between the false-fronted buildings marked with signs reading: 'Nickleson's Bar' – 'Tilly's Tonsorial Parlor' – 'Everett's Dry Goods Emporium' – 'Buck's Place' – 'Bank'.

Passing the horses tied to hitching posts, Caroline again whispered, 'Where's all the people?'

Smoky glanced at a bull's hide hanging as a door to the saloon named 'Buck's Place'. Remembering similar towns in western Louisiana, he said, 'Everybody's probably inside looking out at us.'

Caroline shuddered. 'Do you think so?'

'It's one possibility, mam.'

'Why would they do that?'

'It's how folks act in small towns, mam.'

'But certainly this town is used to seeing strangers. It's on the main road between San Francisco and New Orleans. Strangers must pass through Lead Springs every day of the year.'

Rob repositioned the hat on his forehead, saying, 'Don't forget, mam, that the railroad is changing things. It cuts straight across these parts, taking traffic –'

A gun shot broke the silence; the two horses bolted at the sharpness of the noise; Rob gripped the reins, struggling to steady the disturbed animals.

* * *

A tall, swarthy man in a wide-brimmed black hat and dust-covered clothes stepped from behind the bull's hide hanging from the saloon doorway, levelling a rifle at the buckboard as he moved across the boardwalk.

'Who are you?' Caroline demanded. 'What's the meaning of this?'

The man smiled, his face softening as a straight line of white teeth flashed beneath his bushy black moustache. 'Who are *you*, missy?'

The rakishness of the grin caught Caroline off guard.

'I'm . . . We're from San Francisco . . . The earthquake drove us out . . .'

The man lowered his rifle, saying, 'Now, no earthquake can be all bad that drives a pretty lady like yourself to our parts.'

Flustering at the bold remark, Caroline softened, demurring, 'Perhaps you can help us, sir. We're looking for a ranch.'

'Any particular spread?'

'Rattler Gulch.'

The man's playful smile dropped.

Caroline elaborated. 'I'm told there's a woman there who can give me information about property I'm interested in buying.'

Raising the rifle's barrel, the man's voice hardened. 'There's no property for sale around here, lady. You best keep on moving.'

'Oh, but you must be mistaken,' Caroline insisted. 'I was told specifically to speak to the lady at Rattler Gulch Ranch.'

He squinted one eye. 'What lady?'

'I was only given her first name.'

'Which is?'

'Bess.'

'Black Bess?'

'Do you know her?'

The man pointed the rifle into the air, firing a quick succession of shots and, behind him, men began rushing from the saloon, pouring out onto the boardwalk with pistols drawn, rifles ready.

A stout man wearing a grey Confederate cap called, 'What's the trouble, Jaspar?'

The swarthy man – Jaspar – kept the rifle trained on the wagon. 'This little lady here wants to chew the rag with Bess.'

The man in the Confederate cap asked, 'Did you tell her the old lady has no truck with visitors?'

Jaspar nodded, looking from Caroline to Rob, apprais-ing Smoky sitting beside Petal on the rear seat.

'Where they from, Jaspar?' called a shorter man in a fringed leather shirt.

'San Francisco. The earthquake chased them out. So she says.'

The Confederate laughed. 'Then we better escort them out to the ranch and let Bess show them a little Texas hospitality.'

Jaspar kept a straight face. 'You're right, I reckon.'

Turning to the rest of the men, he called, 'On your animals, boys.'

The men mounted the horses on both sides of the street, taking positions in front of and behind the buckboard.

Rob, snapping the reins, followed Jaspar down the street as Caroline sat rigidly on the bench, looking neither to left nor right.

Behind her on the rear seat, Smoky heard whistles and catcalls rising from the men following on horseback; he turned and saw Petal sitting sideways on the bench, waving at the riders.

Grabbing Petal by the shoulder, Smoky wondered if he had been wrong in insisting she didn't stay at the hotel.

* * *

The countryside to the east of Lead Springs was flat, dotted with scrub pines, the grass burned brown by the sun. Low hills rose in the distance, glimmering purple in the afternoon as the horses trailed a cloud of yellow dust.

Jaspar Jones, riding in front of the team of dappled mares, had not spoken since leaving Lead Springs an hour ago. As they approached a tall wooden gate on the left-hand side of the road, he motioned the other riders to slow down and waved Rob to follow him under the crossbeams of the gate.

Smoky, glancing over his shoulder, saw the trailing riders stop and dismount by the fence.

He leaned toward Rob. 'They're closing the gate behind us.'

Caroline began to fidget and squirm. 'What's going to happen?'

'You tell us, Mrs . . . Winfield!' Rob scowled as he followed Jaspar's horse down a sloping road to a collection of out-buildings built around a dirty yard. 'It's your plan.'

Caroline's voice was a whine. 'Daddy didn't say Bess had so many men working for her.'

Rob had lost all patience with Caroline. 'Why didn't you mention this bunch of hoodlums to us before now?'

'I didn't want to frighten you.'

'Frighten us?' Rob grunted.

Caroline pointed. 'Look!'

Rob and Smoky were already staring at a Black woman approaching the buckboard, a short woman dressed in denim bib-overalls and a red bandana knotted over her wrinkled face.

Caroline whispered, 'That must be her. Black Bess.'

Rob asked, 'She owns Rattler Gulch?'

Before Caroline answered, Smoky sat forward on the seat, complaining, 'You didn't tell us some Black woman owned the ranch we were going to.'

In front of them, Jaspar gestured to Rob to halt the buckboard; the short woman faced them, boots set wide apart, arms folded across the bib of her overalls.

Without taking her eyes from the buckboard, she rasped, 'Jaspar Jones, where'd you find this wagonful of shit?'

'They're from San Francisco, Miss Bess, mam.'

She looked from Caroline to Smoky and Petal. 'Them two niggers too?'

'Yes 'm.'

'What about that milk-fed White boy? Where's he from?'

'All from San Francisco, mam. The White gal says the earthquake drove them out.'

'What they doing messing around Lead Springs?'

'Come to buy land, she claims.'

Bess fastened her shoe-button eyes on Caroline. 'Did you tell that White gal, Jaspar, there's no buyers or sellers in these parts? That we're just takers and grabbers?'

'Yes'm. But she says she wants to talk to you.'

Hooking her thumbs around the braces of the bib overalls, Bess ordered, 'Get down out of that rig, girlie. Let's see how much flesh you got on them bones.'

Smoky moved first, followed by Rob; they helped Caroline step to the ground; behind them, Petal scrambled to clutch onto Smoky's arm.

Bess noticed Petal's quick movements. 'What's the matter with you, nigger wench?'

Petal, shrinking against Smoky, buried her head like a frightened child.

Bess demanded, 'What's wrong with your wench, boy? She some kind of dummy?'

Smoky's voice was firm but respectful. 'Mam, her brain ain't the same since the earthquake. She don't talk much.'

'Good.' Bess nodded. 'I don't like a talkative wench. She might make my boy, Bubba, happy.'

Looking back to Smoky, Bess said, 'You're a fine looking buck, boy.'

'Thank you, mam.'

Studying his body, Bess's little brown eyes returned to the crotch of Smoky's twill trousers. 'You got a lot stuffed in those britches, ain't you, boy?'

'I ain't had no complaints, mam.'

'Ever been sucked by a woman with no teeth?'

'No, mam. Can't say I have.'

'You ain't had nothing till you do.'

Bess moved past Smoky, nodding approvingly as she surveyed Rob, and continued towards Caroline.

She chewed her toothless gums as she studied Caroline's full skirt, pleated bodice, straw hat and ivory-headed parasol. Finally she asked, 'Now what kind of fancy gal have we got here?'

Caroline began, 'Mam, my name is –'

'I don't care what your name is, wench. All I care about is –'

Bess reached for Caroline's skirts, grabbing between her legs.

Caroline pulled back her hand to slap. 'How dare you!'

But Bess moved faster, slapping Caroline across the face, striking her a second time and knocking her to the ground.

Smoky and Rob moved to help her; Jaspar Jones pulled two pistols, warning, 'Back, boys. This ain't none of your concern.'

Standing over Caroline sprawled on the ground, Bess mocked, 'So the little city cat's got spunk, has she?'

Caroline gathered her skirt and shrilled, 'I came here to buy land! You can't treat me like this!'

'I don't care who you are or why you came here, missy. We ain't sellers around here. We're takers and grabbers! And I just grabbed your . . . snatch!'

Her small brown eyes twinkling with mischief, Bess ordered, 'Jaspar, take this little city cat along with the pretty Black boy. Lock 'em up in my shack. Lock the White boy over in the woodshed. I'm going to keep them apart till the auction sale.'

'Auction sale?' asked Jaspar Jones. 'What auction sale, Bess?'

Bess rehooked her thumbs around the braces of her overalls. 'The boys got extra money from the round-up. It's burning holes in their pockets, so why not sell them a few slaves?'

'Slaves?'

Bess ignored the question; grabbing Petal by the arm, she ordered, 'Come along with me, wench. Let's see what Bubba makes of you.'

She shoved her across the yard to a cluster of small tarpaper shacks as Jaspar Jones began separating Smoky, Rob, and Caroline.

* * *

Bubba, a large young man in his early twenties with a headful of nappy black hair and a lighter complexion than Bess, wore bib overalls like his mother.

He studied Petal standing in the middle of the shack's

dirt floor, asking as he circled her in his bare feet, 'What's she doing here, Ma?'

Bess was half the size of her son. 'Bubba, you need to learn two things before you're a real man. First, you need to know how to enjoy poontang. Second, you got to learn how to use your whip.'

'Whip? Can I whip her, Ma?' Bubba's eyes brightened as he looked back to Petal.

'Not her, you big heap of blubber! You're going to *pester* this wench!'

Bubba's round cheeks dropped with disappointment. 'Oh.'

Bess added, 'I've got somebody else for you to whip.'

He grinned. 'I like whipping, Ma.'

Dismayed, Bess shook her head. 'Bubba, I don't know where you get that mean streak. It must be from your no-good Pa. The more I think about it, the more I know how right I was to cut the balls off that bastard and bury him six feet under this ranch.'

Bubba wasn't listening; he was shuffling back around Petal, studying the curve of her hips, the fullness of her breasts straining her pink cotton dress, the soft brown coloring of her arms, neck and face.

Watching him appraise Petal, Bess asked, 'Like what you see, Bubba?'

'She's pretty, Ma. Real pretty.'

'Good. I'm going to leave you two alone to see how well you get along together.'

Bubba understood and, biting his lower lip, bashfully dipped his head, drawling, 'Oh, Ma –'

'Don't you get goofy on me, boy. This is your chance to lose your cherry. So get to work.'

Bubba waited until Bess closed the shack door behind her before he moved closer to Petal, running the palm of one hand across the fluff of her hair, complimenting, 'You're a right pretty gal, Petal.'

Petal stared at him, eyes rounded with fear.

'Don't be scared. I ain't going to whip you.'

She studied his round face, his bulging brown eyes, the spread of his freckled brown nose, his fat cheeks, double chin, thin shoulders.

'You like me, Petal?' he asked as he moved behind her, appraising her buttocks.

She kept staring straight ahead of her, silent like a soldier in review.

'Can we play together, Petal, you and me?'

The question startled Petal; she opened her mouth to speak; she hesitated; finally she repeated one word, 'Play?'

Bubba nodded. 'I'd like to play with you, Petal.'

Her words came slowly. 'Will you . . . marry me?'

He stopped. 'What'd you say?'

'Will you marry me?'

'Marry you? For play? Or for real?'

'Real. Play.' Petal shrugged. 'I don't care. I just don't want to be all alone in the world.'

'Me neither. So how about this? As long as you're nice to me, I'll be nice to you and neither of us will be alone?'

'Really?'

'I promise.' Bubba moved back to her, asking, 'Can I see your titties now?'

'Sure.' She began unbuttoning the front of her dress, unlacing the front of her corset. She felt at ease, even safe with Bubba. It was the first time since the fire that she had wanted to talk, to have a conversation with anyone.

Bubba stopped her hand unbuttoning the dress.

She looked at him in surprise.

Reaching forward, he felt the silkiness of Petal's corset between the tips of his thumb and middle finger.

She watched him as he became increasingly mesmerized by the silky touch, and remembering men acting the same way in the bordello, she explained, 'My undies.'

'Undies? I ain't never seen no undies like this before. I seen dresses. I seen petticoats. I seen drawers. But I ain't never seen . . . undies.'

'Want them?'

He pulled back his hand as if he had been burned. 'Me?'

She nodded.

He protested, 'But men don't have . . . undies. Not like this.'

Petal's voice was matter-of-fact, childlike. 'That don't mean you shouldn't. You're special.'

'Special? Me? Really?'

'To me you are.'

His eyes lowered covetously to Petal's silk undergarment, to the lace decorated with fine pink ribbon. 'Can I really have your . . . undies?'

'Sure. It'll be my present to you. My wedding present to you. You can even wear them when we're alone. In bed.'

'Me?'

'Why not? If you like them.'

Bubba lowered his eyes to his own body. He frowned. 'Ain't I too big to wear . . . undies?'

He glanced at the door, whispering, 'And what if somebody comes in when I am trying it on?'

'I'll keep watch. Don't worry.'

Bubba looked from Petal, to the door, back to Petal again. He said, 'I never met nobody like you before. I like you lots and lots.'

'I like you, too.'

Hurriedly, Bubba bolted the door and began unfastening his overalls while Petal stepped out of her dress and unlaced the front of her corset.

In a few moments, they both stood naked in the middle of the dirt floor, their clothes heaped at their feet except for the lace-trimmed corset. Petal stood facing Bubba, gripping the corset in a wad, rubbing the silk over his naked chest, around his neck, across his stomach, under his crotch, exciting his penis into hardness by the smooth touch.

He giggled, 'See how hard you make me.'

'Hmmm. And you got a big one to make hard!'

'You like big ones?'

'A lot. I always said any husband of mine should have a real big one.'

He lowered his voice, 'You don't mind your husband liking his wife's . . . undies?'

'Oh, no. Fact is, I'd like to see you wearing a corset, your big fat dick dangling down from under the lace. I'll get you your own corset to wear if you marry me. Promise.'

'You're fun!'

Petal looked into his eyes, saying seriously, 'I'm all alone in the world, Bubba. I got nobody.'

'No, you're not alone any more. You've got me.'

Grabbing her, Bubba planted a kiss firmly on her lips, pressing their nakedness together, whispering, 'I ain't never felt so good in, in, in . . . never ever never!'

Petal pulled back from him, speaking as if she were inquiring about a child's new game, 'Have you ever eaten pie?'

'Pie?'

'Hair pie.'

'Is it like mud pie?'

'It's better. Get down. I'll lead you.'

Petal stood back from Bubba and, as he knelt on the floor in front of her, she guided his face between her thighs, ordering him to stick his tongue into the thatch between her legs, to poke his tongue in and out of her expanding pinkness, to suck on her wiry black hair, to chew on her lips, to work his mouth harder on her wet mound, coaching, 'That's right. Eat me. Eat your wife's little pie. Your wife's going to buy a nice pair of undies for you. So eat your wife's potato pie.'

Petal thought of Alicia making love to her, tonguing her vagina; then she saw an image of Smoky's penis flash in front of her eyes. But remembering Bubba's more than generous piece of manhood, she recalled how she had made it grow, become hard, and Bubba promising to marry her. So forgetting about her past, she thought how she was going to concentrate on her husband, a true husband, someone who could be both a woman and a man. What was more, Bubba was the only person who was promising to take care of her. The Lord had sent him to her as an answer. Maybe the Lord had at last given her a home.

Chapter Thirteen

THE SLAVE AUCTION

'*Please* go to bed with Bess,' pleaded Caroline as Smoky paced the floor of the tin-roofed shack where Jaspar Jones had locked them. 'Bess wants you to make love to her.'

'How do you know what she wants?' Smoky's voice was clipped and impatient.

Caroline followed Smoky, hounding, 'Bess said she wanted to make love to you. She grabbed you and told you about . . . doing things to you with no teeth.'

Smoky laughed. 'Don't believe everything an old woman like that says.'

Caroline persisted, 'If she wants to make love to you, you must let her. She'll tell you things she won't tell Rob and me.'

Smoky slowed his pacing. 'Why would that old woman trust me and not you two?'

'Because you're –' Caroline fumbled for the right words. 'You're like her.'

'I'm like her? How?' Smoky's patience with Caroline was wearing thin. 'Say exactly what you mean, lady!'

'Rob and I are White. But you – you're –'

'She'll tell me things because I'm Black? Is that what you're saying?'

'Yes!'

'Lady, do you think being Black is like being in some kind of club?'

'No. Of course not. But –'

'Do you think Black people tell each other all their secrets?'

'Don't get hysterical. I was just saying –'

'Do you think that being Black makes me your slave and you can tell me to do whatever you want me to? Have you plumb forgotten that the Emancipation Proclamation has ever been written? That the Civil War has been fought? Do you think you can say "do this", "do that", and all us niggers will bow and scrape and run and do your fetching? Is that what you think, lady?'

'No. Of course not. But –'

'So what makes you think I'd go to bed with whoever you say anyway?'

'I *am* paying you.'

'To be your bodyguard. But I'm not some whore.'

'Oh, ho! Since when?'

Smoky stared at her, fighting himself to control his anger, reminding himself that he had never struck a woman – not when she didn't want to be hit – and that he wasn't going to start doing it now.

Nodding his head, he agreed, 'Yes. I was working on Pleasant Street when you met me. I was a whore. But that's over now. I started working for you. But you put my life in danger because you don't know what the hell you're doing.'

Caroline also was becoming angry. She faced Smoky, asking, 'Are you standing there and telling me I don't know what I'm doing?'

'We wouldn't be in this pickle if you did. Look at us. Locked up in some little shack. Waiting for some mad woman to auction us off like slaves to a bunch of whisker-faced cowboys!'

'Don't shout at me, Smoky Summers! That old woman has property that belongs to me. Railroad bonds my father bought to give me security for the rest of my life. But Daddy was fool enough to come here when he was hurt. Bess took the bonds away from him and put them under her bed. When Daddy was able to escape, he couldn't get back the bonds. Black Bess had them under her bed and was sleeping on them. Now I must find that bed and get back my bonds. I don't need you saying I don't know what I'm doing because I know very well what I'm –'

Caroline paused; she watched Smoky moving away

from her, crossing to a long box with a sack on top of it.

'Where are you going? You're not even listening to me!'

Kneeling down by the wooden box, he said, 'This is it.'

'What?'

'This is where she put the bonds.'

'I said under a *bed*! Not under some old bag on a box!'

'This *is* her bed,' Smoky insisted. 'This is her cabin. So this is where she sleeps. A corncob mattress. Lots of Southern people sleep on them.'

Lifting the lumpy mattresss from the box, Smoky tossed it behind him and lifted the top of the box, opening it like a trunk.

Caroline looked over Smoky's shoulder as he began digging through the musty contents. Wrinkling her nose, she said, 'Ick! It looks more like some dirty old magpie's nest.'

Clawing through papers, tin boxes, rags, Smoky singled out items. 'A copy of the *Louisiana Picayune* . . . a tobacco tin . . . a button jar . . . a saddle bag . . . some old socks . . .'

'Stop! That's it!' Caroline snatched the saddle bag from the box. She threw back the flap and pulled out a sheaf of blue-and-gold embossed documents.

Smoky jerked them away from her and stuffed them back into the saddle bag. 'Leave them here.'

'Are you crazy?'

Smoky dropped the saddle bag back into the box, pulled some papers and rags over it, and lowered the lid. 'If she looks inside and sees that the bonds are gone, she'll know why we're here and then we'll never get away.'

Caroline meekly answered, 'Oh.'

Getting to his feet, Smoky tossed the corncob mattress back onto the box. 'We've got to pretend we don't know they're here.'

She nodded submissively. 'You're right.'

Smoky softened his voice. 'I didn't mean to shout at you. I'm sorry.'

Caroline shook her head. 'No. You're absolutely right. But you're a gentleman to apologize. Thank you.'

Smoky resumed pacing the floor. 'Now we've got to think of some way to get out of here.'

'You're right,' repeated Caroline, but only thinking about how much she admired Smoky, wondering if she could make love to him. She had never felt so safe, so secure with a man since she had been a little girl with her father. Was her ideal man a Negro? Oh, dear! Why was life so complicated?

* * *

Rob answered the knock on the door of the woodshed where he was locked, across the dirty yard from Bess's shack.

'Come in. You've got the key.'

The door opened on its leather hinges and a woman entered the woodshed, a shawl wrapped around her shoulders, her bare feet crunching across the wood chips as she moved to the chopping block to set down a covered tray.

Removing the cloth from the tray, she picked up a plate of food and a tin cup of coffee, saying, 'Keep your voice low, if you want to ask any questions.'

Rob looked at the half-open door. 'Who are you?'

'Ruth Day. My husband and me lived on a ranch east of here. Sam refused to sell cattle to Bess at her price so she killed him. That was two years ago.'

'You've been here ever since?'

She nodded.

'Why?'

'I'm a prisoner like yourself.' She looked blankly at him. 'You saw how many men she's got working for her.'

'Who are all those men?'

'Cattle rustlers. Thieves. Anything dishonest and low.'

Rob was suspicious. 'How do I know you're not one of them? That she didn't send you here?'

The woman raised one hand, pulling back her hair and exposing an ugly bruise on the side of her face. Rob saw that she was younger than she had at first looked in the ragged old clothing, that she was a very attractive woman with large green eyes, a small nose, high cheekbones.

Distrustfully, he asked, 'What does the bruise prove? Lots of men beat their women. Lots of women enjoy it.'

'Not me. I like a man to respect me.' Ruth dropped her hair. 'But you're right not to trust me. I was a fool to think you would.'

She moved to lift the empty tray from the block.

'No. Wait.' Rob put his hand on her wrist. 'Are the others safe?'

Ruth glanced at the door and whispered, 'The Black girl's with Bubba. He's Bess's son. The White girl and the other man are locked in Bess's cabin. Bess is planning some crazy kind of shindig for supper tonight.'

'We heard her tell that guy, Jaspar, that she's having some kind of slave auction.'

'Slave auction?' Ruth crossed herself. 'Holy Mother of God!'

'Why? What does that mean?'

'The men get bored easy. You and your friends will probably be their amusement for a few nights.' Her eyes fixed on Rob, she added, 'In and out of bed.'

* * *

The cookhouse at Rattler Gulch Ranch was situated at the far end of the dirt yard, a long, peak-roofed shed with a lean-to attached to one end. Two cast iron cookstoves stood in the rickety annexe and the main shed had plank tables running along three sides of its one big room.

Bess ate supper at the center table placed at the head of the other two; Jaspar Jones sat on her left; Bubba sat on her right, with Petal sitting next to him, ignoring the sixteen men at the tables in front of her, clinging devotedly to Bubba's arm and whispering into his ear.

Ruth Day carried bowls and platters of food from the kitchen, huge servings of spare ribs, boiled potatoes, beans and rice, sliced bread smeared with lard.

When supper was over and Ruth began gathering the dirty plates and cutlery, Bess rose from her chair and, pounding her earthenware whisky jug on the table, she shouted, 'Listen to me, you bastards! Listen to me, God damn it to hell!'

Waiting for the room to silence, she began, 'I paid all you sons-of-bitches good money for last week's roundup from Del Rio. Tomorrow you're going to make more money bringing Heinrich's herd back from Lubbock.'

A bald man with a sunburnt face rose from a bench. 'Bess, do we camp down at Lubbock or ride back tomorrow night?'

Bess squinted one eye. 'Willy, you always piss when you should be shitting. Why can't you ask the right question at the right time?'

'Yes 'm. Sorry 'm.' The ranch-hand named Willy Liddle sank sheepishly back down on his bench.

Bess, chewing her toothless gums, surveyed the fifteen weatherbeaten faces gathered around the plank tables in front of her. 'You bastards got more questions about tomorrow's ride? Or are you going to let me get on explaining about the surprise I planned for you tonight?'

Shouts and whoops answered that she should explain the surprise.

Bess hoisted the jug to her mouth, taking long, thirsty gulps, the corn liquor dribbling down her chin. She wiped her face on her sleeve and continued. 'Lots of you yahoos come from the South. Louisiana. Georgia. Arkansas. The Carolinas same as me. You Johnny Rebs knew about the old slave days from folks back home. You heard about the days when a person could lay down money on the table and buy a good buck or nice juicy wench.

'I know about slavery first hand. I was born a slave sixty-three years ago. But I was so mean, so cussed ornery, my master got tired of whipping me and gave me money to get as far away as I could from his land.'

Taking another swig of corn liquor, Bess wiped her

mouth, continuing, 'Tonight I'm going to give you a little show of what a slave auction used to be like in the old days.'

Loud cheers rose from the men, some clanking spoons or a knife against their tin mugs.

'Quiet down, you sons of bitches! Quiet down!' Bess waited for them to silence, explaining, 'I had me a few surprise visitors this afternoon. One is the pretty little colored wench you see Bubba smooching-up alongside me here tonight.'

Petal dipped her head to Bubba's shoulder as he grinned at his mother.

Bess continued, 'I might decide to marry this wench here off to Bubba. But I decided the best way to get rid of the other visitors is to *sell* them! To you!'

Laughter filled the room.

'So this is what I'm going to do.'

Gripping one thumb around a shoulder brace on her overalls, she proceeded, 'In old slave days, an auctioneer stripped down a wench to let interested customers examine her toe-nail to titty. But if I strip down a wench in front of you horny bastards, you'd stampede me to death trying to get your hands on her. So I'm going to –'

She clapped one hand to her mouth, shouting, 'Hey, Charlie! Bring out that fancy piece of poontang!'

The cook, Charlie Tilsbury, a lanky man with a grimy brown felt hat pulled down over his big ears, shoved Caroline Roper from the kitchen, goading her with a long wooden spoon.

Bess called over the men's din, 'You're going to have to take my word for it that this piece of tail is the hottest thing outside of Charlie's kitchen!'

Charlie the cook grinned, nodding his head.

Bess continued, 'The highest bidder gets to have her till morning. To be his own personal slave.'

'Ten dollars!' called the first bidder.

'Ten dollars?' Bess snorted. 'You pay more to hump old Katrina Bahutivich in Lead Springs!'

'Eleven!' offered a second man.

'Eleven?' Bess spat. 'You tight-fisted buggers!'

'Fifteen!' called a third.

The next bid was: 'Twenty!'

'Twenty-five!'

'Twenty-seven and my new pair of false teeth!'

The bids mounted to fifty, sixty, seventy-five dollars, passing one hundred.

Caroline shrank back from the men shouting and waving fistfuls of money, holding both arms across the bodice of her dress as if she were naked.

The bids climbed past two-hundred dollars, mounting to two-hundred-twenty, two-hundred-fifty, two-hundred-and-seventy-five dollars.

A deep-chested voice shouted, '*Five hundred dollars!*'

The room silenced.

A smile on his swarthy face, Jaspar Jones rose from his chair next to Bess and dug into his pocket. Pulling out a fat roll of money, he peeled off ten bills and slapped them on the table.

Pushing back his chair, he strutted around the table, faced Caroline, and extended one arm as if he were inviting her to dance.

Caroline glanced at Bess and, looking back at Jaspar Jones, slapped his face.

Jaspar Jones laughed and, putting one hand around her buttocks, the other under her legs, lifted her from the floor and carried her towards the cookhouse door.

* * *

Charlie Tilsbury returned from the kitchen with two rolls of rope. He was followed by a burly ranch guard, Chris O'Leary, carrying a bundle of woven hemp. Tilsbury tossed one end of the rope over the ceiling beam as O'Leary dropped his bundle to the floor.

Bess, watching the two men work, explained to the ranch hands, 'In the old days, planters used to breed slaves.

A White master went down to the slave quarters and knocked up a nigger wench, giving himself a nice little high-yellow piccaninny to work for him in the field. Because I'm Black, as well as being a gal, I'm getting a pretty coon boy to knock-up a White gal. Or at least give us a good show trying!'

A man called, 'It looks to me, Bess, like you're planning a lynching!'

'I'll lynch your damn neck, Porky Hubbard!' Bess slurred, her tongue thickening from the corn liquor. 'If you look, you'll see O'Leary's brought in a hammock. A God-damned Mexican hammock. He and Charlie are going to string it up from the rafters so we get a good view of a buck pestering the wench!'

She looked to the kitchen, shouting, 'Ruth, get your arse out here, gal!'

Ruth Day appeared in the doorway.

Bess ordered, 'Get over by Charlie, Ruth, or I'll use Bubba's bullwhip on you!'

Ruth hesitantly obeyed.

As Charlie Tilsbury proceeded to knot a rope to each end of the hammock, Bess explained, 'I'm going to match up Ruth with a colored boy who would've been a house-nigger in the old days. Somebody too pretty to waste in the cotton fields.'

Looking back to the kitchen, Bess bawled, 'Boys, bring out that nigger buck with the big dick.'

Two ranch guards dragged Smoky through the kitchen door, pushing him towards Tilsbury and O'Leary.

Bess ordered, 'Shuck off them clothes, boy.'

Smoky looked from Bess, down the table to Petal.

'Can't you hear me?' rasped Bess. 'I said shuck off them clothes. The same goes for you, Ruth.'

Looking at Ruth, Smoky slowly began unbuttoning his shirt; Ruth moved to untie the sash on her faded cotton dress, keeping her eyes to the floor.

'After you two peel off your clothes, hop into that hammock,' Bess ordered. 'We're going to watch you give us a hump show. You better give us a damned good show or else I'll –'

She reached into the pocket of her overalls, pulled out a Smith & Wesson pistol, and fired a shot in the air.

'That's what happens to you,' she explained, 'if I feel you ain't performing up to snuff.'

Excitement was mounting, men rising from their seats, crowding to look at Ruth and Smoky undressing, to get a look at Ruth's breasts, at Smoky's penis.

Charlie Tilsbury waited until Ruth and Smoky were completely naked and, shoving them into the stretched hammock, he and O'Leary began tugging their ropes.

Bess, watching the Mexican-rope hammock rising above the floor like a fish net from the sea, ordered, 'Raise 'em high, boys! Raise 'em up high!'

Inside the hammock, Smoky squirmed and tossed, the hemp burning his skin.

Ruth's legs bumped against his thighs; her knee hit his groin; her breasts squeezed against his chest.

In a tangle of arms and legs, she whispered, 'I wish I could die.'

Smoky tried to give her more room to find a position, saying consolingly, 'Don't worry, mam.'

'But we're supposed to make . . . love!'

'We'll manage something.'

Ruth pressed against him as the hammock rose higher on the ropes. 'You heard what she said about shooting us.'

Smoky offered, 'At least maybe you should know my name.'

'You're Smoky – your friend Rob talked about you.'

'You know Rob?'

Ruth whispered. 'I took supper to him. He's locked in a woodshed across from Bess's cabin.'

'Do you work here?'

Ruth brushed hair from her face. 'My name's Ruth. Ruth Day. Rob will tell you about me.'

Smoky chanced, 'If you see Rob before I do, tell him we

found Caroline's property. But we need some way to escape.'

'Tomorrow's a cattle drive. The ranch will be near enough deserted for three days.'

A pistol shot cracked below them and Bess bellowed, 'Start plugging her, boy, or you'll get an arse full of lead.'

Ruth whispered, 'She won't think twice about killing us.'

Smoky took a deep breath. 'We better start doing something.'

Ruth, knowing Smoky was right, moved her head to his midsection, opening her mouth, taking his penis between her stretched lips.

Smoky took his cue from Ruth's action and moved his head between her naked legs.

Whistles rose below the hammock as Smoky and Ruth lay head to midsection; Ruth used both hands to hold Smoky's hardened penis to her mouth; Smoky buried his working tongue between her spread thighs.

A ranch hand shouted, 'How is it, Ruthie? Does it taste as good as White meat?'

Another voice asked, 'Does he spoil you for a White guy, Ruth?'

Bess called, 'Come on, boy. Don't just lie there like a slug. Start pumping some Black dick into that White bitch.' She fired another shot.

Obediently, slowly, Smoky moved up beside Ruth, easing his penis into her vagina as she rested the soles of her bare feet on the sides of the hammock. Opening her thighs with her hands, Ruth allowed Smoky's penis to drive deeper, wider into her, giving a full view of their copulation to Bess and the ranch hands, hard blackness slipping in and out of wet pinkness.

[illegible] Shirley's [illegible], but was [illegible]

[illegible] The [illegible]

[illegible]

[illegible] killing [illegible]

[illegible] took a deep breath. 'We [illegible]

[illegible]

[illegible]

[illegible] between [illegible]

[illegible]

[illegible] Spencer's [illegible]

[illegible]

[illegible]

[illegible]

[illegible]

[illegible]

Considering [illegible] Shirley [illegible] Both [illegible]

[illegible] the [illegible] things [illegible]

[illegible] of [illegible]

[illegible] out of [illegible]

Chapter Fourteen

THE BULLWHIP

Smoky sat bolt upright on the floor and looked around him in the darkness. He remembered with a start that he had fallen asleep last night in Bess's cabin. After freeing him and Ruth from the hammocks, Bess had led him from the cookhouse, stumbling drunkenly across the dirt yard, waving her pistol in the air, threatening to use it on him if he didn't make love to her as he had done with Ruth. But inside the cabin, Bess had collapsed onto the corncob mattress, gripping the pistol in one fist, the door key in the other, muttering that she'd shove the pistol barrel up Smoky's arse if he tried to escape.

Seeing daylight slanting through the shutters bolted across the cabin's small window, Smoky realized that he had been more exhausted last night than he had suspected, that he had fallen into a deep sleep only a few minutes after Bess had begun snoring. She had obviously risen early this morning and left him in the cabin.

As his mind began to clear, Smoky recalled Ruth telling him about Bess's men going on a cattle drive today.

Moving to the small window, he pressed one eye against the plank shutters, trying to see if the horses were gone from the corral, if Bess's men had already left the ranch. Hopefully she had gone with them.

A clank sounded behind him.

Turning, he heard a bolt slide outside the cabin door; he stood in the middle of the floor, watching the door slowly open, and saw Bess outlined in the low doorway, the bandana knotted on her head.

'Morning, boy.'

'Morning, mam,' Smoky replied, trying to look past her to see if the corral was empty.

Bess sauntered into the cabin, thumbs hooked around the braces of her overalls. 'You ready to tell me what you four were doing in Lead Springs yesterday in that buckboard?'

'Exactly what the lady told you, mam.' Smoky saw the pistol butt poking from her pocket.

'Cut the bullcrap, boy. You don't expect me to believe some story about you coming to Lead Springs to buy a new home after that earthquake chased you out of San Francisco?'

Where was Caroline this morning? Was Rob still in the woodshed? Had Ruth managed to speak to him again and make some escape plan?

'What's the matter, boy? Cat got your tongue?'

Remembering the story Caroline had told him to say, Smoky shrugged, answering, 'Mam, Petal, Rob, and me just work for Miss Caroline.'

Bess cocked her head to one side. 'That Petal wench, she's not as much a dummy as you said she was, boy. Fact is, that wench is getting on right chummy with Bubba. They've been talking together quite a bit since they met yesterday.'

Smoky had seen Petal sitting next to Bess's fat son last night at supper; he had noticed how Petal had clung to Bubba's arm, how attentive Bubba had been to her.

'Mam, maybe your son is the man Petal needs.'

Bess spat on the floor. Wiping her mouth with one hand, she said, 'They ain't the only lovebirds we got around here today. Your fancy White gal spent the night with Jaspar Jones. Jaspar's quite the lady's man when he wants to be. Fact is, they got on so well together last night, Jaspar took her riding with him today.'

'Caroline's gone?'

Bess grinned. 'A hard screwing makes a gal forget her high and mighty ways. After a night in bed with a good man, a woman will tell him anything, boy. Even where she hides her life savings.'

'Then, mam, I suggest you ask Miss Caroline what you want to know.' Smoky fixed his eyes on Bess, insisting, 'I can't tell you nothing.'

'Boy, there are a few things I haven't told you. For instance, Bubba has a bullwhip. But the bad thing about it is he's just learning to snap that long leather cat. He misses his mark quite a bit. He tears up a man's back something awful.'

Appraising Smoky, Bess shook her head, adding, 'It'll be a pity to ruin that pretty body of yours with a bullwhip, boy.'

Smoky blurted, 'Whip me?'

'Damn right!'

'But whipping's over with. Whipping's gone out with slavery.'

'The shit it has, boy. Whipping's a fact of life. So's slavery. Slavery's not finished. Any nigger who thinks so is a damned crazy fool.'

Stepping closer to Smoky, Bess's toothless face puckered into a grimace, and tapping her forefinger on his chest, she said, 'Most niggers are more slaves now than before Freedom Day, boy. You're from the South. You seen niggers with no place to live. No jobs to work at. No food for their young'uns. If niggers do get a job, it's share-cropping, living in a share-cropper's cabin not fit for a dog to crap in. They break their backs picking cotton for the White man. The White man's store keeps them poor. Niggers these days keep shackled to Whitie tighter than any iron chains ever held them in slavery.

'People say bad things about me, boy. That I kill and steal. That I rob and whip innocent people. And I do, boy. I do all them things. And do you know why? Because I ain't ever being no poor-ass slave to no Whitie no more. I was freed once and I'm staying free. This is my land. I aim to keep it mine.

'And I don't like strangers snooping around here, boy. I'm going to whip any man, woman, or child who doesn't give me a damn good reason why he's got a nose to my ground. Even if he's a nigger. A nigger owes nothing to nobody 'cept himself.'

Nodding her head, Bess said, 'So think about that, boy. Think about who you should be loyal to. Yourself or that White gal. You better decide soon if you want to save your Black ass. You decide by the time I come back or I'm going to set Bubba on you with his bullwhip.'

Turning, Bess closed the door behind her, sliding the bolt shut on the outside.

Smoky waited until he heard her footsteps crunch away from the cabin, then, moving towards the bed, he threw back the corncob mattress and opened the box.

* * *

Jaspar Jones galloped out of Rattler Gulch Ranch with Caroline Roper and fourteen men as the sun was rising over the jagged eastern skyline. Riding five miles south to Elephant Mesa, he halted the men, ordering Chris O'Leary to escort Caroline back to the ranch. Jaspar Jones had not told Caroline specifically that he and Bess's men were cattle rustlers; he had only said that it would be dangerous for her to ride with them for the next few days on the cattle drive.

A good horsewoman, Caroline spun the tawny stallion which Jaspar had given her to ride, waving farewell to him one last time as he and the men disappeared in a cloud of dust and thundering hooves.

Mindless of O'Leary riding alongside her to keep her from escaping, Caroline cantered peacefully back to Rattler Gulch Ranch, thinking about Jaspar returning in three days' time, remembering how he had told O'Leary that he would hold him personally responsible if anything happened to her.

Dressed in one of Jaspar's shirts belted at the waist, and a pair of his trousers rolled above her lace-up boots, Caroline ignored the morning heat, considering how she had never before met a man as exciting as Jaspar Jones, the only man ever to appeal totally to her as a lover.

Jaspar had been full of the unexpected.

Caroline's first surprise last night had been the orderliness of Jaspar's cabin. After he had carried her kicking and screaming from the cookhouse, he had dumped her into the middle of his big brass bed and lit a kerosene lamp.

As Caroline cowered in one corner of the bed, Jaspar had paced the floor, commiserating with her about the earthquake that had driven her from San Francisco, complimenting her for having the courage to travel to find a new home, adding that if he were her husband he certainly would not allow her to face the rugged Texas countryside.

Polite, attentive, even debonair in his swarthy manner, Jaspar sank to the edge of the double bed, apologizing for the rustic condition of his cabin.

'A young lady of your breeding deserves better than a shack like this.'

Caroline sniffed, pleased that he recognized her as a person of quality.

He added, 'But this is the best place for you on the ranch, mam. You'll be safe with me here. Oh, yes. I'll see to that.'

Caroline wondered if she should believe him.

Sitting on the edge of the bed, he rested both elbows on his knees, saying, 'I don't regret the five hundred dollars I gave Bess not to sell you to those savages. A lady of quality like you could never survive with those brutes.'

Without turning to her, he soothed, 'Just look at you. Quivering. Shaking. A bundle of nerves.'

She whispered. 'I'm better. Thank you . . . sir.'

He reached for her hand. 'No, I can feel it. You're trembling like a leaf.'

'No, really.' His hand felt dry, firm, comforting.

Lifting her fingers to his mouth, he gently brushed them with a kiss, whispering, 'You're just like a little doll.'

Caroline, feeling more relaxed the more he talked,

eventually rested her head against his shoulder, confiding that she was pleased to be with him, away from Bess and the other men.

Jaspar, turning his head to her, lowered his mouth, lightly kissing her lips, increasing the pressure as she responded.

Pulling her towards him, he moved his tongue between her lips, exploring the warm cavity of her mouth with his tongue as his hand began to move across her body.

Caroline stopped his fingers on the top button of her dress. 'No . . . please.'

'I only want you to relax. You can't stay dressed and awake all night.'

She pulled back. 'Will I *sleep* here?'

'It's the only place you'll be safe.'

'But –'

He held one finger to her lips. 'Don't. I want to protect you. I would feel responsible if I allowed you to be taken away and something happened to you.'

'You *are* kind.' Caroline gazed into his dark eyes and, looking up, she saw how handsomely his black curly hair tumbled over his forehead.

'Now get yourself comfortable.'

Jaspar resumed unbuttoning her dress, giving her a kiss for each button he undid.

As she scrambled under the top sheet, Jaspar moved to turn down the flame and undress in the darkness. Caroline saw his nakedness by moonlight, not protesting as she admired his tightly muscled back, the smooth contours of his buttocks, the flash of a thick penis curled over his scrotum.

Waiting for him to join her in bed, she felt a devilish urge she had never known before, hearing an inner voice telling her that she did not know if she was going to live or die, to escape or remain a prisoner here, so why not risk making love to a man who was so complimentary to her, so appealing to her, a man whose body she could not fault?

Feeling the mattress sink as he climbed into bed, she gave a deep sigh, telling herself to accept life like a grown woman, not to be a frigid, terrified little girl.

As moonlight streamed through the window over the bed, Jaspar moved between Caroline's legs, petting her blonde hair against the pillow as he smiled down at her.

Looking up at his eyes, his thick moustache, his flashing white smile, Caroline realized that a dark Latin-type lover like Jaspar – not Smoky – was indeed her ideal man, someone who knew how to treat her like a goddess.

Jaspar's love-making was like nothing Caroline had ever known. Each sexual gesture was accompanied by a tender kiss, an embrace, a compliment, some word or phrase complimenting her beauty, her taste, her courage.

Torn between the gentleness of his voice and the thrill of his muscular body pressing between her legs, Caroline remembered that he might be a thief, possibly a cattle rustler, and the thought increased her excitement, making an orgasm course through her body, slickening her feminine channel for his phallus.

He gripped her tightly on both shoulders, securing a strong hold to plunge his phallus more fully into her warmth, his knees planted between hers.

Caroline submitted to his manly pressure, enjoying the way he was dominant yet considerate, giving her more pleasure than she had ever known in bed, surpassing even the image of men in her masturbation fantasies.

Breaking the rhythm of his drives, Jaspar ejected himself and moved to explore her body with his mouth.

Lips. Eyes. Shoulders. Neck. Breasts. Caroline abandoned every part of herself to him. She squirmed on the sheets as he nibbled her toes. She tossed and quivered as he licked her inner thighs. She gasped as he gobbled her nipples and returned to driving the blunt head of his penis inside her clutching warmth.

Caroline remembered he was possibly a common thief, a bandit, a brigand, and she thrilled at the idea of being with him. The next thought to cross her mind was that she might only be attracted to men who were dangerous. Oh God! What chance of happiness did she have if that were so?

Despite his role as Bess's foreman, Jaspar showed only respect – and passion – for Caroline throughout the night. They had hated to get out of bed early this morning to leave for the cattle drive. And remembering how Jaspar had given her his clothing to wear, Caroline realized with a shock that she and O'Leary had passed through the gates of Bess's ranch, that they had already ridden the five miles back from Elephant Mesa, and she had spent the entire time in a sensuous daydream about Jaspar making love to her.

Coming out of her trance, she saw an ugly sight in the dirty yard.

* * *

Smoky stood facing a post planted in the dirt yard in front of Bess's cabin; thin leather cords bound his wrists around the post; his shirt was torn from his back and the flesh on his back was ripped, dripping with blood.

Bubba stood behind Smoky, gripping a leather bullwhip in one hand as Petal hovered behind him, nervously biting her fingernails and watching Bubba strike Smoky with sharp, hard lashes.

Pulling the whip over the shoulder of his bib overalls, Bubba squinted his bulging eyes and threw its tip forward, drawing another streak of blood across Smoky's spine.

Smoky tightened with the sting. He jerked back his head as a new ladder of scarlet appeared on his torn flesh.

Bubba laughed like a child, pulling the whip towards him across the dirt, crying, 'You're my slave, nigger! You're my very own slave to play with like I want!'

Snapping the whip with his right hand, Bubba aimed again for Smoky's shoulder blades. But missing the target, he curled the leather above the trousers encircling Smoky's waist.

Caroline galloped angrily towards Bubba; she reared her stallion, screaming, 'Stop it! Stop it right now!'

Chris O'Leary galloped behind her, trying to keep her from interfering with Bubba. But Caroline reared her horse, frightening O'Leary's animal, making him drop his rifle, and she turned her stallion to face Bubba. Leaning from the saddle she snatched the whip from his hand.

'Damn you!' cried Bubba. 'Damn you, White bitch!'

Gripping the whip's butt, Caroline flailed it at Bubba, shrilling, 'I'll show you what this feels like!'

Bubba held up both hands, running from Caroline, crying, 'I'm going to tell my Ma! I'm going to tell my Ma!'

'Tell her!' screamed Caroline as she chased him down the yard, snapping the whip at him. 'Tell her and I'll whip her too!'

As Bubba ran towards the far shed, O'Leary galloped behind him; Caroline turned the horse, seeing Petal also trying to escape.

Dancing the frisky horse in front of Petal, Caroline demanded, 'Why didn't you try and stop him?'

Petal froze, staring up at Caroline.

Caroline steadied the animal. 'How could you stand by and let him hurt Smoky? Don't you know Smoky was the only one who wanted to help you?'

Petal looked from Caroline on the stallion to Smoky slumped motionless against the post.

Caroline raged down to her, 'I would have left you on a cinder heap in San Francisco! But Smoky insisted on bringing you with us! The least you can do is keep that big lummox from whipping him to death!'

Petal, looking one more time at Smoky, lifted the long hem of her dress and dashed down towards the far end of the yard.

Hopping from the stallion, Caroline rushed to the post.

Smoky's head hung to one side, his back smeared with

blood, the leather cord having worn the skin raw on both his wrists.

Hurriedly untying his hands, Caroline wailed, 'Are you going to live?'

Smoky groaned.

Tossing the leather cord to the ground, she helped him to stand upright, begging, 'Oh, forgive me for getting you into this mess. Believe me, I'm sorry. I'm so sorry.'

Smoky opened his mouth. 'I got the . . . bonds.' His voice was barely audible.

Caroline gaped at him.

Leaning against the post to keep from collapsing, Smoky repeated, 'I got the bonds.'

She whispered, 'Where?'

He gave his crotch a limp pat. 'Here. My pants.'

The sound of a horse racing from the far end of the yard attracted their attention; turning, they saw Ruth and Rob galloping towards them on a black mare.

Rob reined the mare, jumped to the ground and ran to Smoky. 'We couldn't come sooner, old friend. Ruth had to find us a horse.'

Sitting astride the big animal, Ruth looked anxiously over her shoulder. 'Talk later, Rob. Bubba's gone to bring Bess from the cow barn!'

Rob pulled off his shirt and tied it around Smoky's neck like a cape, protecting his back wounds from the harsh sun. Putting Smoky's arm over his shoulder, he helped him toward Caroline's horse, saying to Ruth, 'You girls ride together.'

Caroline stared from Rob to Ruth, suddenly bewildered.

Positioning Smoky's foot in a stirrup, Rob explained, 'Ruth says there's a noon train from Lead Springs.'

Ruth moved forward on the saddle for Caroline to mount behind her. 'There's a woman in town who'll hide us till the train comes.'

Rob mounted the stallion in front of Smoky to keep from rubbing against his back as they rode.

Caroline, taking a deep breath, glanced back down the

length of the yard. What should she do? Wait here for Jaspar? Or should she leave and chance never seeing him again?

* * *

Caroline's words echoed in Petal's head as she ran down the dirt yard – the chastisement for allowing Bubba to whip Smoky, how Smoky had been the only one who had wanted to help her. The sharp rebuke lifted a fog from Petal's mind. Caroline was right. Petal thought, 'Why didn't I stop Bubba?' She realized she had to start asserting herself over Bubba, not only to save Smoky but to secure a home for herself here, and she was going to have to do it quickly.

Reaching the cow barn at the end of the yard, Petal looked around the cool darkness and spied Bubba with his mother in the far corner, their heads together in a deep conference.

Walking directly towards them, Petal grabbed Bubba by a shoulder brace of his bib overalls.

Bess shrieked, 'What the hell you doing, wench?'

Ignoring Bess, Petal demanded, 'Bubba, you love me or not?'

Bess stepped forward, repeating, 'What the hell you doing with my boy?'

'Shut your mouth, old woman,' Petal ordered, seized by a fury she never knew she possessed.

Looking back at Bubba, she demanded, 'You love me or not?'

Bubba's eyes protruded from their sockets as he looked from Petal's angry face to the shock on his mother's face. He knew she was surprised that someone dared speak to her in such a way.

'It's either her or me,' Petal threatened. 'So are we going to be man and wife or not?'

Bess grabbed the other brace of Bubba's overalls, pulling him away from Petal. 'Boy, we're wasting our time here when I should be getting my pistols. You came here telling me that the blonde bitch took away your whip and made you stop lashing that nigger boy. Let's go teach them a lesson.'

She began dragging him to the barn doors.

Petal followed, ranting, 'Are you willing to forget everything we talked about, Bubba? Your happiness? The things you like doing? The things we both like doing?'

Bubba looked over his shoulder at Petal, confusion in his eye, as Bess pulled him from the barn.

Petal ran after them, knowing this was her chance to get a home and she wasn't going to lose it.

'Bubba,' she called, 'it's either your Ma or me, Bubba! I'm better for you than she is, Bubba! You know it! You know it!'

Petal glanced beyond the corral, seeing Bess's cabin. She knew that if Bess got her pistols, Smoky's chances of escape would probably be lost. So would her chances of forcing Bubba to rebel against Bess.

Running ahead of them, Petal threw open the cabin door and looked around frantically for the pistols.

Chapter Fifteen

TRAIN DAYS

Katrina Bahutivich, a red-faced widow with straw-colored hair and a cheery disposition, settled her unexpected guests into the parlor of her small house beside the railroad tracks in Lead Springs. Tossing a collection of embroidered pillows and rag dolls off the plush divan by the window, Katrina made room for Smoky to lie on his stomach. Then she produced a can of herb salve to spread on his wounds. Pushing Rob toward a settee against the opposite wall, she moved to drag two chairs from the kitchen for Caroline and Ruth to sit on. Ruth stopped her, sitting instead beside Rob on the settee while Caroline continued pacing the small parlor, wringing her hands, wondering if she was making the right decision by leaving Texas and not waiting for Jaspar to return from the cattle drive.

As she worked, Katrina chattered, 'When it rains it pours. I usually don't get company in the morning. But Paul Hogan appeared five minutes before you folks knocked on the door. You must excuse me for not making a pot of fresh coffee right away. Knowing Paul Hogan, my business with him won't take very long. I'll be finished in a few minutes and able to be a better hostess to you.'

Ruth had explained to Rob, Smoky, and Caroline before entering Katrina's house that the chubby, cheerful woman had once travelled the Texas Cat Track as a prostitute. After marrying a railroad engineer, she had settled down in Lead Springs and given up her profession, but after her husband died, she had resumed entertaining men in the small house beside the railroad tracks.

After Katrina had disappeared into the bedroom adjoining the parlor with her morning customer, Caroline lifted the can of healing salve from the table. Smoky had given her the railroad bonds from his trousers and she thought that the least she could do to repay him for his loyalty was to put medicine on his lash wounds.

As the bed began to creak in the next room, Ruth started to hum, nervously looking around at the decor in Katrina's parlor, at a cuckoo clock, at the embroidered cushions, commemorative china plates hanging on the wall.

Rob, elbowing Ruth, asked, 'So how do you know this Mrs Bahutivich?'

'Sam – that was my husband's name – he knew Katrina's husband.'

'She seems like a nice woman.'

'Hmmm. Very friendly.' Ruth relaxed slightly. 'Very honest about life.'

Smoky lay on the divan, his cheeks resting against his crossed hands, eyes closed and grimacing as Caroline tended his wounds.

Rob called, 'Smoky, I understand you and Ruth did some work together last night.'

Smoky opened his eyes.

Rob continued. 'Ruth told me this morning that Bess took a few pot shots at you two with her pistol.'

Smoky raised his head from his hands, seeing Ruth nervously fidgeting next to Rob.

Rob said, 'When Ruth and me were making plans to escape, she told me about Bess forcing you and her to do something last night that maybe I should know about.'

Smoky understood. Ruth was obviously smitten with Rob – and Rob with her – but she was worried about him discovering that she and Smoky had made love in the hammock in full view of everyone.

Hoping to protect her yet not wanting to lie to Rob, Smoky answered, 'You didn't see much of Bess at the ranch, Rob. Not like us. So you didn't see how she keeps a pistol right on the supper table beside her knife and fork. She uses it to make sure she gets all the trimmings with her supper.'

'Supper?' Rob's forehead wrinkled.

Smoky, resting his head back on his hand, closed his eyes, explaining, 'That's what Ruth did. Serve supper. I was brought in later to help.'

'Serve supper?' Rob looked at Ruth. 'Was that what you did?'

'Yes. After I brought your tray to the woodshed.' Ruth dipped her head, glancing gratefully at Smoky.

Rob pressed, 'Why did you tell me I might not approve?'

Smoky interrupted. 'You have no idea how bad those men talked in that cookhouse. Not fit for a decent woman to hear.'

Caroline interrupted, saying in an icy voice, 'Can we please not talk about last night? I'd rather forget about that dreadful place.'

'No disrespect to you, mam,' Rob said, reaching for Ruth's hand. 'But this lady and I are making plans for the future so I'd like to clear a few things.'

Caroline frowned, dipping her fingers back into the salve can.

Rob explained, 'Ruth and me had a good talk this morning. Ruth's had a hard time surviving on Bess's place but she still knows a lot about decent living. And ranching. I have to set my roots someplace so I figured that if I can scrape together enough money, I might buy a little farm and Ruth here can help me run it.'

At that moment, Katrina hurried back from the bedroom, clutching a floral kimono around her waist, 'Now let's see about this poor boy's back.'

She stopped when she saw the amount of salve Caroline had applied.

'Honey, what do you think you're doing here? Frosting a cake?'

Caroline looked bewildered.

Taking the can from her hand, Katrina explained. 'You've got to rub it in, honey. Not *smear* it!'

Timidly, Caroline said, 'I didn't want to hurt him.'

'Hurt him? Pooh! Men are tough as old boots, honey.

You better learn that fast or you'll never hold onto a man.'

Caroline's eyes welled with tears, and looking at Rob and Ruth, she fled to the kitchen.

'What did I say wrong?' asked Katrina.

Ruth rose from the settee. 'You must forgive us, Katrina. This waiting around for the train has us all a little bit nervous.'

'Relax! Don't worry! It was a good idea you had to come here. Bess will never think of looking for you at my house. She disapproves of me as much as I disapprove of her.'

'I hope you're right!' Ruth glanced to the window.

'Of course I'm right!' insisted Katrina. 'Bess might be queen bee on her ranch but, honey, she's outnumbered here in town. It may sound like I'm bragging but nobody's going to let her ride rough shod over me.'

Rob said, 'You've been in Lead Springs a long time, mam?'

Stepping to the window, Katrina looked down the wide dirt street. 'I first came to Lead Springs on the Santa Fe Stage in '82. I was travelling to 'Frisco when the stage broke an axle on the outskirts of town. Us passengers had to traipse into town and wait until they got it mended.

'Old Jake Cartwright started chatting to me at the Silver Dollar Saloon. It ain't there no more. But Jake had eleven girls working upstairs for him in those days. He invited me to make it an even dozen. I said "yes" and he opened the annexe – this little house. It was my idea to do some advertising for him.

'The train was just starting to run through Lead Springs in those days. Three times a week. Tuesday, Thursday and Sunday. On train days, I'd lie right here in this window, propped up on this very divan, ready to catch the attention of the gentlemen as the train chugged and puffed into town.'

Losing herself in memories, Katrina explained, 'That's how I met my Frank. He was an engineer on the *Amarillo*. He fell madly in love with me the first time he saw me. He said I looked like some little kewpie doll in a toyshop lying here in my window.

'We got married a week later, the biggest wedding the Cat Track ever saw. A circuit judge performed the ceremony. I had eight bridesmaids all with fresh flowers and ruffled white parasols. Old Jake Cartwright donated the champagne. Frank bought this little place from Jake and we made our home here for fourteen wonderful years. I stopped entertaining gentlemen callers but we had a constant string of visitors travelling back and forth from 'Frisco to New Orleans. Ah, those were the days when this street was really a part of the Cat Track, some of the liveliest tom-cats and prettiest pussycats passing back and forth right through this very parlor.'

A train whistled in the distance.

Katrina sighed, 'Ah, the past!'

Rob and Ruth jumped to their feet; they hurried to help Smoky from the divan as they called for Caroline, shouting excitedly that it was time to leave for New Orleans.

* * *

Seven hundred and fifty miles to the east of Lead Springs, a husband and wife sat on the back porch of their small farm house in northern Louisiana.

The time was evening, the sky was painted lavender, deepening to purple as day blurred into night. The rural stillness was cut by the chirrup of crickets, and the babble of a small creek rushing over its rocky course beyond the kitchen garden.

The man was Warren Rickers, dressed in a faded shirt and trousers, seated in a rocking chair beside his wife. His cinnamon-brown face was handsome, his black hair touched with white at the temples.

Gemma Rickers was a small woman with high cheekbones, her dark gleaming eyes showing she was still a very forceful woman.

Having been married for more than forty years, Warren Rickers knew when Gemma was troubled, and he broke the evening's silence, saying, 'You're worried about Smoky. I can tell. But that telegram he sent says he's on his way home.'

The telegram from California had eased Gemma's worries about her grandson, Smoky, and her brother, Jay, surviving San Francisco's catastrophic earthquake. But in the week since the telegram had arrived, Gemma had developed new anxieties.

Staring into the night, she said, 'So many things could happen travelling home from California.'

'Travelling?' Warren shook his head, holding his stocking feet flat on the porch as he rocked. 'You and I, we did our share of travelling when we were young, Gemma. Travelling all the way here from Pennsylvania in the year right after the war. Neither one of us knew what we'd find here.'

Reaching for her hand, he mused, 'Remember how rundown this place was when we first saw it, Coffee Cup?'

Gemma remained silent, unmoved by her husband's memories, his use of a favorite old nickname for her.

Her voice was stern when she spoke. 'You had to work hard all your life, Warren Rickers.'

'And you managed a few chores yourself, girl.' He added, 'They still aren't over.'

'A home doesn't take care of itself.'

'Neither does a hungry old husband.'

Gemma wasn't listening. She had stopped rocking and was staring across a distant field.

'Warren, look,' she said. 'What's that light up there towards High Hill?'

Warren leaned forward on his rocker, studying the darkening sky where Gemma pointed, a distant flicker against the tree-covered mountain.

Gemma rose from her rocking chair. 'Isn't that . . . fire?'

Not answering, Warren stood beside her.

The light in the distance moved against the fading light,

its color building like the flames of a blaze.

Warren offered, 'It could be some brush fire. From men clearing fields.'

'Not at High Hill,' Gemma shook her head. 'Nobody's worked that land for years.'

Warren knew that fact was correct. But he didn't want to admit that a fire might also be the sign of trouble, a clash with certain White people they had been fearing in recent months.

Gemma asked, 'Didn't you say, Warren, that you heard riders on your way in from milking?'

Warren nodded. 'Coming from Belrose.'

Gemma held both hands to her chest, whispering as if she were saying a prayer, 'Oh, Lord, don't let our Smoky come home to more grief!'

Standing side by side on their porch, Gemma and Warren Rickers remembered the last time that the Ku Klux Klan had torched a home in Longchamp Parish, that the Klan didn't cause trouble only for Negroes.

PART THREE

BASIN STREET

Chapter Sixteen

COMMON LAW

Smoky hurried along North Basin Street, listening to the sing-song cries of the New Orleans street vendors – 'I got oysters! Get your fresh oysters!' 'Delicious rice fritters right here!' '*Café noir! Café au lait!* Like a good woman! Hot all night! Hot all day!' – intermixed with the cacophony of trolley cars, the clip-clop of horse traffic, horns blasting on new automobiles.

Pleased to be back in the humid, lazy, decaying, happy-go-lucky atmosphere of New Orleans, Smoky moved quickly along the boardwalk, glancing at tall granite and wooden houses set back from the street, their bay windows swagged with rich curtains, palm fronds drooping gracefully inside extravagantly furnished parlors. Less than a year ago, Smoky had been turned away from the back doors of all these bordellos but, now, he had a job – if only for one night – in one of the biggest houses on this stretch of Basin Street called The Line.

Twenty-four hours had not yet passed since Smoky, Rob, Ruth and Caroline had arrived at the Canal Street Terminal from Texas. Caroline had taken them directly to the Louisiana Purchase Bank on Royal Street, giving her letter of credit to the bank manager, receiving a large quantity of cash, and paying Smoky and Rob their promised wages.

Smoky had gone from the bank to the Canal Street post house to find out about catching a stage home. To his dismay, he found that all wagon transport north was cancelled until further notice. As no trains ran to Longchamp Parish, he realized he would have to spend most of the money Caroline had paid him to buy a horse. That would leave him with no money to buy presents for his grandparents, and nothing to save for his future.

Leaving the post house dejected, Smoky had remembered the letter of introduction which Elizabeth had given him to show to her friend, Mattie Hayes, on Basin Street, to use in case of such an emergency.

Now, hurrying away from Mattie Hayes' house, Smoky turned off Basin Street, moving down St Ann Street, walking into the French Quarter, enjoying the aroma of freshly baked croissants, the scent of coffee and hibiscus floating from behind high brick walls, looking at the elaborate iron-work galleries overhanging the narrow boardwalks – banquettes.

Passing bow-fronted shop windows, Smoky thought of how Mattie Hayes had offered him a job in a special show tonight at her bordello after reading Elizabeth's letter. Mattie had not divulged what Elizabeth had written in the letter. Nor had she explained anything about the show except that the entertainment would be held after midnight in the bordello's basement, that the other performers would be female, and that the audience was very select, very, very rich.

Rushing now to keep a rendezvous with Rob and Ruth in the French Quarter, Smoky wondered if he should tell them about his temporary job on The Line.

Remembering how Rob had stopped interrogating him about what he and Ruth had done in the cookhouse, Smoky decided to keep his mouth shut about any public performances. Rob and Ruth were obviously becoming more than just good friends. Why should he make Ruth uncomfortable by reminding Rob to ask more questions about the depraved ways of Rattler Gulch Ranch? And why should he mention whorehouses, reminding Rob about working on Pleasant Street? He would let bygones be bygones.

Jackson Square was alive with flower pedlars and entertainers crowding the fronts of the sprawling Pontalba buildings flanking the square. The spires of St Louis Cathedral rose majestically above the muddy Mississippi, a riverboat's horn blasting in the distance.

Enjoying the activity, Smoky passed the front of the Cathedral, hands in his pockets, asking himself if he had done the right thing by going to Mattie Hayes' house.

Was the money he would get for tonight's show worth becoming involved again with a brothel? True, he would not be working there as a whore but, nevertheless, he would probably still be entertaining people in some sexual way.

Slowing as he moved from Jackson Square, heading down Chartres Street to where Rob and Ruth had rented a furnished room, Smoky remembered when he had worried about being exploited by White people for the size of his penis, how he had rationalized working on Pleasant Street, comparing himself performing as a prostitute to Uncle Jay working in a black face in vaudeville.

Was such a comparison fair? Smoky wondered. Or was he no better than some alley cat, having little or no morals? Did he do what he wanted in life, finding excuses to quiet his guilt?

Could a man be too greedy for money? Was quick money from prostitution like a drug? Would he never be able to escape the lure of fast money? Or did money have nothing to do with his attraction to prostitution? Was he merely depraved? If so, would he ever be able to live on a farm, away from decadent city life?

There would be no answers to any of these questions, Smoky knew, until he returned home, going back to the isolation of Longchamp Parish, and seeing how long he could stay with his grandparents.

And would he also learn answers at home to other questions, suspicions about his mother, his father, what they had done themselves when they had come to New Orleans as young people?

* * *

The taste of spirits did not appeal to Smoky but he

politely, even cheerfully, accepted the whisky Rob poured for him to toast their future. Ruth did not join the small celebration. After inquiring how the salve was healing Smoky's wounds, she returned to packing clothes she and Rob had purchased that afternoon on Canal Street. They were planning to leave town early tomorrow morning to visit her sister in Arkansas and begin the hunt for a new home.

Rob and Smoky, seated at a wicker table on the room's louvered gallery, reminisced about past weeks and people they had met.

One boot resting on his knee, Rob agreed, 'For all Caroline Roper's high and mighty ways, she's not a bad gal.'

Smoky had noticed that Caroline had changed in the short time in which they had left San Francisco and arrived in New Orleans; he asked, 'Why didn't she want to go back to Fort Worth for her suitcase? She left a fortune's worth of clothes at the hotel. But suddenly they weren't important to her. Nothing was important to her. If I hadn't seen her in California and known she was alone, I'd swear she was lovesick.'

'Caroline Roper? Lovesick?' Rob shook his head. 'Getting to New Orleans with those railroad bonds was all she could think about. It was more important to her than going back to Fort Worth and collecting her luggage.' Rob grinned. 'It's a good thing we didn't leave Petal at the hotel. She'd still be there, too.'

Smoky revolved the whisky tumbler between thumb and forefinger. 'I wonder if it was wrong of me to insist on Petal coming with us in the buckboard. She might have been safer staying in the hotel. She'd never have met Bess's kid that way.'

'Stop feeling guilty about Petal. You did enough for her. Who knows? Maybe she played a bigger part in our escape than we'll ever know. She might have kept old Bess from chasing us into town.'

Smoky realized that Rob was right in not worrying about Petal. Changing the subject, he asked, 'Didn't Caroline have a big business meeting with the railroad company this afternoon?'

Rob pulled out his pocket watch. The time was a few minutes past three. 'It should be happening about now.'

'Let's hope she gets what she wants.'

Rob lifted his glass. 'To all of us. May we all become rich and prosperous and –'

Ruth stuck her head through the doorway, ' – and happy!'

Smoky joined the toast, gulping down the whisky.

Rob and Ruth laughed as Smoky coughed, the whisky burning his throat; wiping tears from his eyes, Smoky laughed along with them, remembering the times he had made love with them – with Rob in a foursome on Pleasant Street; with Ruth in the hammock in the cookhouse – and he was grateful that the three of them could still sit peacefully together as friends, laughing, having a good time.

* * *

Ruth stood arm-in-arm with Rob on the gallery above Chartres Street, watching Smoky amble down the boardwalk toward Jackson Square.

'Poor Smoky,' she said. 'He seems so alone in the world.'

'He's got his family,' Rob offered, remembering how fondly – and frequently – Smoky talked about his grandparents in northern Louisiana. 'He's going back home and that's probably the best place for a kid like him. He doesn't have a mean bone in his body. People tend to take advantage of easy-going fellows like him.'

'He needs somebody. He shouldn't be alone.'

'Give him time, give him time. His day will come.'

Ruth sighed. 'I want everyone to be as happy as me.'

Remembering the conversation he and Smoky had had a

few minutes ago, Rob asked, 'Did you notice something odd about Caroline on the train? Like she might be lovesick?'

Ruth teased, 'She was probably upset she didn't catch you.'

'Me? A lumberjack? No, I'm not fancy enough for a gal like her. If anything, she's lovesick over some smooth-talking slick-billy she met at Bess's place.'

'Please can we not talk about Bess? I want to forget about her and her ranch forever.'

'Do you believe in love at first sight?'

'I'm serious, Rob. I never want to talk about that place again – even if it's only to discuss Caroline Roper's problems.'

'Who's talking about Caroline Roper? I'm talking about us. How I fell head-over-heels in love with you when I first saw you.'

Ruth remembered how she had brought Rob a food tray into the woodshed, and she murmured, 'I was so ragged, so torn, I'm surprised you paid me the slightest bit of attention.' She ran her hands appreciately over her new dress; it was bright and colorful but, most important, clean.

Rob leaned forward and, pulling back her long auburn hair, kissed her cheek. The bruise had disappeared from the side of her face, and, in the past two days, her skin had become radiant, her eyes had got back their sparkle, and her hair had become luxuriant, tumbling down to her shoulders, smelling of fresh shampoo.

Rob whispered. 'I have a confession to make.'

She frowned. 'Not the past again.'

'Does this morning count as the past?'

Ruth blushed. She guessed what Rob was referring to: they had made love as soon as they had checked into the room this morning.

Pulling her towards him, he whispered, 'I want to be with you again. Right now.'

She smiled.

He asked, 'You too?'

She nodded.

'Why didn't you say so?'

Her cheeks dimpled with a grin, a blush coloring them.

'We must tell each other these things, honey.'

Gripping her hand, he pressed it to his crotch. 'Feel that?'

She nodded.

'Well?'

She looked at him, gaining bravado. 'Well what?'

'Is this a one-sided affair, woman?'

Reaching for his hand, she pressed it to the skirt of her new dress, holding it between her legs.

'Sorry,' he said. 'That's not good enough. I want better.'

Sighing, she lifted her skirt, placing the tips of his fingers on her thin underpants, the fabric moist from excitement.

Working his finger into her mound, Rob murmured, 'Does this embarrass you?'

'No.'

'Am I too bold?'

'I never want you to be anything different. I don't want us ever to change. Not in any way.'

'Not even to get married?'

'I'm happy exactly as we are. Forever and ever.'

'You know what they say about people who live together and aren't married, don't you? They say they're joined by common law.'

'With you, Rob Johnson, nothing could ever be common.'

Ruth sank her head against his shoulder, grateful that she had found such a kind, generous, unique man. He was handsome, but more important, he was optimistic. Her days married to Sam Day had begun happily enough but their life had quickly become drudgery, a burden for both of them, making Sam bitter about the future. It was as if his murder had been the logical conclusion to a long, heartless period of bad luck. The subsequent months at Bess's ranch had made Ruth despair that she'd never know happiness again. She had lived there like a sleep-walker, barely existing, but Rob's appearance had snapped her out of what seemed like a bad dream, making her realize that life did have its surprises, that prayers could be answered. Now she wanted to do nothing except satisfy her new husband, common-law or otherwise.

Rob wrapped both arms tenderly around Ruth, pleased that they could be so straightforward with one another. Ruth did not question his past. She did not ask him where he had worked, how he had made a living in San Francisco, whom he had loved before meeting her. Rob was grateful to have found such an open-minded woman. He believed that – unlike the many people he had encountered on Pleasant Street – neither of them would ever have to visit a whorehouse looking for something they couldn't find in their home, whether it was love, friendships, or fantasies.

* * *

After darkness fell over the French Quarter, encompassing the slate roofs, the spires of St Louis Cathedral outlined by a deepening blue, Caroline lay on a four poster bed in her suite at the St Charles Hotel on Royal Street. Her middle finger curled between her spread legs, she squinted her eyes shut, trying to picture a tall man with broad shoulders . . . curly dark hair . . . a flashing smile . . .

Stopping, she jerked down the hem of her nightdress. She threw back the sheet. She hopped out of bed.

Damn it!

She had a fortune! The railroad bonds were going to secure her future! But what good was it being rich without having the man you loved?

Looking at the four poster bed sitting in the middle of the elegantly furnished suite, Caroline remembered how much happier she had been with Jaspar Jones in his cabin on Rattler Gulch Ranch.

Turning to the directoire bureau, she began pulling open drawers, flinging newly purchased clothes onto the floor.

Yes, she would go back to Texas. She would try to find Jaspar. She had found her ideal man once. Why lose him?

Chapter Seventeen

SMOKY ROW

'Ladies and Gentlemen, it's showtime again in Mattie Hayes' cellar and tonight I'm taking you on a flying carpet to Turkey!'

Mattie Hayes, a short, buxom woman, had a round face with yellow ringlets piled on top of her head. Wearing a long black lace gown trailing to the floor, she clutched a fringed shawl around her shoulders, her stubby red fingers ringed with diamonds.

Standing in front of multicolored silk cushions strewn across an Oriental carpet, Mattie faced a small audience of men seated on gilt chairs dotted around the candlelit cellar. A few ladies were seated in side alcoves, sheer curtains protecting their identity but allowing them a view of the cellar's small stage.

As a piano tinkled *In A Constantinople Garden,* Mattie continued, 'We've all heard stories about harems and how a Sultan keeps eunuchs to guard his many wives and concubines. Tonight I'm going to tell you the story about a Sultan who forgot to look down a eunuch's pants.'

Laughter spread across the cellar.

Mattie moved to the left of the gauze curtains hanging behind her, alongside the pair of tall iron candelabra flanking the colorful heap of silk cushions.

In the shadows, her voice continued, 'Many years ago, in a land faraway, a Sultan brought a new eunuch to his harem . . .'

As piano music rolled, Smoky stepped through the billowing curtains and stood between the tall candelabra.

Wearing a red satin turban twisted with pearls, he held his arms high across his naked chest, his bare feet positioned outwards, jutting his midsection forward, a skimpy gold loincloth bulging with his penis and testicles.

Offstage, Mattie's voice explained, 'As you can imagine, the harem girls went wild over this new boy in town . . .'

Two women undulated onto the stage, slim, white-skinned prostitutes wearing their long blonde hair cascading down their backs, their breasts uncovered, sheer harem pants betraying dark patches of pubic hair.

Small bracelets jangled on their wrists and ankles as they danced around Smoky, dipping, swaying, bending to the music as Smoky remained motionless, his head high, proud, unsmiling.

Mattie resumed, 'Word spread through the harem that something big was coming up . . .'

A third, fourth, fifth, and sixth girl appeared through the pastel curtains, joining the dance around Smoky, writhing, swaying, their fingers slithering over his body, caressing his biceps as Smoky slowly sank to the cushions, closing his eyes, the girls removing his loincloth.

Smoky lay naked on the cushions as the girls began licking his arms, legs, feet, running their tongues up and down his abdomen and thighs, adoring his expanding penis, wetting it with darting tongues.

Mattie explained from the shadows, 'Meanwhile the Sultan decided to see what was up . . .'

A light appeared behind the curtains, illuminating a man wearing a turban and long robes who slowly raised a knife in one hand as he watched Smoky and the prostitutes.

The piano music grew *furioso* and Mattie explained, 'The Sultan's first reaction was to kill the new eunuch . . .'

The girls gripped Smoky's penis, six hands holding the organ upright, their fingers working, squeezing, gripping its jutting firmness.

Mattie said, 'But the Sultan – being a queer fellow – decided to have a little fun too . . .'

The man behind the curtain lowered his dagger and, pulling open his robe, reached for his own penis, beginning to masturbate as he watched the prostitutes taking turns sucking Smoky's organ, alternating their mouths on the crown of the phallus.

Smoky, having never made love to more than two women at one time, forgot about the audience and began enjoying the sensation of six females gratifying him.

The girls also seemed to be enjoying themselves, their touches becoming more gentle, more genuine, smiling as they looked at him.

His head propped up on the heap of silk pillows, Smoky looked down his chest at the girls by his penis, one girl sucking the crown, two other girls moving their mouths on opposite sides, occasionally kissing each other, the erect penis between their pressing lips.

It felt good, too, having two women pleasuring his testicles, gently sucking his scrotum as if it contained two delicate eggs.

As he watched the four girls gathered around his crotch, another pair of girls moved up his chest, beginning to chew his nipples, a girl on each side, both teasing the nipples with their mouths, gently biting the small copper buds with their glistening white teeth.

The girls soon began turning him over on one side and took positions in front of and behind him on the carpet.

As two girls continued to pleasure his penis and scrotum, two others crouched behind him and began chewing on his naked buttocks, gently working their mouths over the fullness of his round, brown moons.

Smoky began to gasp, an orgasm building with the sensations, and to keep him from exploding his seed, the girls again turned him over on the carpet.

As the girls continued ravishing Smoky on the pillows, turning their love-making towards one another when they suspected Smoky might be about ready to reach an orgasm, other prostitutes appeared from behind the curtain, moving between the guests' chairs, their nakedness visible through diaphanous silk robes.

The orgy soon spread from the stage to the audience, and as guests began shedding their clothes, Mattie stepped to one of the dimly-lit alcoves.

Sitting on a chair beside a finely-dressed woman, she asked, 'Lizzie, do you have anything like this out in 'Frisco?'

Neither Elizabeth nor Cory replied. They both stared transfixed at the six women gathered around Smoky.

* * *

It was almost two o'clock in the morning when Smoky finally climbed the stairs from the cellar to Mattie Hayes' bedroom. Hardly able to keep his eyes open from fatigue, he nevertheless wanted to collect his pay before leaving the house. From Basin Street he would go to the stable on Levee Street where he had located a chestnut mare for sale and had agreed on a price with the owner. He would sleep for a few hours in the hay loft there before setting out for home.

Rapping lightly on Mattie's door, Smoky listened to voices drifting from the parlor below and remembered Elizabeth's house on Pleasant Street. He was glad to be going home. He had had enough of prostitution and bordellos for a while.

When nobody answered the door, he reached to knock again but the door opened, his fist stopping in mid air.

Elizabeth stood in the doorway. She flung both arms around him, squealing, '*Surprise!*'

Smoky returned the warm hug, looking past her shoulder, seeing Mattie and Cory Roper beaming at him from the garishly decorated bedroom.

Elizabeth led him towards a pink marble-topped table, explaining, 'Cory had business to attend to here so I thought, what the hell? Why not tag along? It's been years since I've been in New Orleans.'

Cory shook Smoky's hand, telling him that reconstruction work was progressing on Nob Hill, but that they weren't yet near the point of rebuilding the house.

His voice lowering, Cory added, 'Do you know what happened to my daughter, Caroline? We went to the hotel from the station. But they told us she checked out only a few hours earlier. Is anything wrong?'

The announcement surprised Smoky. 'She could be there. But I haven't seen her since this morning.'

'Oh, you know Caroline!' Elizabeth offered gaily. 'She probably had a fight with the hotel and checked out. We'll find her tomorrow.'

Mattie stepped forward, handing Smoky an envelope. 'Before I forget.'

Smoky took the envelope, feeling what was unmistakably money sealed inside.

Elizabeth asked, 'When are you going home?'

'As soon as I get a few hours' sleep.'

'Our timing's just perfect.'

' "Smoky".' Mattie considered the name. 'It's not an unusual name. But neither is it common.'

Winking at Elizabeth, she asked, 'What does it remind you of, Lizzie?'

'Smoky?' Elizabeth shook her head. 'I've never known anybody else named Smoky.'

'No. Not a person. A place.' Mattie looked at Cory, teasing, 'Has Lizzie here ever told you about her early days on Smoky Row?'

Elizabeth forced a laugh. 'Oh, that funny old street.'

' "Funny old street"?' gasped Mattie. 'You called it the "wrong side of town".'

Smoky glanced from Elizabeth to Mattie. 'Where's Smoky Row?'

Mattie explained, 'On Burgundy Street. Between Bienville and Toulouse. It used to be the old redlight district for colored girls in New Orleans. But you know Lizzie. She always ends up where she shouldn't be.'

Smoky could tell from the expression on Elizabeth's face

that Mattie Hayes was saying something she shouldn't be.

He chanced, 'That's where you knew my mother, wasn't it?'

'Smoky, please. Not now.' Elizabeth reached for his hand. 'I told you. I was friends with your mother and helped at your birth. But let's leave the rest –'

'That's why I'm called "Smoky", isn't it?' he asked. 'I was named after the . . . wrong side of town!'

'Smoky!'

'My mother was one of the colored girls who worked there, wasn't she?'

'Oh dear.' Mattie nervously gripped her shawl, asking, 'What have I started now?'

Smoky turned back to her. 'You said it was on Burgundy Street? Between Bienville and Toulouse Street?'

Mattie looked to Elizabeth for help.

Elizabeth conceded, 'Fine. I won't deny it. You would have found out anyway. Just promise me you don't tell your grandparents who told you.'

Smoky pushed, 'What about my father? Where does he fit in?'

Elizabeth lowered her voice. 'I told you in San Francisco, Smoky. I didn't know your father very well.'

'What happened to my father? How did he die?' Smoky persisted. 'I know my mother died in childbirth. But how did my father die?'

'He was killed.'

'How?'

'He was shot in a fight.'

'Who shot him?'

'A man named Willy. They called him Willy-the-Whip.'

'So why did they fight, this Willy-the-Whip and my father?'

Elizabeth glanced at Mattie.

'Why did they fight?'

'Willy was a . . . pimp.'

'My father was a pimp too.' Smoky's words weren't a question.

Elizabeth dropped her head, again trying, 'Smoky, please. This isn't the time nor the place . . .'

Smoky was tired as well as upset. He knew too that Elizabeth was right. This was not the moment to discuss his background.

Only wanting to get away from here, to be by himself, Smoky looked at Cory, saying, 'Mr Roper, I don't know where Caroline is. All I know is that she got the bonds she wanted from Texas. She paid Rob and me for the work we did for her and said she was going to the hotel. That's all I know.'

Lifting the envelope of money at Mattie, he said, 'Thank you, Miss Hayes, mam, for giving me a job on the spur of the moment.'

Stepping towards Elizabeth, he said, 'You've done a lot for me. I won't be forgetting it.'

Kissing her lightly on the cheek, he squeezed her hand, adding, 'And I won't be bothering you no more.'

Elizabeth began to sob as Smoky gently closed the door behind him.

* * *

Smoky Row – what was left of it – was no more than a line of small wooden houses, mostly 'shot-gun cottages', peak-roofed and fronted by shallow porches. Children's toys littered the ramshackle boardwalks; an old man slept on a pallet in a frontyard; garbage lay in the gutter. To Smoky's eye, the four blocks stretching between Bienville and Toulouse Street looked no different from the rest of Burgundy Street, from any of the derelict residential blocks in the French Quarter, certainly not like some notorious redlight district for colored prostitutes. Standing in the dawn's faint light, Smoky thought how this short stretch of a road had so drastically affected his life, had touched the lives of people he did not even know, and the voices of its long-ago inhabitants sounded in his ear, young Black girls calling to passers by:

'Ever had Black pussy, mister? Best Black pussy in town!'

'Want a good time? Good time waiting right here with your name on it, sweet potato.'

'Want to go to Heaven or rather to Hell? You got fifty cents and I give you a little bit of Heaven. You got a dollar and I give you a whole lot of Hell.'

Smoky's mother must have been one of those girls.

Chapter Eighteen

LONGCHAMP PARISH

Smoky galloped between the dark shapes of water oaks, riding the young mare at an open run, hoping to reach the town of Junctionville, Louisiana, before nightfall.

Fortunately, the day was cool, not humid, and he did not have to worry about the animal lathering in intense heat. He also took regular stops to avoid over-extending the young mare's endurance. At the town of Centipede, he watered her and purchased bread, cheese, and beer for himself from a tin-roofed store. Sitting on its sloping porch, he broke off chunks from the crusty loaf and guzzled the cool beer, refreshing himself for the next stint of hard riding.

Reaching Junctionville as the sun was sinking beyond the jagged silhouette of Meacham's Swamp, Smoky stopped at a livery stable on the edge of the small lumber town, an establishment owned by a stoop-shouldered Black man who lived with his large family in a small house next to the stable.

The stable-owner studied Smoky, drawling, 'Your face is familiar, boy. Didn't you come through here on the public stage?'

Smoky's grandfather had taught him that to remember a man's name often meant the difference between receiving a warm or cheerless reception, and he answered, 'That's right, Mr Washington. I did travel through on the stage. But they told me in New Orleans that the stage stopped running here.'

Leading Smoky's horse into the stable, Washington replied, 'Stopped over two months ago.'

'Why?' asked Smoky, following. 'Not enough customers?'

Washington lowered his voice. 'You remember the driver? Young Johnny Robinson?'

Smoky indeed remembered Johnny Robinson, a Black man barely older than himself, a father of three children and descendant of an old Louisiana slave family.

Washington explained, 'Some white man wanted Robinson's job so they killed him. Killed him in cold blood and now they're waiting for people to forget about it before they start running the stage again. I can tell you who did the killing, too. It was the Klan. That Ku Klux Klan. That's who killed Johnny Robinson.'

Smoky had forgotten the fear which the Ku Klux Klan held over Black people in the parish, the group of White business men and farmers who dressed in White hoods and rode at night doing harm to Black families working to get ahead in the world. The Klan wanted life to return as it had been in the slave days.

Washington produced a feedbag of oats for the mare, asking in a lighter voice, 'So where were you gone so long, boy?'

Smoky stood at the wooden barrel, pumping water. 'Out to California.'

'California? That's where they had them that big earthquake, ain't it?'

'Yep, and I got caught right in the middle of it.'

'Then you seen yourself some big sight.'

'I seen enough, Mr Washington, to last me a lifetime.' Smoky held his head under the water pump as he worked the squeaking handle, thinking of women who paid to be humiliated, of old men bossing a bedful of lovers, of a lesbian hand-cuffing him and threatening to cut off his cock and balls with a pair of garden shears.

Washington agreed, 'There's some dang fool things happening in this crazy world all right.'

'Enough to make me come running back home.'

'Fool things happen around here too.' Washington shook his head muttering, 'Dang Klansmen.'

Smoky was sorry Washington had mentioned the Klan;

it was like hearing about a serpent raising its head in a land which he had been hoping and planning on being his Eden.

Washington asked, 'Many Black folks out there in California?'

'Mostly White folks. A lot of Chinamen, too. Yellow men they brought over from China to work the gold mines.'

'Them Whities, they sure do like making slaves out of all kinds of colored people, don't they?'

Washington lifted a curry brush from a peg, asking, 'You find any of them gold nuggets for yourself out there in California, boy?'

'Afraid not. Somebody beat me to all of them!'

'You didn't do too bad coming back home with such a fine looking animal.'

'Oh, I managed to save a few pennies, Mr Washington. I managed to save a few pennies from odd jobs here and there.'

Smoky asked Washington a few idle questions about his own business and family, questions to which Washington replied with quiet, easy-going answers. He said, 'The only complaint the wife and me have is over our oldest daughter, Shelaine. She's a handful of trouble but nothing a good husband in marriage can't settle down.'

Washington showed Smoky the loft where he could sleep for the night, saying that he would tell his wife to fix him a supper tray. Eating a heaped tin plate of sow belly, rice, beans, and collard greens, Smoky felt drowsy, ready to sleep, but he had promised Washington to tell his children about California, about the night that the earthquake struck San Francisco.

Washington, his wife, and their eleven children sat in a semi-circle on a pile of straw in the stables as Smoky recounted how he had been walking along a street when he had heard a roar coming from deep inside the earth, a growl like a dragon trapped in some underground cave.

'Were you scared, mister?'

Smoky looked at a small boy with a shaven head and

little protruding brown ears. 'Good and scared.'

'Did you run?' asked his brother.

'Fast as my two feet could carry me. But I had to watch where I ran because a city that big has buildings six, eight, ten floors off the ground and they were falling down all around me.'

'I bet they don't build high buildings like that no more!' offered another brother.

A chubby girl with a headful of pigtails tied with brightly colored rags asked, 'What happened to folks living up on top of such tall places?'

'They got out! Lickety-split!' Smoky proceeded to tell them how the fire had spread through the city, how the people had to escape in crowded boats across the Bay.

When Washington decided that his children had asked enough questions, he shooed them off to bed, thanking Smoky for the evening's entertainment. 'It ain't often a well-travelled man passes through these parts,' he said. 'Least of all, not a man willing to stop and share stories with the family and me.'

* * *

Smoky climbed the ladder to the hay loft, stripped off his clothes and, stretching out in the night's coolness, wondered if any of the Washington children would ever leave Longchamp Parish to seek their fortune in the outside world. Or would they all stay here, living a life little different from their folks?

Almost asleep, he heard a noise on the ladder leading from the floor below him.

Reaching for his trousers, he saw a shape rising up the ladder, the frizz of hair telling him that it was a woman.

He whispered, 'Who is it?'

'Shelaine.'

The name meant nothing to him.

'Shelaine Washington,' she called, moving across the straw. 'I wanted to thank you for tonight.'

Smoky remembered a buxom girl among Washington's children, a girl he had guessed must be eighteen or nineteen years old. He also recalled Washington saying he was having trouble with his eldest daughter.

He asked, 'Does your Daddy know you're out here?'

'No.'

'You might get us both in trouble if he finds out.'

'He won't hear. He's asleep.'

Smoky felt a hand on his thigh as Shelaine whispered, 'You're sure a pretty boy.'

'You're a nice looking gal,' he said, remembering how he had noticed earlier that Washington's eldest daughter had stared at him all through the story-telling.

He added, 'But I don't think you should be out here.'

Her mouth pressed against his lips – its taste warm, sweet, inviting – as she grabbed his naked crotch.

Pulling back her head, she whispered, 'I've felt big peckers before. But – oh my!'

The touch excited Smoky but he still wondered if he should send her back to the house or, instead, should he enjoy her nicely rounded body, satisfy the lust he himself felt. The choice became more difficult when she moved her head down to his crotch, her mouth encircling his penis.

Putting both hands under her arms, he laid her back onto the hay and fell against her warm body, trying not to think of her mother or father as he sank himself into her waiting heat.

A fulsome girl, Shelaine Washington cradled Smoky between her legs, responding to his stirring penis, her vagina perfectly sized for Smoky's generous proportions.

Rolling across the hay with her, Smoky fondled her large breasts, listening to her sigh, driving one leg between her legs, driving another leg between her legs, sinking himself farther, deeper, warmer into her clutching femininity.

When Smoky lay on his back, Shelaine lay astride him, looking down at his face as she squeezed, leaned side to side, working her thighs to get the full benefit of his manhood.

Enjoying him, she whispered, 'I bet travelling around the country, you've seen all kinds of different things.'

Smoky looked up at her. 'Gal, you sure this is okay?'

'Daddy's asleep. That's all he ever does. Sleep. He don't know what I do. He don't know what I like.'

He gave his penis a quick bump up inside her. 'You like this?'

'Uh-huh'. She looked down at him, grinning. 'And more.'

'What more you like?'

'You really want to know?'

'I asked, didn't I?'

Leaning towards her dress piled on the hay, she reached into one pocket.

Dropping something in Smoky's hand, she said, 'That's what I like.'

Smoky, looking in the moonlight, saw two leather thongs.

'Boy, you know what they're for?'

'Uh-huh.'

'That surprise you?'

'What surprises me is how come you're taking this chance with me?'

'You got that look in your eye, boy. That look of a man who's got ladies chasing him all over the place.'

'And if I did?'

'That means you're used to being spoiled. You're used to sluts like me chasing you. Wanting you. Needing you.'

Smoky understood more clearly.

Looking at Shelaine Washington, he said, 'You're pretty old for your age.'

She held his eyes. 'Some folks say I'm a slut.'

'Does it bother you what folks say?'

'I like it. I like it a lot.'

Smoky remembered Pleasant Street, recalling how the White woman, Barbara Lowry, had wanted him to call her a 'slut', had wanted to be humiliated and abused. Barbara had paid for it. This country gal had the same hunger and no money. Should she be deprived?

He said, 'If your Daddy wouldn't hear us, bitch, I'd knock the holy hell out of you.'

She squeezed her thighs, feeling his penis hard between them.

Smoky, assured now of the sort of treatment she wanted, quickly grabbed her by both shoulders. He lifted her off him and, pushing her down to the hay on her back, bound one leather cord around her wrists.

Holding her down in the hay, he bent to her feet and bound her ankles together.

Kneeling above her trussed in the leather, he ridiculed, 'You're a dirty slut for coming out here like you did.'

Her voice was cautious, reverential. 'I saw your prick tonight when you were telling stories. I saw it was so . . . big.'

'Prick-hungry slut!'

'I love big cocks.'

'Dirty bitch.'

'You've got one of the biggest ones I've seen. I wanted it so bad when I saw it.'

'This is all you get of me, bitch.' He spat at her.

She gasped.

He spat again. Raising her head, she opened her mouth.

Smoky spat a third time, his saliva hitting her mouth. She swallowed it. He spat on her forehead, her cheeks, rubbing the saliva across her, saying, 'You're lucky your Daddy's nearby because, gal, I'd beat your ass raw for being such a slut!'

She lifted her bound hands towards him. 'Please! Please can I at least *see* your prick?'

'No.'

'Please!'

Kneeling above her, he bobbed his hard penis temptingly in front of her eyes.

She opened her mouth.

Smoky whipped her face with the penis sneering, 'Bitch.'

She tried to kiss it.

He moved back.

She crawled after him, trying to kiss the tip of his swollen penis.

Smoky kept moving across the hay, leading Shelaine, criticizing as she crawled, 'Look at you! Just like a bitch dog in . . . heat!'

Bellying across the floor with arms and legs trussed together, she begged, 'Please . . .'

Smoky grabbed her by the hair and, rolling her onto her back, threw up her arms.

Lying down on top of her, he drove himself into her vagina, pressing one hand over her mouth, saying, 'I bet you give your tail to every man who passes through here, don't you, slut?'

Groaning, nodding her head, Shelaine worked her thighs for Smoky's penis.

He continued taunting her, abusing her, feeling her working more feverishly below him, her orgasms flowing in torrents.

When he was ready to explode his own orgasm, he pulled out from her womanhood and, kneeling above her face, shot his seed in long arcs above her head, pushing her down to the hay as she repeatedly tried to catch the warm seed with her mouth.

Fifteen minutes later, she had dressed and crept down the ladder. Smoky was fast asleep.

* * *

The next morning Smoky awoke with the rooster's crow. Three children brought him coffee and fresh bread. After paying Washington for the meals and stabling, he gave each of the children a dime and mounted his horse. Not seeing Shelaine Washington this morning, he waved goodbye to her little brothers and sisters and set out on his early start.

Heading north-east from Junctionville, Smoky decided it was not necessary to ride as hard today, not as fast and strenuously, as he had done yesterday. He would reach home by late afternoon even if he travelled at a leisurely pace.

Familiar sights began telling him he was coming closer to home: share-croppers looked up from the long bags they dragged between the rows of cotton and waved at Smoky passing on his mare; a small wooden cross stood crookedly at Crow Forks Junction, a commemoration to Black people killed there many years ago; smoke curled from the chimney of the little house at the Dasher Place, a farm once owned by an old woman named Biddy Hen but now worked by two men, Ken and Paulie.

Looking at Ken and Paulie's neat farm, Smoky thought of his Uncle Jay, wondering if Ken and Paulie were lovers as Uncle Jay and Marc might be? Were people in Longchamp Parish really no different from the outside world? Remembering Shelaine Washington last night, he guessed that people were pretty much the same everywhere.

* * *

The town of Bossburg had changed little since Smoky had first gone there as a child, and it had not changed at all since he had last seen it. Quiet, run down, tucked into a forgotten corner of the Louisiana wilderness, the farming town seemed only to get a little more dilapidated, a little more grey, a little more weathered by sun, wind and rain.

Riding down the short main street, Smoky saw Bernadette Hite, a share-cropper's widow, holding the reins to a scrawny mule, her pretty daughter, Angel Pie, sitting alongside her in the wagon.

Smoky tipped his hat to the fat Black widow. 'Morning, Mrs Hite.'

'Morning, Smoky,' she answered as if she had just seen him yesterday, and elbowed her nineteen-year-old daughter to speak.

Smoky lifted his hat a second time, calling to the pretty girl, 'Morning, Miss Angel.'

Angel Pie nodded, shyly gripping her mother's arm, only turning to look at Smoky when she thought he had passed, grinning widely when he caught her looking at him.

Smoky next saw the lawyer, Quentin Vaughn, coming down the front steps of Fowler's General Store.

'Morning, Mr Vaughn.'

'Morning, Mr Summers.'

Mr Summers? The proper title, the use of a surname, surprised Smoky. Why would a White man – especially an important man like a lawyer – address him as 'mister'? Was the new little mare so impressive? Smoky told himself not to forget to mention this incident to his grandparents.

Thinking about his grandparents, Smoky trotted through town, wondering if he should stop at the general store to get some kind of gift for them. He had not purchased anything in San Francisco or New Orleans.

Considering the idea, he thought, 'But why go all the way across the country, clear to the Pacific Ocean, and wait until I get back to Bossburg to buy them a present? It doesn't make sense.'

Instead of a present, perhaps he could do something special for them. Build something for them. Do something. Something very, very special. But what? What would they appreciate? What did they need?

Quickening his gallop, Smoky climbed the hill on the far side of town, remembering how miserable he had felt when he had left New Orleans. The memory reminded him again of his mother and father, of the fact which Mattie Hayes had inadvertently let slip in her bedroom.

The closer he got to home, the farther away the street called Smoky Row seemed to be, and the less despondent he felt about the facts he had discovered about his background, his tie to the Black prostitutes' red-light district. He was willing to forget Smoky Row temporarily.

Cantering down a hill lined with poplars, Smoky saw the

gate to his grandparents' farm and his stomach leaped with excitement.

Patting the mare's neck, he said aloud, 'Here we are, old girl. This is home.'

Then he saw Teddy running towards him down the grassy road, the brown and back dog barking at Smoky and the horse.

'Teddy! Don't you know me any more, fella? Hey, there, boy!'

The dog, recognizing Smoky's voice, lowered his front legs to the dirt, shaking his haunches back and forth, wagging his tail as Smoky kept talking to him.

The barking brought Smoky's grandmother from the house. She stood by the fence, drying her hands on her apron, her head erect as she looked up the driveway.

Smoky knew at that moment he could not mention anything about his mother to his grandparents. How could he hurt people he loved so much?

* * *

Thick slices of smoked ham. A platter of golden fried chicken. Smothered pork chops. Candied yams. Collard greens. Fried corn. Potato salad. Gemma complained she had not had enough time to fix a proper supper as she heaped more food on the kitchen table for Smoky and his grandfather.

Talking between mouthfuls, Smoky asked questions, answered questions, repeated how happy he was to be back home. And he was.

Finishing his third helping of red cabbage, he called to his grandmother at the oven, 'You heard from Uncle Jay?'

Gemma hurried a pan of fresh cornbread to the table. 'A letter came a few days after your telegram. He sent an address where he'll be in Seattle.'

Warren sat opposite Smoky; he had eaten lightly this evening, a coffee cup and saucer placed on his plate.

He suggested, 'We can write to Jay now and say you made it back home.'

Smoky took another gulp of buttermilk and, wiping his mouth, asked, 'What's the news here, Grandad?'

Warren spooned honey into his coffee. 'High Hill went up in smoke last week.'

Smoky's fork paused. 'Burnt?'

'Plumb to the ground.'

'Anybody hurt?'

'Killed Mrs Summers.'

Smoky felt a chill. 'Mrs . . . Summers?' He thought of the man who had been his father, Alain Summers.

Gemma clanked a bowl behind him. 'Marisse Summers kept to herself. We had nothing against her.'

Marisse Summers? Smoky pictured the straggly blonde woman he used to see riding in a big, oldfashioned carriage when he was a child, always a big Black man driving the carriage, a man who didn't come from these parts.

How did Marisse Summers fit into his life? Was now the time to ask his grandparents for the story? Should he also tell them that he had found out about Smoky Row, had heard that his mother had gone to New Orleans to be a prostitute, his father a pimp?

Instead, he helped himself to more potato salad and kept his voice light and chatty. 'So how did the fire start?'

Gemma came back to the table. 'Let's talk about you being home.'

She was purposely avoiding the subject. Smoky knew it was not like his grandmother to gloss over unpleasant facts. He knew she was a lady who faced problems and solved them. So why was she avoiding talking about High Hill? About Marisse Summers? The fire and her death?

Warren's voice brightened, also seeming to want to avoid the subject of High Hill. 'So how long are you going to be staying home this time, Mr Gad-about?'

'Warren! Stop it!' scolded Gemma. 'You make it sound as if this is a hotel.'

The porch door rattled.

'Who's that?' whispered Gemma, looking over her shoulder. 'I didn't even hear a horse on the drive. Or Teddy bark.'

Warren pushed back his chair from the table, and, as Gemma moved to stand behind Smoky's chair, they listened to Warren's greeting. 'Evening Mr Vaughn. Smoky said he saw you this afternoon.'

A deep Louisiana drawl replied, 'Mr Rickers, I hope I'm not interrupting you folks.'

'You're just in time for coffee and a bite to eat.'

Vaughn doffed his straw hat as he came into the kitchen. Nodding to Gemma, he said, 'Evening, Mrs Rickers.'

'Mr Vaughn.' Gemma produced a chair.

Not sitting, Vaughn held out his hand to Smoky. 'I come to bring you good news, young man.'

Shaking the lawyer's hand, Smoky looked quickly at his grandmother and grandfather, seeing that they were as puzzled as he was.

'I don't know if you've heard about the accident a few nights ago at High Hill.'

Warren put his arm protectively around Gemma. 'We were just talking about it, Mr Vaughn.'

Vaughn offered, 'It's sad that any person should come to such an awful end. But all's not bad news.'

Looking back to Smoky, he said, 'As executor of Marisse Summers' estate, I've come to inform you, Mr Summers, that she has named you her sole heir.'

Gemma stepped forward. 'Named?' Her tone was challenging.

Vaughn nodded. 'Bequeathed.'

Smoky looked at his grandparents, speechless.

Vaughn explained, 'I have papers here saying you not only inherit High Hill but a sum in excess of seven hundred thousand dollars, as well as Marisse Summers' jewels, her furnishings, livestock, insurance, all her earthly possessions. Mrs Summers was a very rich lady, rich from her own family as well as her first husband's family. She was far wealthier than anybody around here ever imagined, which makes you – as her recognized grandson and sole beneficiary – a very rich young man.'

* * *

Junior Dehasset lay fully dressed on the big oaken bed in the master bedroom at Belrose Plantation. Trying to calm his mind over the disturbing fact he had just learnt only a few minutes earlier, Dehasset watched Sophie French twisting, turning, fornicating herself on his plantation-made love dolly, a foot-long phallus stretched with horse leather. But for all Sophie's movements – sighs, gasps, simulated ecstasy – Dehasset could not forget the shocking news he had been told in the library.

Earlier this afternoon, three men had ridden from Bossburg to Belrose with news that Warren Rickers' grandson had inherited High Hill Plantation. The visitors had been Judd Gillman, Dave Cooper, and Dwight Pine. Junior had received them behind the locked doors of his library, and Judd Gillman had said, 'You promised us that burning High Hill would rid us of nigger lovers.'

'It was meant to. Marisse Summers died. But so what?'

'Her will's been made public. She left her place to Warren Rickers' grandkid.'

Junior had sat staring blankly at Gillman.

Gillman had continued, 'Joined with the Rickers farm, that coon kid now stands to own one of the biggest places in the Parish, if not *the* biggest. Even bigger than Belrose. So think about that!'

Junior's answer had been a nervous belch.

Mopping perspiration from his forehead, he had answered, 'How was I to know what was in that old lady's will? It's your fault for not running Quentin Vaughn out of the Parish a long time ago. I can't do everything for you God-damned knuckleheads!'

Judd Gillman, as speaker for the men, had refused to let Dehasset shift the blame onto them. He had stood in front of Junior's desk, insisting, 'We're not here to discuss what we should've done. We're here to discuss what we got to do. Public opinion's turned in favor of old lady Summers. Just like we warned you it might. Nobody likes to see a poor old widow killed. So the Klan's got to lie low for a while. That's how we still feel. More than ever.'

'I'll think of something,' Junior had promised. 'I'll think of some way to stop these niggers owning the world.'

After Gillman, Cooper, and Pine had ridden away from Belrose, Dehasset still had not come up with an answer to the dilemma of a Black family becoming the largest landowners in the parish.

Thinking about Quentin Vaughn keeping the details of Marisse Summers' will a secret all these years made Dehasset angry. A legal document could easily have been switched. Changed. Altered. Now it was probably too late for that. But it wasn't too late to make Vaughn pay for his negligence, an act which Dehasset considered to be false loyalty.

The most important matter to settle, however, was what should happen to Smoky Summers. Dehasset's oldest rival in the Parish was the boy's grandfather. Warren Rickers had made him look a fool too many times since the Rickers family had first come here many years ago. An old score had to be settled once and for all. But how? Where? When?

Looking at the foot of the bed, seeing Sophie slowing her copulation with the love dolly, he bellowed as a diversion for himself, 'Open up that hole of yours with that dolly, bitch, or you won't be able to take my meat.'

Sophie – used to Dehasset's lies about the size of his manhood – told herself that it was not his penis she was preparing herself for. She too had heard that Smoky Summers had come back from California. She did not know how she was going to do it, but somehow she was going to get to see him, to learn if Smoky had any ideas about how she could escape Junior Dehasset's dreadful clutches.

Picturing Smoky's pretty face, his athletic body, his

nice, gentle ways, she derived increasing pleasure from the leather phallus, pretending that she and Smoky were married, that he was planting babies deep inside her.

And the thought of having Smoky's babies gave Sophie the idea of going to see his grandmother. She could confess her love for Smoky to Gemma Rickers. Would Smoky's grandmother play cupid?

Chapter Nineteen

A MASTERING PLACE

Smoky's mind was a whirlpool. One moment he considered inviting Rob and Ruth to help him farm High Hill. The next second he imagined giving the land to his grandparents. They could live in the big house and he would fill it with servants and they would never have to work again. He thought about marriage, about having a big family. But who would he marry? Angel Pie Hite? The mere thought of the pretty young girl with large brown eyes and rounding hips made his penis swell. But he realized that Angel Pie probably couldn't read or write, that she had probably never owned a pair of shoes in her life, and he heard his grandmother telling him: '*Don't marry some pretty young thing just because she makes your blood boil. What kind of mother and wife will she make?*' Thinking about marrying a woman who was only physically attractive to him, Smoky wondered if his newly inherited fortune would make him useless, a layabout, a no-good man who went through the world with no ambitions, seeking physical pleasures, thrills, excitement.

Remembering how quickly he had jumped into bed with strangers on Pleasant Street, how readily he had performed on Basin Street, how easily he had humiliated Shelaine Washington, Smoky lay in bed in his room down the hallway from his grandparents and wondered if he was already on the path to perdition, if his newly inherited money would seal his downfall. Perhaps he should put all his inheritance in a bank and leave it there and live the life of a frugal but decent man. Perhaps he should ignore the big house at High Hill and stay here on the farm with his grandparents, living as he had done all his life. But did that mean he was running away from responsibilities? Did he secretly want to be a little boy forever? And what about the church? What about giving money to Reverend Calvin Lee Hines? Should he make a big donation to charity? Try to wash away a few sins?

Tossing, turning, fretting, sighing, scratching nervously throughout the night, Smoky was relieved when morning finally came and he could go downstairs to breakfast.

His grandfather, seated at the table, announced that it might be a good idea for Smoky to visit High Hill today. He offered to go along with him.

Smoky jumped at the offer, inviting his gradmother to come with them. They could take the wagon.

Gemma declined. 'No, you men go by yourselves.'

Smoky did not see her nod approvingly at his grandfather.

* * *

'You travelled all the way 'cross country?'

'And back again.'

'Did you stick your feet in the Pacific Ocean?'

'Close enough.'

Smoky remembered the night that he had sat with Elizabeth at the end of the Jackson Street Wharf, how the two of them had talked for the first time about his mother. He had not told his grandparents that he had met Elizabeth; he had not once referred to his mother since he had been back home. After the lawyer, Quentin Vaughn, had left the house last night, Smoky's grandmother had said that he was probably tired and that the best thing for him to do was to try and get some sleep. Kissing him goodnight on the forehead, she took her Bible upstairs to her room.

Warren Rickers, having admired the new mare but without asking how Smoky had got money to buy such a fine animal, rode alongside him on his roan. They kept to the Parish Road which circled Benteen Mountain, Teddy following, barking at squirrels, snapping at the droves of yellow grasshoppers hopping through the tall dry grass beside the road.

Resettling his straw hat, Warren announced casually, 'You other grandad and me were neighbors for over forty years but nobody could have been more of a stranger. I met him only once in my life. And that wasn't exactly a very friendly occasion.'

The announcement stunned Smoky.

His voice low and easy, Warren continued, 'Herc was his name. Short, I guess, for Hercules. He was a big man. Fine looking. Darker skinned than you or me. He was a man who didn't smile much. He worked as overseer for Phillippe Summers. That was Marisse's husband, Phillippe, a Creole from New Orleans.

'The story goes that Marisse Summers moved Herc into the big house after Phillippe went off to war. But some folks say that Phillippe had a say about Herc moving into the big house from the slave quarters. There were always strange toings-and-froings at High Hill. No doubt about it, Marisse Summers enjoyed a Black man in her bed. That's how she came to be your grandmother, Herc being the father of her son, Alain.

'A Frenchman came from New Orleans and challenged Herc to a duel over Marisse. Their reason was some personal matter and nobody knew much about it. Although your grandmother – my sweet Gemma – never did admit it, I always suspected she had something to do with that Frenchman coming to High Hill. But that's another story for another time.'

As the two horses travelled side-by-side between the towering spires of pine trees, Warren continued, 'Herc had his eyes on our land. He began conniving with White men in Bossburg to get it. A road through our property would give High Hill direct access to the Parish Road. They wouldn't have to go around the mountain like you and me are doing now. High Hill would double in value, not being so remote.

'Herc teamed up with White men to run us out and get our land. That's when the Klan came after me one night. It's queer now to think they're the ones who killed Marisse Summers and put High Hill in your hands.'

Smoky asked, 'Why would the Klan want to kill Mrs Summers?'

'Who knows? She's always had a dark-skinned man in tow. Even lately, in her old age. The Klan probably decided it was time again to make an example of some nigger-lovers, and Mrs Summers was the only one they could think of.'

'The Klan's leader is Junior Dehasset, isn't he? Over at Belrose?'

'All I'm willing to say about Junior Dehasset, son, is that he seems to have had a personal grudge against me since we first came here.'

'Why?'

'It began with me stopping him whipping Black boys. It just seems that when there's no Junior Dehasset in Longchamp Parish, there's no Klan here either.'

Without turning to Smoky, Warren asked, 'You ready for trouble yourself, son?'

The question caught Smoky unawares. 'Trouble?'

'Without naming names, there are White folks who aren't going to take too kindly to you inheriting all this land. Whether they've been indirectly responsible for it or not.'

Smoky gave a deep sigh.

'Course, son, you don't have to accept it. You can put the land up to public auction. Let some White farmer buy it far below value.'

'Are you serious?'

'I'm just saying, that's one thing you can do.'

'Do you think that's what I should do?'

'Son, it's hard when a Black man gets money. He's got to think "Dare I do this?" "Dare I do that?" or, "Am I going to upset this person if I buy that thing-a-ma-bob?"

'When a White man gets money, he says, "Whoopee,

look at me! I'm rich now!" But not a Black man. Not if he wants to stay healthy. Now, mind you, I'm not saying that's right or wrong. I'm just saying that that's how things are and we aren't going to change them overnight.'

Smoky held the reins in one hand, head down, bobbing to his horse's easy gait. 'What should I do, Grandad?'

'I wish I could tell you, son. I wish I could tell you. All I can say is that it's good this didn't happen before you grew up. When you were a kid. You're a man now. Your months working in New Orleans, your time out west in California, that probably made you more of a man. You've seen things. Good and bad.'

Smoky did not comment.

'How much you know about mastering, son?'

Smoky looked at his grandfather. 'Mastering?'

Warren Rickers held himself high in the saddle, a proud man, his voice relaxed as he explained, 'High Hill was always what I called a "mastering place". A master ruled the roost there. But the master wasn't always White. Phillippe and Marisse Summers put Herc on a pedestal there. It was no well-kept secret that both of them enjoyed mastering in their love-making. Do you know what I mean, boy, by mastering in love-making?'

Smoky nodded, disbelieving that his easy-going, retiring grandad was actually speaking to him about domination, submission, pain in love-making, all the goings-on of a bordello.

Warren continued, 'The slave business in the South, that fed the whole mastering ways people have these days in the privacy of their bedroom. It put people on the track of dominating one another, using whips, naming slaves, worshipping masters. Men and women, husbands and wives, all kinds of folks, they want to be masters and slaves. And it's my idea that those ideas got fuelled by America's old slave days.

'Black people were good field slaves in the old days. They were strong, hard workers. I also figure that that's why a Black man knows how to be a good master when

White people like the Summers bring him into the bedroom. Men like Herc know about power. Strength. He learned it at the other end of the whip so he knows how to use that old whip. Herc became a strong master. Marisse became his love slave. Their son, Alain, he was a master, too, I guess. And I reckon that our Emmy – your own Mama – she was Alain's love slave. Least, Alain got a mean hold on Emmy and treated her no better than some slave.'

Keeping his voice level, Warren elaborated. 'I don't know if Alain and Emmy ever got married. We've never seen any documents or papers saying they did. After they left here together in his bright little red buggy one morning, we never seen them again. Your grandmother finally went down to New Orleans looking for them. But she found things there that broke her heart. Plumb broke the woman's heart.'

The gate posts to the left of the Parish road were stone, ivy obliterating the brass plates proclaiming 'High Hill'. Smoky did not give the posts a second glance; he was thinking of his mother leaving home, his grandmother going to look for her in New Orleans.

Passing between the posts at an easy pace, Warren said, 'Smoky, your grandma is a good woman, a fine woman with a smart head on her shoulders. She's a fair-minded woman, too, and she has a saying she strongly believes in. *"If you give a child life, then give it to him. Don't hold onto it like a fishline."* That's how we tried to raise you. But who knows? Maybe it's wrong.'

Smoky's voice was almost a whisper. 'I appreciate it, Grandpa.'

'Son, we haven't talked much to you about your folks in the past. I don't know if that's right or wrong either. I don't know if it's right or wrong to tell you everything all at once or in short doses. I personally think it's best for facts to come out in bits and pieces, us telling you when you're ready to know, when you *want* to know.'

Smoky shrugged, unable to speak.

'But your grandmother and me figured you should know something about the Summers family being you're inheriting their land. Being you're becoming the master of High Hill. Your grandma and me discussed us having this talk.'

'Grandad?'

'Son?'

'Do you think the Klan will start trouble?'

'I do. And when you least expect it.'

'You said Junior Dehasset came after you. How did he cause trouble for you, Grandad?'

'Promise me you never ask your grandmother that question. Gemma's biggest scare in the world came from Junior Dehasset. Her biggest heartbreak was losing our daughter. But her biggest scare was from that . . . bastard.'

Smoky recognized the hatred in his grandfather's voice, a tone he had never before heard him use, and it gave him the first germ of an idea.

Warren reined his roan, pointing ahead of him, saying in his usual drawl, 'There it is, son. There's High Hill.'

Smoky, looking up a slope, saw a large house on the crest, its walls crumbling, its windows broken and jagged, the floors collapsed, most of the timbers burnt or blackened by fire. The breeze gently flapped a white hood from a nearby poplar tree, a pillowcase with eye-slits, a sign of the Klan.

Smoky's idea took root.

* * *

Gemma, finishing the morning's breakfast dishes after Smoky and his grandfather left the house, washed the few dirty clothes which Smoky had brought home and, after hanging out the laundry to dry, went into the parlor and sat down in a chair with her Bible.

After reading from Corinthians, she closed the old book and sat with both hands folded on its well-worn Moroccan cover, thinking again about Smoky's news, wishing that she could rejoice with him, celebrate with him for becoming a rich man.

But she could not rejoice. She considered Marisse Summers' action to be the cruellest, most selfish thing in the world.

Jealousy. Hatred. Greed. Smoky would be seeing all the worst traits of people. And all because of new and sudden wealth.

Why hadn't Marisse given them some little clue that she was going to name Smoky in her will? That she planned to make him a rich man? They could have made proper preparations. Perhaps sent him north to school. Prepared him for an environment where it would be easier for a rich man – a rich *Black* man – to find his peers, to cope with everyday life.

Gripping her hands in frustration, holding her eyes shut, Gemma wished she could be more useful to her grandson at this moment in his life. In younger days, she might have thought of something courageous to do, might have been able to take him into the outside world herself. But now she was old, cautious, not brimming with the fight of younger years.

Smoky had an adventurous spirit, true, but where could he meet his equals? Who was there to educate him? To introduce him to friends befitting his new status? Her brother Jay? No, Jay was too old. Jay lived too much like a gypsy.

But Smoky had to go somewhere. He couldn't stay here in Longchamp Parish. Continuing living here would make too many men jealous. Not Black people. But White people. The same people who had murdered Marisse Summers would sure enough try to kill Smoky.

Gemma jumped when a hand touched her shoulder. Opening her eyes, she saw Smoky standing in front of her.

'Grandma, you're crying.'

Embarrassed, Gemma tried to choke back her tears.

Smoky bent forward, wiping a tear from her cheek, saying, 'Don't cry, Grandma.'

Touched by the concern in his voice, Gemma clutched him, begging, 'Don't let them come and get you too, baby. Don't let them come and get you too.'

Smoky, wrapping both arms around her, tried to sound cheerful, to ingore what she was saying. 'Don't worry, Grandma. Everything's going to be all right. Don't worry.'

Continuing to hold his arms consolingly around her, Smoky realized that the time was right to start preparing the groundwork for his plan.

Cheerfully, he said, 'Dry that pretty face of yours and tell me a story.'

Sniffing, she said, 'Story! You've got some way with you, child. You got some pretty way with you, I declare.'

'No, really, Grandma,' he protested, squatting in front of her chair. 'When Grandad and me were up looking at High Hill, I started thinking about the time you and me went to Belrose to see Sabrine Crowley.'

Gemma nodded, drying her eyes, glad for Smoky to be distracting her mind.

Almost like a child, he pleaded, 'Tell me about Belrose, Grandma. What it looked like inside. How big the rooms were, where the kitchen was. And parlor. And bedrooms. I know you remember. I know.'

Gemma, pleased at the diversion, began reminiscing about the big house at Belrose Plantation, about the days when its master and mistress had been her friends, Sabrine and Cramer Crowley, before the plantation had passed to Junior Dehasset.

* * *

In Texas, Jaspar Jones arranged for four beer kegs and three cases of whisky to be brought from Fort Worth to Rattler Gulch Ranch to celebrate his marriage to Caroline Roper. Bubba insisted on paying for half the refreshments because he was marrying Petal on the same day. The wagonful of beer and whisky was followed by brightly-dressed women on horseback and in carriages, town prostitutes anxious to join the ranch-hands in the big, weekend-long celebration.

Sunflowers, bachelor buttons, and cactus flowers decorated the tables in the cookhouse. Reverend Stokes from Lamb of God Baptist Church in Lead Springs officiated at the ceremony. Caroline wore an ivory silk gown which she had brought from New Orleans. Petal had sewn a ruffled dress from the bolt of white organza which Caroline had given her for a present. The ceremony was brief and simple, and after the newly-weds retired to the grooms' respective cabins, the guests began a drunken revelry.

Liquor flowed freely, beer washing down whisky, the town women dancing on the tables, the men twirling one another in square-dances as Cy Gibbons played fiddle and Bob Barber shouted dance calls.

Dancing soon gave way to abandoned activity, the heat making women strip off their clothes, groups of two, three, and four couples crowding under tables and in corners, prostitutes plying their trade, ranch-hands sating their lust.

Bess listened to the shouts and squeals of laughter from behind the locked doors of her shack. Petal had locked Bess in the cabin a week ago and she had long since ceased screaming and pounding on the walls, accepting the fact that her son – goaded by Petal – had led a mutiny against her.

In Bubba's cabin, Petal stood naked beside the bed, looking down at Bubba wearing the gift she had made him for their wedding night, a lacy camisole and frilled small-clothes cut from the same fabric as her bridal gown.

Petal, appraising Bubba dressed in the feminine underclothes, teased, 'You're no longer tied to your mama's apron strings. You're a husband and a pussy for me, aren't you, Bubba?'

Bubba glanced at the bolted door, nervous about being discovered wearing his cherished new gifts.

Petal teased, 'Shame on you. A man dressed like a pussy! Shame!'

Bubba rubbed the tips of his fat hands over the contrast of the black hair matting his chest and the smoothness of the frilly clothing.

Petal threatened, 'Should I punish my husband for being a pussy?'

Bubba reached for his crotch.

Petal nodded her approval. 'That's right! Play with your pussy, bitch. Play.'

Bubba's penis was growing, protruding long and thick from the lacy top of the small-clothes.

'What a big pussy you have!' Petal teased, watching Bubba's hand working his penis.

Petal, remembering how Alicia had spoken to her when they had been lovers on Pleasant Street, pushed out her furry patch towards Bubba's face, ordering, 'Eat me, bitch. Open your mouth and . . . eat me!'

Bubba raised his head from the pillow, moving his mouth towards Petal's crotch, anxiously running his tongue around her furry delta, poking the slit, finding the moisture, working for the candy taste of its sticky reward.

Petal ordered, 'Roll over, bitch.'

Bubba rolled onto his stomach.

Reaching for a black leather belt on the floor, Petal gripped one end of the belt in her hand, snapping it across Bubba's hirsute buttocks, saying, 'Now, I'm going to make you pay for being a pussy.'

Bubba pumped his hips in excitement, displaying his buttocks high as a target in the air, groaning, gasping, whining as Petal snapped the belt against him, moaning, 'Thank you . . . thank you . . .'

Across the dirt yard from Bubba's cabin, Jaspar and Caroline lay side by side on Jaspar's brass bed. Boxes, bags, and valises littered the plank floor around the bed. Chairs and tables were heaped with clothes, shaving equipment, shoes and boots. Jaspar and Caroline planned to leave Texas tomorrow morning, travelling west to California to make their home on Octavia Street.

Caroline still did not know where she had got the courage to return to Texas and propose marriage to Jaspar. She had been greeted by a surprise when she had arrived here, Petal and Bubba having imprisoned Bess in her cabin, holding her captive as they ran the ranch.

Jaspar was surprised that Caroline had come back to Texas. She had confessed to him that the story she had told about being married, of looking for a new home, had been a lie. Jaspar was flattered at being pursued by such a pretty girl, someone who was not only fifteen years his junior but a proper young lady who was also very rich.

Lying next to her in bed, he smoothed her hair against the pillow, confessing, 'I don't know what I'll do for a living when we get to San Francisco.'

'We'll see when we get there.' She snuggled against his muscular body, not believing her good luck in finding a man she considered to be ideal, the sum total of everything she had ever wanted.

'You might have to support me.'

'I don't mind.' She kissed his bicep, thrilled that her husband was so finely muscled.

His black eyes danced. 'You don't mind having a poor husband?'

'I don't mind if you don't mind.' She ran her tongue over the brawny cap of his shoulder.

He laughed, 'Oh, I don't mind!'

They had spent much of their time in bed since Caroline had returned to the ranch. Jaspar had noticed new, little telling things about her, how she frequently opened her eyes during love-making, stealing glances at him, as if she wanted to make certain it was him, it was her, it was them truly making love – together.

Deciding it was time to take her a step further in sexual knowledge, Jaspar pulled away from her and stood on the mattress.

He looked down at her, gripping his penis in one hand,

his fingers working the foreskin back and forth, holding his eyes on her as he asked, 'Are you ready for more of this, Mrs Jones?'

She looked up at him.

Holding his eyes on her, he complimented, 'You look very good down there, Mrs Jones.'

'And you look very good up there, Mr Jones.'

'Above you.'

She nodded. 'Way above me, Mr Jones.'

'I'm going to keep you down there, Mrs Jones.'

'I need to be down here, Mr Jones.'

Deciding she was ready to be taken further in her sexual education, he ordered, 'Get on your knees.'

She obeyed.

Putting one hand behind her head, Jaspar pushed her mouth towards his penis, saying, 'Open wide.'

Her lips parted, her eyes closed.

'Nice and slow . . .'

Closing her lips around the fat crown of Jaspar's phallus, Caroline continued to follow his instructions.

'Back and forth. Back and forth.'

Caroline moved her head forward; she brought her head back, her mouth full of thick penis.

'Watch those teeth.'

Enjoying her first experience of fellatio, Caroline quickly relaxed, breathing through her nose, slicking his phallus with saliva, making the act easier, more comfortable, less choking for her.

Without warning, Jaspar withdrew his penis from her mouth.

She looked up at him, bewildered.

'You like sucking cock?'

She nodded.

'You want to do it more?'

'Please.'

Reaching towards a nearby chair, Jaspar lifted his shaving mirror from the assortment of objects.

Standing back above Caroline, he pushed his phallus

into her mouth, and as she hungrily resumed sucking him, he held the mirror beside her face.

'Look at yourself sucking cock.'

Caroline opened her eyes, seeing the reflection of the hard phallus protruding from her stretched lips.

'See the cocksucker.'

She continued looking in the mirror, enjoying the sight.

'See the lady sucking the cattle rustler's cock?'

Caroline resumed working her mouth back and forth, keeping her eye on the mirror, her fantasy at last a reality.

* * *

Caroline had left a letter for her father at the Royal Street bank and, after reading it in front of the teller's brass cage, Cory hurried back to the St Charles Hotel and showed it to Elizabeth in their luxurious mezzanine suite.

Elizabeth read the neat lines of blue ink as Cory paced the carpet, finally lowering the piece of cream parchment to her lap, saying, 'I can hardly wait to meet this man who's managed to get your daughter to chase after him. He must be something!'

Cory threw up his arms. 'A cowboy who works for Black Bess! And Caroline says she hopes to persuade him to marry her!'

'The girl's got guts. That's all I can say. The girl's got guts.'

'But I planned on a big wedding for Caroline. A cathedral wedding. A European honeymoon! The works!'

'That's what *you* wanted. Did you ever ask Caroline?'

Cory slowly shook his head.

Elizabeth turned to the silver service on the table next to her chair. Pouring a cup of coffee for Cory, she added sugar, saying, 'You must try not to worry. She'll bring her cowboy to meet you when the time's right.'

'But what if something happens to her?'

Elizabeth poured herself a cup. 'I know it's not a very

original idea, but "Nothing chanced, nothing gained".'

Bending over her shoulder, he kissed her neck, asking, 'Don't you ever get tired of being right?'

'Me? I always say you're the smart one!'

'Ho *ho*!'

'I'm not joking,' she protested. 'I loaded myself down with bogus titles and false illusions and all kinds of unnecessary baggage over the years. But you put me on the right path. Oh, sure, I've got a nose for making a quick buck. How to make an extra dollar here and there off my girls . . . and boys. But that's only business.

'No, Cory Roper. It's you who's the bright one. I always say that. And do you know who else has had an effect on me? Recently?'

He looked at her.

'Smoky,' she said, explaining. 'For years, I barricaded myself with pins and scarves and high-buttoned collars to hide what I was. But what could Smoky do to hide what he was? Nothing! Black people have to face the world and say that they're no different from anybody else. And they're *not* different! No more than a Jew! Or an Irishman! Or a Dago! Or a Kraut! Everybody's the same because we're all on this earth together. Even us . . . whores!'

Cory stared at Elizabeth, asking, 'What are you saying?'

'That I have to be more truthful. Not only about who I am, but what I say to other people about themselves. I realized that fact the other night at Mattie's house when I saw how upset Smoky was. I had told him a few facts about his mother in San Francisco. But only a few facts. I should have told him everything. How his mother was like a slave to his dad even if he never married her. That she loved him heart and soul. Walked the damned street for him. I should have told the kid, too, that I was there in the whorehouse where he was born. That he was brought into the world to the sound of knife clashes and snapping whips and gun shots. Hell, he's got a brain. he's got a mind. He doesn't need me to protect him, to mother him, no more than I need him protecting me!'

'What about me?' Cory asked meekly. 'Can't I protect you?'

'You?'

'If you agree to be Mrs Cory Roper, I'll protect you twenty-four hours a day.'

'Is this a proposal?'

Sinking to one knee in front of her gilt chair, he grasped her head, promising, 'In the best old-world tradition.'

She raised one eyebrow, teasing, 'I warn you, I don't want a cathedral wedding either.'

They fell laughing into each other's arms.

Chapter Twenty

THE PERFECT GIFT

Smoky, having decided on the perfect thing to do for his grandparents as a homecoming gift, planned to begin accomplishing it shortly before dawn. He remembered a school teacher once telling him that people slept deepest during those hours, and so he thought that his plan would go best at around four o'clock in the morning. He would also have the darkness of night to cover his actions.

Going to bed at the same time as his grandparents, Smoky slept fitfully despite his carefully laid plans. He awoke. He dozed off again. He awoke, checking the time on the clock next to his bed.

Finally, he rose and dressed, careful not to make any noise. He was certain he had not raised his grandparents' suspicions about his plan – they would never suspect he'd do such a thing – but he did not want to alert them by clattering a chair across the floor, or screeching a drawer.

Carrying his boots in one hand and a change of clothes in the other, he shut the bedroom door behind him and moved stealthily down the hall, descending the stairs one by one.

In the kitchen, he found all the necessary objects he had spotted last night while he had been drying the dishes for his grandmother – the butcher knife, the raw stewing meat, the towel.

Outside, the air was fresh, increasing Smoky's alertness. There was no question of going back to bed and forgetting about his plan.

Opening the back gate, he told himself that the job would be over in a few minutes if he succeeded; closing the gate, he tried not to think of what would happen if the plan failed.

Two bits of stewing meat quieted Teddy in the barn. Stuffing the rest of the package of meat into his pocket, he crammed his extra clothing into a saddle bag and began saddling the mare, softly coaxing her not to nicker or stomp in the stall, promising he would soon give her a name, a nice pretty name.

Telling Teddy to be a good boy and to stay inside the barn, Smoky led the mare to the yard, closed the door behind him, and crossed the edge of the yard to the grassy shoulder of the driveway.

Smoky waited until he reached the Parish Road to mount the animal. He was anxious to get on his way but feared that the sound of hoof beats might carry to the house.

The butcher knife wrapped in the towel and tucked into his belt, Smoky rode eastwards at a slow pace, heading towards Belrose Plantation.

* * *

Reining the mare in a poplar copse across from the main gates to Belrose, Smoky looked up the cypress-lined drive and saw the white pillared house luminescent in the early morning darkness, an open gallery fronting the house, no sign of lights in any of the windows.

Knowing it would take longer to walk up the drive than to ride the mare, Smoky had nevertheless decided to lose time rather than risk being observed on a horse.

Tying the mare in the poplar copse, he dashed across the road, passed through the gate, and hurried past the cypress trees towards the big house.

Sabrine Crowley had welcomed Smoky and his grandmother at the front doors of Belrose, Smoky remembered. Pulling the package of meat from his pocket, he instead skirted the house, moving toward the back of the pillared breezeway connecting it to the kitchen. The staff cottages and workers' cabins – the old slave quarters – lay well in the distance.

The rear door was not locked. Smoky was not surprised. Who bolted doors in the country?

Listening to the stillness inside the dark house, Smoky softly clucked his tongue, whispering, 'Here, boy . . . Here, girl . . . Here, puppy, puppy, puppy . . .'

Sure enough, nails clicked across tile, and the large, dark shapes of two dogs moved toward him.

Petting the animals, listening to them gobbling the meat he fed them, Smoky made his way across the serving room, noticing the dogs' bed against the far wall as he moved.

Emerging in the main hall, he saw two matching doors exactly as his grandmother had described them, one to the parlor, one to the library.

Beside Smoky, a staircase rose to the upper floor. He climbed the carpeted steps, approaching the overhanging balcony.

Facing him at the top of the stairs was a pair of double doors. He hoped his hunch was right, that Junior Dehasset had taken the most important bedroom in the house when he had become plantation master.

Crouching at the corner of the banister, Smoky looked at the other doors facing the balcony. They were all shut. The rooms behind them were empty or, if not, hopefully the occupants were fast asleep.

Stepping up to one of the master bedroom's double doors, Smoky pressed down the handle. It did not budge. His heart beat quickened but he told himself to remain calm, not to panic.

Moving flat against the other door, he tried the second handle and, gently, it moved in his hand.

Pushing open the door, Smoky heard the sound of heavy snoring. He smiled. Men snored when they slept on their backs. Face upwards.

Closing the bedroom door behind him, he accustomed his eyes to the darkness, seeing a large wooden bed cornered by four carved posts. A White man lay on his back in the bed, a corpulent man with a bushy grey moustache. Smoky had seen the man enough times to recognize him as Junior Dehasset.

Reaching towards his belt, Smoky felt the towel wrapping the butcher knife.

Freeing the knife from its towel scabbard, Smoky surveyed the room for small tables, chairs, stools, anything which he might kick over when he left: escape was more important than entry.

Standing above Junior Dehasset, Smoky looked down at him, realizing that this was his last chance to change his mind. Murder was a terrible crime. Probably one of the worst offences against the Lord's Commandments.

And was he really doing this for his grandparents? Did he truly believe that killing Junior Dehasset was a substitute for not having the time to buy a present for them in San Francisco or New Orleans, for not bringing home a souvenir dish? A hand-painted plate? A nickel bag of salt water taffy?

Remembering how selfish he had been in the past, how he had talked himself into becoming a male prostitute on Pleasant Street, Smoky realized that his own life would be safer, easier, without Junior Dehasset alive. So why not admit it?

Looking down at Dehasset on the bed, he saw how helpless he looked, eyes shut, mouth open, hands crossed on his chest – a defenceless victim.

But had not Dehasset taken his own defenceless victims? Had he and the Klan not caused trouble for his grandparents? Killed Marisse Summers? Hundreds of other people in the Parish? So why should one man be allowed to take victims and another not be allowed to stop him?

The plunge was fast, strong, determined. The long, sharp blade quickly severed the wind pipe, slicing the throat ear-to-ear, cutting cords and muscle, crunching bone, and a warm, dark liquid began gushing from the flesh, fresh blood reminding Smoky of butchering pigs on the farm.

Stuffing a corner of the bedsheet into Dehasset's gurgling mouth, Smoky held down his hands on his chest with one strong grip as the body tossed, turned, pushed.

Waiting for the corpse to stop convulsing, Smoky yanked off a linen case from the pillow. He wiped the blood from his knife on it and, holding the pillowcase in front of him, quickly slit two eye holes. Turning, he mounted it on one of the bed's posts, hoping this crude sign would be taken as a clue.

Moving toward the door, wrapping the knife back into the towel, Smoky stepped out into the hall and looked down to his feet to make sure that he was not trailing blood, leaving any tracks.

Hurrying down the steps four at a time, he tossed the rest of the meat at the dogs in their bed and, once outside the house, he did not stop running until he reached the poplar copse.

Wanting nothing more in the world than to rush back to his grandparents' house, he knew he had to think about the future. He headed in the opposite direction from home.

* * *

Gemma shook Warren from his sleep.

'Wake up. He's gone.'

Warren, regaining consciousness, seeing that the bedroom was dark, asked, 'What's the matter? What time is it?'

'He's gone,' repeated Gemma.

'Who's gone?'

'Smoky. I looked in his room and he's gone.'

'He probably went for a walk. He probably couldn't sleep. Now will you please come back to bed and let the boy be.'

'No. Something's wrong, Warren. Believe me. I have a feeling. I know something's wrong.'

Warren knew Gemma's feelings, her premonitions, and as they were often correct, he wearily threw back the sheet and reached for his clothes. 'All right. I'll go have a look.'

The parlor was empty. The kitchen showed no sign of Smoky. Crossing the porch, Gemma and Warren went outside into the darkness and crossed to the barn to look for him.

Gemma stood next to Warren in front of the stall where Smoky kept his mare. It was empty.

'I don't like it,' she said.

Scratching his head, Warren insisted, 'I still say he got restless and went for a ride.'

'Something's the matter. I don't care what you say. Something's the matter.'

Warren, wrapping his arm around her, said, 'I can't go back to sleep now. Why don't you come inside and fix me some coffee?'

Gemma and Warren sat facing each other at the kitchen table as dawn lit the morning sky outside the window. They spoke in low voices, discussing how good Smoky looked after all his travels, how calmly he seemed to be accepting the fact of becoming a near-millionaire, how well he had listened to the story about his other grandfather, Herc, being a slave at the time that Marisse Summers had first brought him into her bedroom.

The hours of early morning slowly ticked by, Gemma going to the window to check the driveway, returning to the table. It was past time for Warren to begin his morning chores, for Gemma to start her work. But they remained sitting at the table, drinking coffee, watching the clock show six o'clock, seven o'clock, eight o'clock, nine o'clock, nine-thirty . . .

Gemma confessed, 'I hope you're right, Warren. That the boy's gone for a ride. I admit, it's a big load for him to bear –'

Teddy's barking interrupted her; Gemma rushed to the window, seeing a horse galloping down the drive.

Hurrying outside, Gemma and Warren ran to the gate at the end of the wooden walk.

Gemma recognized the rider halting a black horse in the

yard; she whispered, 'It's that wench from Belrose. Dehasset's fancy girl.'

Sophie French reined the animal, calling excitedly, 'They killed Junior Dehasset! Junior Dehasset's dead!'

'Junior Dehasset?' Warren held protectively onto Gemma. 'Somebody killed him?'

Looking down from the horse at Gemma and Warren, Sophie announced, 'Davey found his body when he took in his breakfast tray. There was a hood stuck at the foot of the bed. Davey rode to town fast and got the Sheriff. The Sheriff came and says he don't know what to think. It looks like it could be the Klan's work.'

Gemma and Warren exchanged glances; they both knew that Sheriff Laird rode with Junior Dehasset in the Klan.

Gemma stepped forward. 'Did the Sheriff send you here to tell us this news, miss?'

'No . . .' Sophie looked anxiously at the house.

'So why did you come here?'

'Your grandson's back home from California, ain't he?'

'Yes.' Gemma's eyes sharpened.

'I know you don't approve of me, Mrs Rickers. I know you think bad of me for living so snug with a White man like Junior Dehasset. But I had little choice. He would've killed me or done something awful. So please give me a chance now. Believe me. I ain't a bad girl. And I come to you because I got concern for Black people same as you do.'

Gemma said, 'That still doesn't answer my question why you came here, young lady.'

Looking around her, as if there might be eavesdroppers, she leaned forward in the saddle, confiding in a lower voice, 'Fact is, I think the Sheriff was pleased to see what happened. It's no secret in the Parish that Junior Dehasset headed the Klan. It's no secret either that the Sheriff also took midnight rides with them. But they fought lately, Junior and the Sheriff. I heard them. A lot of White men think Junior did wrong burning out High Hill. So I figures that the Sheriff's happy to shush up Junior's killing –'

Gemma interrupted angrily. 'I don't want to listen to gossip and theories, young lady. Just tell me why you came here this morning with this news.'

Sophie stared boldly into Gemma's eyes, saying, 'You're a hard woman, Mrs Rickers, but people respect you. Black as well as White people in the Parish. They respect what you do and what you say. The good people.'

'And?' Gemma was not mollified.

'I want you to put in a good word for me with your grandson.'

Gemma, not shrinking from the girl's boldness, said, 'My grandson can make up his own mind about whom he sees or doesn't see, young lady.'

'Well, you tell him I came here. You tell him I brought you this news about Junior Dehasset. You let your grandson know I've got a few decent bones in my body, however I might have spent the last few years. That's all I ask of you, Mrs Rickers. To put in a few good words for me with Smoky. He'll be settling down soon and I'd make him a good wife. I'm free now to marry.'

Looking one last time at the house, she turned her horse and galloped down the driveway.

Watching her disappear, Warren said, 'Junior Dehasset's dead.'

Gemma sniffed. 'I'll believe it when I see his grave.'

Warren continued, 'And that wench came here hoping to feather her nest with Smoky. Well, if that ain't the dickens.'

'She's looking to make her nest at High Hill! That's what a hussy like her wants! A nice, big fancy home now that she's going to be out in the cold!'

Warren was still exuberant about the news. 'It's like some awful thing has been lifted over our heads, Gemma. Some awful thing that's been hanging over us for years and years and years.'

Gemma looked at the driveway. 'I wish that boy would

get home. If the Klan *is* riding the road, I don't want him out there by himself.'

Warren pulled Gemma to his chest. 'We won, Coffee Cup. We won.'

'It's not over yet.'

'No. But we out-lasted Junior Dehasset. He didn't drive us out like he swore. We won.' He hugged her tighter.

* * *

'You're up early.'

'I went for a ride.'

'So early?'

Smoky sat down on a chair next to his grandmother by the kitchen table, looking across the table to his grandfather, saying, 'You told me yesterday about a road connecting this place to High Hill. I went up to see how big a job it would be to make it.'

Surprised, Gemma asked, 'You been to High Hill?'

'Hmmm.' It was not a lie. He had gone there to wash in the creek, to change his clothes and bury the bloodstained clothes deep in the earth.

Warren said, 'You missed some big news.'

'What's that?'

'Junior Dehasset's dead.'

'Dead.' Smoky felt his face suddenly tighten, his throat go dry. 'When? What happened?'

'The Klan killed him. So the Sheriff's saying.'

Smoky had not been prepared for this announcement. He stammered, 'The Sheriff's . . . been here?'

'No.' Gemma quickly added, 'That's the other piece of news.'

'What other news?' Smoky felt light-headed, as if he might faint, more nervous than he had felt all morning.

Gemma explained, 'A wench from Belrose came here. She told how one of Dehasset's servants found him in bed. So she didn't lose no time in high-tailing it over here to impress you with the big news.'

'Impress me? Why . . . *me*?'

Gemma rose from the table, shaking her head. 'Boy, sometimes I wonder how you made it back home from California in one piece, you're so innocent. But then, maybe that's why you're such a good boy. You're not bad looking. You're even-tempered. And now when word's out that you've got a few pennies in your pocket, you're surprised when wenches start riding wild animals to this place trying to win your attention. My, my, my.'

'Just a minute now. Hold it.' Smoky, regaining confidence, wanted to get the facts straight. 'Junior Dehasset's dead and the Sheriff says the Klan killed him?'

'So that fancy gal claims.' Gemma reached for her apron.

'Why do they think the Klan killed him?'

'Because they left a hood as a sign on his bed.'

Warren suggested, 'Don't go asking questions that don't concern you, son. Just be glad that the old devil's finally gone.'

'Warren!' Gemma shamed. 'Have some respect for the dead!'

'Respect?' Warren stared disbelievingly at his wife. 'That man made hell on earth for us for over forty years, Gemma, and you tell me to have some respect?'

Putting a skillet on the cookstove, she argued, 'Junior Dehasset's facing his Maker. So we must pray for him. We must pray for everybody facing the Lord. Whoever they are.'

'Grandma?'

'No more questions now, son. It's almost time for dinner and I still haven't fixed you men your breakfast.'

'Grandma, I was only going to ask you to pray for me, too. I've done a few bad things myself lately. I think I need a few of your prayers.'

'Bad? You've come home. That's all that matters to us.'

Smoky smiled to himself. He would add the perfect gift to his list of sins.

THE END

THE HOUSE AT 3 O'CLOCK
by Rupert Gilchrist

First in the *Slaves Without Masters* Series

The Civil War over, the Deep South is a smouldering and bloody shambles, with four million negroes, unshackled from their chains, seeking work, food, shelter from defeated and vengeful white Confederates . . .

Gemma and Warren Rickers, a young black couple, arrive in Longchamp Parish, Louisiana, to claim a plantation bequeathed to them by a white widow. They find the community engaged in a clandestine plot with Confederate officers – a plot with a horrible twist – to reinstate slavery. Despite themselves, Gemma and Warren become entangled in an appalling web of intrigue, perverse lusts, cruel dominance and cringing submission – a decadent world of sexual cravings, lit by the flaming crosses of the hooded riders in the night . . .

0 552 12161 4 £1.50

A GIRL CALLED FRIDAY NIGHT
by Rupert Gilchrist

Second in the *Slaves Without Masters* Series

Emmaline Rickers, daughter of Gemma and Warren, whose shocking story was told in THE HOUSE AT 3 O'CLOCK, takes a stagecoach to New Orleans in search of her freedom – as a prostitute.

This, the second volume in the scorching new series "Slaves Without Masters", plunges the Rickers family ever deeper into the turbulent times following the American Civil War. Emmaline's story concerns the forbidden love she shares with the heir to High Hill Plantation, Alain Summers, a selfish young man who conquers her with his sadistic love-making, ultimately selling her pleasures to other men, so as to finance his own unbridled passions . . .

0 552 12425 7 £1.95